THE PRESERVE KILLER

A LUCA MYSTERY
BOOK 14

DAN PETROSINI

Copyright © 2023 The Preserve Killer by Dan Petrosini.

All rights reserved.

No part of this publication may be reproduced, distributed, or transmitted in any form or by any means, including photocopying, recording, or other electronic or mechanical methods, without the prior written permission of the publisher, except in the case of brief quotations embodied in critical reviews and certain other noncommercial uses permitted by copyright law. For permission requests, contact dan@danpetrosini.com

Print ISBN: 978-1-960286-14-7
Naples, FL
Library of Congress Control Number: 2023903986

OTHER BOOKS BY DAN

THE LUCA MYSTERY SERIES

Am I the Killer

Vanished

The Serenity Murder

Third Chances

A Cold, Hard Case

Cop or Killer?

Silencing Salter

A Killer Missteps

Uncertain Stakes

The Grandpa Killer

Dangerous Revenge

Where Are They

Buried at the Lake

The Preserve Killer

No One is Safe

SUSPENSEFUL SECRETS

Cory's Dilemma

Cory's Flight

Cory's Shift

OTHER WORKS BY DAN PETROSINI

The Final Enemy

Complicit Witness

Push Back

Ambition Cliff

1

———

MY FEET SQUISHED IN THE MUD AS I WALKED IN THE Cocohatchee Creek Preserve. Yellow crime scene tape and a pair of officers came into view. I stopped short. My heel lifted out of a shoe. Setting it back, I wriggled it free and surveyed the wooded area.

The low hum of traffic coming from the interstate wasn't the thing breaking the serenity. Marring the nature scene was a body. It was in direct violation of the park's mantra: "Take Only Pictures and Leave Only Footprints."

Pulling on gloves, I considered the location. The body had to have been dumped here; the chances of an argument spiraling out of control in a park seemed remote. I approached slowly.

The corpse was propped against a bald cypress tree. "Looks posed, doesn't she?"

Derrick said, "I don't know. Maybe she leaned against it, trying to get up."

"If she was fighting for her life, she'd be crawling."

Her white shirt was covered in blood. I studied the body. What had happened to her?

The woman was in her mid to late thirties. Shoulder-length blonde hair framed a wrinkle-free face. Nothing flashy or expensive about her clothing and open-toed shoes. "Where's her pocketbook?"

"Good question."

My gaze landed on her lap. There was something under her hand. A vibration ran across the base of my skull. I leaned down. "What's that? A case for glasses?"

"Yeah, that's weird."

I stood and looked in the direction we'd come. "Here comes Gianelli." Cameras hanging off each shoulder, the crime scene photographer flashed the peace sign. "Bilotti is here too."

As Gianelli wrapped his hair into a ponytail, I said, "Do me a favor and document her lap and hands. She's holding what looks like an eyeglass case. I'd like to see it as soon as possible."

"No problem, Frankie."

As he clicked away, I knelt, examining where her back met the tree. "Her pocketbook is wedged behind her."

Derrick came over. "Weird."

"This scene was staged."

"What could be the message?"

"We'll find out soon enough, if there is one."

Gianelli turned to me. "You're good to go. I grabbed twenty shots."

I looked behind me; Bilotti was twenty yards away. "Thanks."

As I extended my arm to reach for the case, Bilotti said, "Hold on, Frank. Don't touch anything."

"She's holding a case; I need to see if it means anything."

"Once I'm through, you can disturb the body."

"Gianelli documented—"

Bilotti arched his brows. "How many homicides have we worked together?"

"Okay, okay. Do what you have to."

"Why, thank you, Frank."

"To me, it looks like it's been staged."

"It may have been."

"Do your thing. We're going to talk to the guy who found her."

We introduced ourselves to Mike Breem, a wiry sixty-year-old. Wearing worn jeans and a baseball cap embroidered with a sea turtle, he said, "I can't believe it. People these days are just crazy. It's so disappointing."

Disappointment was getting a steak raw instead of medium. "What were you doing when you discovered the body?"

"I'm here all the time."

"Why?"

"I monitor the gopher tortoise population."

"Why do you do that?"

"They're a species of special concern. If it weren't for people like me, they'd be wiped off the planet."

He was a turtle expert. I wanted to ask him if it was true that they could live longer than humans. "That's good of you. Now, how long were you in the park before finding the body?"

"About an hour."

The park was only four acres. "As far as parks go, this place is small. What were you doing all that time?"

"I was watching a burrow."

"A burrow?"

"Where the tortoises live. They lay their eggs, and it's fascinating to see their babies emerge."

"Oh."

"Did you know that the sex of a tortoise is determined by the temperature of the dirt where the eggs are buried?"

"That's interesting. So, how did you come to find the body?"

"I always scour the park, looking for signs of new burrows. It gives me an idea of the size of the population."

"I see. What did you do when you saw her?"

"I couldn't believe it. At first, I thought someone was resting or hurt, but as I got closer, I saw the blood. I yelled, but she didn't respond, so I called nine-one-one."

We'd listen to the call. It would give us clues as to whether Turtle Man was telling the truth. Derrick took his contact information, and we walked back to the body.

Bilotti was writing in a notepad. "How's it going, Doc?"

"Your assumption appears correct; I believe she was posed."

"Time of death?"

"At this point, I'd put it four to six hours ago, but we'll firm it up with the autopsy."

It was 10:30 a.m. I asked, "Stabbed to death?"

"Yes. Three wounds in the thoracic region. You can examine the case."

I put my fingers around her left wrist and slipped the brown case off her lap. There was blood on the underside of her forearm. As I stood, I wondered if she'd tried to fight off her attacker.

The old case felt empty. Expecting to see a pair of glasses, I opened the case. "Uh-oh."

Derrick peered over his monitor as I walked in the office. "What did the sheriff say?"

"Not much, but I think he agrees it could be a serial killer."

"Why else would he have left the cutout with the number one on it?"

"Remin's worried about the optics. Doesn't want to panic the public. He doesn't want it publicized."

"What about processing the case and paper?"

"He called them while I was there. The lab is on it."

"It's going to be a key piece of evidence."

I shrugged. "Maybe, but if numbering the victims is the killer's thing, we have to keep it under wraps."

"Yeah, if we catch him, we'll use it to verify it's him."

"Not if—when, we nail the bastard."

"A hundred percent."

My desk phone rang. It was a brief conversation. I slammed the phone down. "No prints on the case or paper."

"The killer is careful."

"Most serial killers are."

"Where are we starting?"

"No cameras at the park or witnesses, other than Turtle Man. You check him out and I'll dig into the victim."

MELISSA WRIGHT's pocketbook didn't contain her phone. Was it another sign of the killer's cautiousness? In her wallet was a driver's license, a ticket for the cleaners, twelve dollars in singles, and a business card belonging to Jonathan Ong, a real estate agent.

I fingered the card. With a hot real estate market and what seemed like a quarter of the population selling homes, was there meaning to it?

Wright's address was listed as 3939 Francis Ave. It was in a neighborhood south of the Naples Airport, off Airport Pulling Road. She wasn't wearing a wedding band, but that didn't matter. Cohabitation without marriage was approaching 70 percent.

Melissa Wright was thirty-eight. My stomach lurched at the thought her family was waiting at home. I prayed she didn't have a child. Encouraged no one had filed a missing person report on her, I headed out.

As a private jet descended, I turned right before Alice Sweetwater's Bar and Grille. Francis Avenue was lined with one-story block homes on narrow lots. A silver Honda Civic sat in Wright's driveway.

Holding my breath, I rang the bell. Nothing. I knocked and still no answer. Circling the house, I looked in windows. No evidence there was anyone else living there. I sent a text to Derrick to get a forensics team out here.

Cupping my hands, I looked inside the Honda Civic.

Sitting on the passenger seat was a book. I tapped a number into my cell. "I'm about to begin the autopsy, Frank."

"I know, Doc. But can you check if she's pregnant?"

"Of course. Why do you ask?"

"Wright has a copy of *The Best Baby Names of 2022* in her car."

"Hmmm. I'll check. It'll be in the preliminary report."

"How long is it going take you to do the autopsy?"

"Any more interruptions and—"

"Sorry, Doc. Just wanted to give you a heads-up."

"That's fine, Frank. I expect to complete it sometime this evening."

WRIGHT'S NEIGHBORS told us she worked at the Hyatt House, a hotel on South Fifth Avenue, opposite Tin City. With traffic whizzing by, most over the speed limit, I wondered what it was like to stay there. I pulled in and parked.

The hotel was on an island. I peeked around the back. The Gordon River stretched out beyond the pool. The location had incredible access to the Gulf of Mexico, and it was no surprise that Captain Joey D Charters operated a football field away.

Paul Norris was the hotel's general manager. Tall and thin, with a shock of white hair, I pegged this as a second career for him. "I can't tell you how shocked we are. Melissa was a wonderful woman. A pleasure to work with."

"What were her responsibilities here?"

"She was the assistant general manager. We actually have three people with the same title."

"What were her duties?"

He smiled thinly. "Whatever came up. This is a business

with zero predictability. You really never know what will come up when you arrive at work."

We had that in common. "Can you provide specifics on her day-to-day?"

"She'd work the front desk when needed, you know, during crunch times, when people are checking in. Melissa was good with people." He frowned. "Her associates are devastated."

"Was there an incident with a guest or coworker, anything that could have spiraled out of control?"

"No, Melissa's strength was her ability to defuse a situation."

"Can you elaborate?"

"Guests sometimes have unrealistic expectations. Rates during the season are quite high, and people feel, well . . . let's just say they can become irate over the tiniest detail. Melissa would settle them down. She'd talk to them, assure them they were appreciated. She'd comp them a dinner or lunch if it was warranted, at Latitude 26, our restaurant."

"Even-tempered?"

"Oh yes. She'd been here two years and never raised her voice."

"Do you know if she was in a relationship with anyone?"

"She was seeing a nice man, Bobby, uh . . . Bobby Ryan. Yes, that's it."

"Do you know how I can get in touch with him?"

3

———

THE DRAPES WERE DRAWN IN THE FAMILY ROOM, AND THE kitchen plantation shutters were closed. The house wasn't only dark, it was silent. Not a good sign.

I tiptoed into the master bedroom. Mary Ann was asleep. I changed and sidled up to the bed, whispering, "Mary Ann. Are you all right?"

She stirred, opening her eyes. "Hi."

"What's going on?"

She squinted. "Bad headache."

"Headache, or a flare-up?"

She shrugged. It was an MS attack.

"When did it start?"

"Midmorning."

"You didn't say anything when I called."

"You had a homicide to deal with."

"That doesn't matter. You come first. I need to know what's going on."

She forced a smile.

"Did you call Dr. Gentile?"

"Yes, she said it should fade away and to call her if it got severe or lasted more than five days."

"That's it? You have to live with pain?"

"There's not much they can do."

"For all the money we're spending on the experimental drug, you should be running marathons."

"I'm sorry it's so expensive. I don't have to get it."

"No, no. It's working a little. I'm just frustrated."

Her eyes welled up.

I reached for her hand. "I'm a jerk. Sorry. I can't imagine how frustrated you must be."

Her lip quivered. "Sometimes . . ."

"Everything is going to be fine; we'll get through this together."

She closed her eyes. Tears leaked out. I climbed onto the bed, spooned her, and closed my eyes.

"Mom? Dad? Is everything all right?"

I propped myself on an elbow. "Yeah, Mom had a headache, and I was beat. We fell asleep."

"Are you okay, Mom?"

"Yes, my headache's gone. I think the nap helped."

I swung my legs off the bed. "Jessie, get the True Foods menu. Mom likes it there; we'll order something to pick up."

"Yummy, I'm starved."

When Jessie left, I said, "You feel okay?"

"Yes, the headache is ten times better."

"You see, I still got it."

She shook her head and got up. I could tell she was feeling better by the way she moved. It was a relief, but the roller-coaster ride was getting old.

<hr>

I HUNG around the house to make sure Mary Ann was still feeling good. She pushed herself to get in the pool. She did half the number of laps, but it meant she was recovering. I kissed her and headed to Fort Myers.

Derrick called as I hit Corkscrew Road. He was unable to locate a next of kin for Melissa Wright. Her parents were dead, and she was an only child. I asked him to contact the Hyatt House to see if they knew what state she may have emigrated from and to look for aunts and uncles.

The door behind me hadn't closed, but a salesgirl was already in motion. She flashed a wide smile. "Welcome to MINI Cooper of Fort Myers. Are you interested in a particular model?"

"I'm here to see Bobby Ryan."

"Oh, I'll get him. Can I tell him who you are?"

"Frank Luca."

As I waited, I couldn't decide whether I liked the wide racing stripes running up the hood of a red convertible. The cars were cute but small. I wouldn't want Jessie tooling around in one.

Ryan was tall and handsome. He stuck out his hand. "Mr. Luca?" He searched my face as we shook. "I'm sorry, but were we working on a car?"

I lowered my voice. "I'm with the Collier County Sheriff's Office. I'm here about Melissa Wright."

"Melissa? Did something happen to her?"

"Can we talk outside?"

We stepped into the parking lot. "What's going on?"

"You don't know?"

"Know what?"

The way his eyebrows rose, had me questioning his sincerity. "Melissa Wright was found murdered."

"Oh my God. Where? How?"

"Her body was discovered in the Cocohatchee Creek Preserve."

"Coco what?"

"Cocohatchee Creek. It's a park off Veteran's Park Drive."

"What happened to her?"

"She died of stab wounds."

He shook his head. "That's terrible. Who the hell did this?"

"I was hoping you had some ideas."

"I can't think straight. Right now, I'm, I'm in shock."

"What was the nature of your relationship with Ms. Wright?"

He shrugged. "We were friends."

"Romantically involved?"

His brown eyes darted around. "Look, I'm married. It's over, but my wife can't find out about it."

He should have thought of that before breaking his vows. "We'll keep the information confidential. When is the last time you saw her?"

"Oh, I don't know. A couple of weeks or so."

I took that to mean no more than five days. "How long did you know her?"

"Around a year or two."

"When did the relationship end?"

"About a month ago."

"Did she have family in the area?"

"Not that I know of."

"Where was she from?"

"Michigan. Grand Rapids, I'm pretty sure."

"Friends?"

"She kind of kept to herself."

"You never double-dated?"

He face scrunched up. "No. We didn't do stuff like that."

I knew the stuff they did do. "She had to mention someone. Tell me."

"She used to go to that bar up the street from her house, Alice Sweetwater's. Never got the name though."

"How often did she go there?"

"I don't know. She'd grab something to eat there. She liked the outside bar area."

"Did you go with her?"

"No. Never."

"Who do you know could have done this to her?"

"I don't know. Honestly, I'm just trying to process this."

"I understand. If you think of anything, no matter how small, here's my card."

"I will. And if you need a MINI Cooper . . ."

"They're nice, but not for me."

"You'd be surprised. They're great cars, a lot of fun to drive."

"How long you been working here?"

"Six years."

"Where'd you move from?"

"Nowhere. I was born in Estero."

A Southwest Florida native, and he didn't know how to pronounce Cocohatchee?

4

───────

The bar by Wright's house was about as far south as you could get from Fort Myers. I checked the picture I'd taken of Jonathan Ong's business card. He worked for the Willis Group, a boutique realty outfit. Their Mercato office would break up the drive. I made an appointment.

A heavy flow of traffic weaved its way through Mercato. I never imagined having to circle around looking for a place to park. After passing one at the far end of Whole Foods, I created a parking space and put credentials on the dash.

The Willis Group worked out of a storefront next to Design West. The interior-design firm was the place to go—if you had twenty thousand for a sofa. I glanced at the pictures of homes for sale hanging in the Realtor's window. Half of them had Sold badges on them.

Wondering how long it took them to sell, I walked in. A perky saleswoman went to a bank of private offices, and Jonathan Ong appeared. He was wearing a dark blue suit with pencil legs. It was trendy but looked too small.

His jet-black hair had just been cut. "Mr. Luca. How can I assist you today?"

His smile collapsed when I introduced myself. "The sheriff's office? Oh, is this about Mrs. Morrow's eviction?"

"No. Melissa Wright."

"I'd appreciate some help. I don't know who that is."

"She had your business card in her wallet."

His smile came back. "I'm a Realtor. We're always handing out cards. There's nothing to it."

"She was found murdered yesterday."

"Oh my God. Really?"

"Yes. I need to know how she came upon your card."

"I didn't have anything to do with whatever happened."

Taking out my phone, I showed him a picture of Wright. "Do you recognize her?"

"Hmmm. She looks familiar. Where does she live?"

"On Francis Avenue by the—"

"Oh, now I know. She's renting that house. Sally Johnson owns it and contacted me about selling it. I went there a week ago to preview it for her. It's not really the type of property our firm handles."

"You met Ms. Wright there?"

"Yes. She was very nice and asked for help finding a rental, but we're not really into doing rentals. It's just not worth the time."

"Was anyone else there?"

"No, just her."

"And what day was this?"

"I think it was Tuesday but let me check." He dug out his phone to confirm. I took down the information for the owner of the home and left.

Alice Sweetwater's parking lot was half full. Maybe it was the pink flamingo in the middle of their sign, but Jimmy Buffet popped into my head as I climbed the stairs to the eatery.

A long oak bar dominated the brightly lit room. An old-fashioned cash register and the mirrored backdrop shifted the feel from 'Margaritaville' to a Colorado mining town. It didn't last long; my eyes settled on a marlin hanging over the kitchen's entrance.

The bartender was chatting with two men holding beers. I signaled, and he slid over. "What can I getcha?"

Explaining, I showed him a picture of Wright. "You know this woman?"

"Yeah, she comes in from time to time, but she sits outside. We got a bar and some high-tops out back."

"She come alone?"

"I think so. Why?"

"Is someone manning the bar outside?"

"Yeah, Philly's back there."

It was another long bar, this one covered by a cranberry canopy. Five guys, all smoking, sat at the far end. A fan behind the bar was blowing the smoke my way. I stepped back as the potbellied bartender waddled over. "What'll you have?"

I flashed my badge and passed him my phone. "Looking for information on this woman."

"Oh yeah, that's Mary or something. She comes in every now and then. Sits over there all the time." He pointed to a corner table with a leaning blue umbrella.

"She come with anyone?"

"I don't think so, but ask Sheila; she's the server." As if on cue, the door swung open, and a woman with platinum hair and two platefuls of food appeared. "Sheila, this cop needs to talk to you."

"One second, hon." She set the plates down. Eyeglasses swinging from a beaded chain around her neck, she came over. "What can I do for you, hon?"

Showing her the photo, I said, "This is Melissa Wright. She comes in a lot, doesn't she?"

"She's pretty regular. Nice gal."

"She ever come in with a friend?"

"Not that I know."

"Any men?"

"No, but I know she was tangled up with somebody married."

"And how do you know this?"

"She was down one night, maybe three months ago. Melissa's a one-and-done girl, and that night she had three drinks."

"Why was that?"

"It was slow that night, and you know, us girls, we gotta stick together."

"She tell you the name of this man?"

"Nah. It didn't matter; they're all the same. They promise you champagne, but it never comes. It's always tap water."

I had to think about that, silently repeating to remember it. "She ever mention any friends?"

"She worked downtown at the Hyatt. Check with them."

"And you're certain she never came in with anyone?"

"Yep."

"Any time she had an argument with someone?"

"No. She wasn't the type. Melissa was sweet. That's why that guy was walking all over her."

"You know of anyone that would do harm to her?"

Her eyes widened. "What happened? Don't tell me somebody did something to her."

I delivered the bad news and thanked her.

On the way out, I stopped to read a quote from Virginia Wolfe: "One cannot think well, love well, sleep well, if one has not dined well." As someone who got grumpy when hungry, Wolfe had a point.

5

———

IT WASN'T EASY RESISTING THE URGE TO CALL BILOTTI. I made a deal with myself as I drove to the office; if he didn't call by the time I got there, I'd call. It took me twenty minutes to get to the municipal complex on Airport Pulling Road.

Parking, my cell rang. "Hey, Doc. What's going on?"

"Sorry it took so long. But a transformer blew, and the—"

Though I didn't like the expression, it tumbled out of my mouth. "No problem. What do you have?"

"Ms. Wright was pregnant. It was early. I'd estimate it at approximately twelve to fourteen weeks."

"Sorry to hear this. What else?"

"She had three stab wounds, one of which penetrated her right ventricle. She couldn't have lasted more than an hour, and the fetus likely died soon afterward."

"Bastard. The weapon, was it a knife?"

"Yes. It appears to be one with a serrated edge, with a blade approximately eight inches in length."

"Any idea of the killer's height?"

"Assuming the stabbing occurred while the victim was standing, I'd put him or her at five foot six to ten."

"Time of death?"

"Based on stomach contents, I'd place the time of death, somewhere in the two thirty to five a.m. range on January sixteenth."

"Was she killed at Cocohatchee Park?"

"I believe so. But I agree on the staging."

Score one for Luca. "Anything else?"

"No drugs or alcohol in the initial screening, but we're running a full tox panel."

"Any fibers or hairs that could have been left by the killer?"

"Nothing, except the victim had blood on the inside of her forearm. It doesn't match the wound patterns. It could be when the attacker withdrew the knife, droplets of blood became airborne."

"Any matter under her fingernails?"

"They appear to have been trimmed recently, but we scraped, and it's with the lab."

"Was she sexually assaulted?"

"No, but based upon minor abrasions, I'd estimate she had intercourse within forty-eight hours before her death."

"That might help."

"I'm going to transcribe the autopsy, and I'll have the preliminary report to you as soon as I can."

I breezed into the office. "Just spoke to Bilotti. Wright was pregnant."

Derrick said, "Damn. That's sickening."

"We begin with her male friends. A waitress at a bar she went to said she was dating a married man."

"Bobby Ryan is married."

"He sure is. And that's where we're going to start."

"What did you think of him?"

"Tough to say; he's a sales guy. One thing was, he was

born down here but made like he didn't know how to pronounce Cocohatchee."

"I don't know, Frank. Half the people I run into never say Immokalee the right way. Indian names are tough."

"I don't buy it, not a local." I reached for my ringing desk phone. "Homicide, Detective Luca."

"Frank, it's Eddie. Somebody called in a body at Baker Park. An officer patrolling Bayfront responded, and confirmed it's a female, mid-thirties, by the kayak rack."

"Did it look like it was staged?"

"They didn't say."

"All right, we're on the way. Tell them to shut down the park."

I slid behind the wheel and said to Derrick, "You ever been to Baker Park?"

"No, we've been meaning to go. You?"

"Been a couple of times. It's a nice place, with trails and water access."

"Maybe we'll take our bikes. I heard the Baker family donated a couple of million to get things moving."

"Must be nice to have that kind of dough."

"They really throw it around, getting their name on every-thing, like the hospital, but it's for good causes."

Why couldn't they send some my way? Wasn't paying two grand for an experimental drug a worthy cause? "Leaving a legacy must be important to them."

"Or seeing their name in public."

"We all need recognition, but it seems overdone."

A marked car blocked the entrance to Baker Park. He moved up, and we scooted up a long driveway, parking by the main building. I'd remembered a kayak rack to right, but an officer led us a quarter of a mile, on a concrete path that changed into an elevated boardwalk.

The sun roasted my back. Rounding a turn, the Gordon River stretched out on both sides of the walkway. A second officer was standing guard at an opening, just before the river's western bank.

"She's down below."

We donned gloves and booties and took the short staircase. I stuck my hand out to stop Derrick and took in the area. The body wasn't visible. A picnic table was to the left, and just beyond it, a ramp for launching kayaks and paddleboards. The access was via a path that disappeared behind a stand of mangrove bushes.

Blocking part of the view was a rack filled with yellow kayaks. "All right. Let's see what we have."

Sitting up, the body leaned against the rack's waterfront side. It was hidden from the main path, but anyone using the ramp or on the river would see it. It was a curious detail, leading me to believe she was placed there at night.

The body's long, dirty-blonde hair was tousled, obscuring her left eye. A large, bloodstain marred the chest area of her pink, satiny blouse. My eyes drifted to her lap. "She's got another eyeglass case."

6

———————

Sheriff Remin didn't disappoint me. He made no attempt to smile. Grunting, he thrust a chin toward a chair.

"It's not good news, sir. We have a serial killer on our hands."

"Are you certain?"

"Yes. He or she left another note, with the 'number two' in another eyeglass case."

"It could be a copycat."

"Unless there's been a leak, we never released the fact the killer was numbering his victims."

The lines in Remin's forehead deepened.

"The MO is the same, and I spoke to Dr. Bilotti. He needs to do the autopsy but believes the same kind of knife was used, and—"

"All right. All right. We need to shut this down, ASAP. I don't want media attention here. They get ahold of this, and this place will be a ghost town."

"We'll be as discreet as possible. But it's going to get out. The new victim was Dr. Sarah Bigham. She had a practice on Piper Boulevard and was well known. Bilotti knew her."

"We need to identify the link between these women."

"We're working on it."

"I hope we don't have someone indiscriminately killing people."

"That makes two of us, sir."

Connections were as important as physical evidence in solving a homicide. They provided a road map leading to the killer. Random killings were more challenging to figure out.

"What do you have in the way of persons of interest?"

We didn't have anything, and after Remin ran away with what I had developed in the Pine Ridge Lake case, I was reluctant to share hard data. "It's early, sir. As soon as I have something, you'll be the first to know."

"I'm going to need something for the press release. Something hopeful, a message instilling confidence."

It didn't bother me one bit to see him uncomfortable. I could have told him I was heading to the doctor's home after this chat but said, "We'll do our best."

"You need additional resources, come to me."

No matter how many times I drove along Gulf Shore Boulevard, the homes always impressed me. It was the reason people believed only the super rich lived in Naples. I called it the Bentley factor. People noticed a Bentley or Ferrari when they saw one but not the scores of Toyotas on the road.

I turned onto Third Avenue South. Dr. Sarah Bigham lived by the beach and restaurant-lined Fifth Avenue. The leafy neighborhood was called Olde Naples and was expensive.

A patrol car sat in the driveway of a one-story structure painted blue, with a detached garage. It was a modest, older home and not yet renovated. The homes on either side had their storm shutters down. It had nothing to do with a hurricane; their owners were out of town.

Looking across the street, I was relieved to see trash cans by the curb. I started up the driveway, eyes settling on a sign stuck in her lawn. The doctor had been selling her house. I stopped short. The Realtor was Stephen Ong.

Was it "the" connection or "a" connection? Ong had claimed the passing of his business card was purely routine. We hadn't followed up with the owner of the house Wright had been living in. It didn't appear important. Ong's story was believable. But was it a mistake that led to the doctor's murder?

Pulling my phone out, I called Derrick. "I'm at Dr. Bigham's house, and it's up for sale."

"Don't tell me Ong is the Realtor."

"He sure is."

"Coincidence or not?"

He knew I didn't believe in coincidences. "Get ahold of the owner where Wright lived. I think it's a Mrs. Johnson. Check the murder book; it's in there. See if she asked Ong to take a look at the house."

"Got it."

"And dig into Dr. Bigham. We need background on her."

"I'm on it."

I signed in, put gloves on, and found the right key from the doctor's pocketbook. The house was too dark, with low ceilings and a chopped-up floor plan. It was built in the sixties, when Naples was a sleepy village and didn't feel like Florida to me.

Dr. Bigham was a busy woman, excusing the lack of housekeeping, but I wondered if there was a clue hidden in the messy state of her home. Was the housing market so hot that home buyers were willing to look past it? Or was this livable home being sold as a teardown?

The kitchen sink had a couple of days of dishes. I pulled open drawers, finding the junk drawer on the third try.

Scooping out a handful, I sorted through rubber bands, pens, and a stack of coupons. How many Bed Bath & Beyond coupons did anyone need?

I moved to the master bedroom. An unmade poster bed dominated the room. The drawer in her nightstand was packed with a Bible, tissues, a bottle of Excedrin, an oral retainer, and at the back, a can of pepper spray.

Like a gym membership, if all you did was buy a deterrent, you got nothing from it but the feeling you'd taken action.

The closet was jammed with clothes, none male.

Stephen Ong kept popping into my head. I decided to send an experienced team in for a thorough search and went into a bedroom serving as the doctor's office. Two large pictures caught my attention. One was a skeletal depiction and the other a poster identifying every muscle in the human body.

I looked at a certificate hanging between them. It was a medical degree Bigham had earned fourteen years ago. Approaching a dark wood desk stacked with files, I tripped on the edge of an area rug. Steadying myself, I pushed the burgundy leather chair aside and rummaged through the drawers.

Nothing was obvious, but it never was. I was preoccupied and that wasn't good. I took a deep breath and tried to identify why. It wasn't Ong. We'd work that. Trying to pin it down, I headed out of the den.

A door to the right of the family room caught my attention. It led outside, to a short path connected to the garage. I opened the garage door and stopped dead in my tracks.

7

MIND RACING, I HOPPED IN MY CAR AND SAT THERE. WHAT were the odds? MINI Coopers were around, but they weren't common. I Googled how many were sold each year. It was lower than I thought, about ten thousand a year of their two-door model in the entire country.

Dr. Bigham's was a 2019, and the license plate holder advertised MINI of Fort Myers. It didn't matter if Bobby Ryan was the salesperson or not. The opportunity to meet was solid. The doctor wasn't married. She was a couple of years older than Ryan. I couldn't see her dating him, but what did I know about attraction?

I put the car in gear and drove off. We had two men who knew both women. It was time to dig in and see which one it was. The decision was who to start with. Tossing around the pros and cons, my cell rang. It was Bilotti.

"Hey, Doc. You have something on Dr. Bigham?"

"I didn't even start yet. It's hard to believe she was killed so brutally."

"She was a nice lady?"

"Only met her a couple of times. But I liked her."

"Was she any good?"

"She's gone, Frank."

"It might help the investigation."

"Let's just say there are better practitioners in the area."

"Did she get in any trouble, medically?"

"No. Nothing like that. I realize expectations for doctors are higher than most, but the reality is there are good doctors and others less so."

"Got it. Why'd you call?"

"Concerning Melissa Wright. The blood on her arm, turned about to be hers."

"Damn."

"The lab completed the DNA workup on the fetus. When you identify a suspect, it could be related to a motive."

"Don't you know the pay is a lot lower for detectives?"

Bilotti chuckled. "After all the interfering you do, I thought you'd appreciate the reciprocity."

It would have been too easy to have the killer's blood. I knew the best plans went awry when violence erupted, but whoever was behind these deaths was careful. They left a clue, but it was a conscious choice. The eyeglass case was more taunt than lead.

The pregnancy could be something, but we'd need to get DNA samples from possible fathers. At this point, we had Ryan and Ong as persons of interest. Ryan was married; if he wasn't using protection, he was reckless, but men thought with their willies, not their heads when it came to sex.

Turning into the parking lot, I blew off Derrick's call. I'd be in the office in two minutes. A flash of lightning broke up a darkening sky. Out of reflex, I counted the seconds waiting for thunder. My hand reached for the doorknob as a crack of thunder sounded. It'd been five seconds. The lightning was a mile away.

One foot in doorway, Derrick jumped up. "Dr. Bigham had a restraining order on a Micky Carbo."

"When was this?"

"A year ago."

"He have a record?"

"Assault, but back in 2010."

"Still, he's got a temper and is violent."

"What do you want to do?"

I told him about the MINI Cooper. "We start with Ryan."

"Yeah, and the landlord—the lady, Johnson—she confirmed asking Ong to look at the house."

"That doesn't mean much. He met Wright. Anything could have happened from there."

"He could have wanted something out of her she wasn't willing to give."

"Seen that movie too many times. Look, you develop what you can on this Carbo character. I'm heading back up to Fort Myers to talk to Ryan."

Standing next to a white convertible, Ryan was chatting with a customer. He opened the driver's door. The woman looked inside and shook her head. "It's nice, but I don't need a special interior; it's too expensive."

"I have a used one coming in on a trade. It's a real beauty, only twenty thousand miles. Let me run some numbers on it."

"I don't know . . ."

"When can you bring the Audi in for an appraisal?"

"Maybe Monday."

"Great. I'll see you then."

Smiling, he shook her hand. She headed for the door and Ryan turned around. His shoulders sagged when he saw me. He rebounded quickly. "You change your mind about a MINI?"

"Maybe. There's a red one outside." I headed for the door and Ryan followed.

The door swung closed. "You never gave me your business card."

He pulled one out of his chest pocket. "Here you go."

"Thanks."

"You liked the red one?"

"Maybe. But what about Dr. Sarah Bigham."

His face darkened. "I heard what happened. What a shame."

"What happened?"

"She was murdered, wasn't she?"

"Yes. How did you know her?"

"She was a customer, bought a Cooper S. Electric Blue, loaded with options."

"How long ago?"

"Gee, about a year or maybe more. I can check."

"When is the last time you saw her?"

"Not for ages."

"Were you and her in any kind of relationship?"

"What do you mean?"

"Were you screwing her?"

"Me?"

"Yeah, you."

"I'm married."

"You were married when you were with Melissa Wright, weren't you?"

"Yeah, but—"

"Speaking of Melissa, did you know she was pregnant?"

"She was? I-I didn't know."

"Are you the father?"

"No."

"You willing to give a DNA sample for comparison?"

"DNA? What for?"

"To see if you're the father."

"I told you, I'm not."

"How do you know?"

"She was on birth control pills."

"They're not a hundred percent effective. Will you give us your DNA?"

"Hey, I don't like the direction you're going in. It feels like you're trying to frame me for her murder. I didn't do anything."

"Then you have nothing to fear."

"You know what? I'm done talking. I think I need a lawyer."

I felt he did too. Still holding the business card he gave me by a corner, I slipped it into a plastic evidence bag. It wasn't ideal but he'd left his touch DNA on it, and we'd find out if he was the father of Melissa's dead baby.

8

———————

THE SIGN SAID, PARADISE PERFECTED. IT WAS A CATCHY phrase, but the reality was, living in Naples Square would cost you at least two million. The collection of buildings were in the coastal contemporary style and close to Fifth Avenue. They were calling it downtown, but though nice, the feel wasn't anything like Old Naples.

Wondering if Stephen Ong had gotten in early or received a discount for bringing buyers in, I hit his bell. Wearing blue slippers and a silk robe, the Realtor opened the door. He looked at my shoes for a long second before saying, "Come in, Detective."

"Nice place."

"It's the new Naples. Contemporary, yet elegant."

He forgot overpriced. "Good location, but is it quiet here?"

"Absolutely. With impact windows, you don't hear anything."

Unless you were sitting on your lanai. "They do the trick."

I followed him into the kitchen. White on white. The backsplash had a slight gray tint to it, and the tile was laid in a herringbone pattern.

Nothing marred the quartz countertops, except a stainless-steel, commercial espresso machine. He was either a minimalist or a neat freak. Six stools were set up around the island, and steps away was a glass-topped table with seating for eight.

I couldn't imagine Ong hosting that many people without taking a Valium. He pulled out a stool, and I took one a seat away, saying, "You knew Dr. Bigham?"

Ong said, "I'm starting to think I'm bad luck or something."

The question wasn't about luck. "When did you first meet Dr. Bigham?"

"At an open house. It was for Realtors; I don't do the public type any longer."

The way he said public, was odd. If he didn't like people, he was in the wrong business. "Where and when?"

"About five to six months ago. I had a listing to die for on Seventh, and she wandered in. I told her it was for Realtors only, but she was so nice, I gave her a quick tour."

"And from there?"

"She was checking the market out before deciding whether to list her house. It was a savvy move on her part."

"Where was she going to move to?"

"She wanted something more secure. More than just a gated community but something with restricted access and cameras in the public areas."

"Did she have a particular concern about her safety?"

"Something seemed to be bothering her."

"Can you be more specific?"

"I wish I could, but she was a private person."

"Did she mention a concern about someone?"

"Nothing specific, but anytime we were together, she seemed to be looking over her shoulder, if you know what I mean."

"As if to see if it was safe?"

"Exactly. Even when we went to view a listing, she'd be hesitant to wander around. I like to leave a client to their own discovery of a property, but she'd want me to go through a home with her."

Bigham was a single woman. In my view, she was prudent. But Naples was a safe place to live.

"Did she ever mention a Micky Carbo?"

He closed his eyes for a second. "No. The name doesn't ring a bell."

"Where were you Monday night and yesterday morning?"

"Me?"

"Yes."

"That was Tuesday, right?"

He was buying time. "Yes."

"Oh, I was at a friend's house for dinner. Then I came home."

"Who's the friend?"

"You don't believe me?"

"Belief has nothing to do with it. Tell me who you were with."

"Sal Takeya."

I took down his contact information. "And Wednesday morning?"

"I was at work."

"What time did you get in?"

"Around nine. You're treating me like a suspect or something. It's unbelievable."

"I'm sorry, Mr. Ong, but I have to do my job."

"I guess so."

"Last question, why did you take the listing on her house?"

"What do you mean? Her house was a knockdown, in a great location, and she would have to buy something." He smiled.

I'd check his alibi, and see if his smile had staying power.

FINISHED WRITING A REPORT, I hit print, and went to the printer. Derrick was on the phone with the Plain City Ohio Police Department. Mickey Carbo had moved there after serving nine months for assault and battery. He lived in Ohio for two years before returning to Florida.

I picked up the sheets of warm paper as Derrick hung up. "They have anything on Carbo?"

"Looks like the entire family are troublemakers. Carbo got into two fights while he was there. He wasn't arrested, but his brother and father were."

"Like father, like son."

"Any weapons involved?"

"No."

"Women involved?"

"Doesn't seem to be, though it could have been over a woman."

"We need to see if he has an alibi."

"You want to go see him?"

"Not right now. But soon."

"You want to see where it goes with Ryan and Ong first?"

"Somewhat, but we can't wait; there's a killer out there. Get Sullivan to keep eyes on him."

"Okay."

"And what's going on with Bigham's phone records?"

"Judge Williams signed the warrant, and I forwarded it to Verizon."

"Stay on them. You never know what might show up."

"I'm the rash that won't go away."

I stood up. "And push the lab. Remin said he was going to tell them processing Ryan's DNA was a priority."

"I got it. Where are you going?"

"Something about Ong is bothering me. He's hiding something."

I WEAVED my way through the window shoppers and pushed through a door. The perky woman greeted me again. She smiled. "Welcome to the Willis Group."

I flashed my badge, and her smile disappeared. "Is Stephen Ong in?"

"No, he's doing a photo shoot."

"Who is the office manager?"

"We don't really have one."

"Who keeps track of who is working when?"

"We're flexible. Agents can work when they need to."

"You don't monitor when they work?"

"No. Oh, except when you work the floor. There has to be an agent here when we're open."

"Who worked the floor Tuesday?"

"I did. I do most times. I'm the rookie."

"What time were you here?"

"I always get in at eight thirty."

"Was Stephen Ong here?"

"No. He came in just after noon."

"Are you sure?"

"Yes. He bought me a salad from Bravo, for lunch, like, ten minutes after he got here."

9

———

Hustling to the car, I pulled my vibrating phone out. It was Derrick. "Was just going to call you."

"Ryan's DNA matches the Wright fetus."

I stopped in front of the Narrative Coffee Shop. "The last thing a married man needs is a baby with another woman."

"Bingo. Didn't he say she was on birth control?"

"He sure did. It's possible Wright stopped taking it to trap him in a relationship—"

"And he got pissed and killed her."

"It's happened before."

"It takes a heartless bastard to do something like that."

I said, "I didn't figure Ryan for that. I thought he could've lost it when he found out someone else impregnated her."

"Jealousy can be deadly."

"Yeah, did forensics finish up with Bigham's house?"

"They had a problem with the van. It broke down on Collier Boulevard."

"You kidding me?"

"They're still down there."

"I'm going to swing by. Call Ryan and get him in tomorrow. He said he wants a lawyer; let's see where that goes."

A WHITE VAN blocked the driveway. I walked up to it. A placard from the Collier County Sheriff's Office was sitting on the dash. It was a rental.

The door to the garage was open. I headed for it. A tech in protective gear was hunched over the trunk. "Hey, how's it going?"

"Frank. How are you?"

"Hoping you're going to make my day."

"We collected several fibers and three different hair samples out of the interior."

"That's it?"

"Car was clean. The dealer must have detailed it when it was serviced."

"It was serviced?"

"Yes, the receipt was in the glove box."

"From MINI of Fort Myers?"

"Yes."

"When?"

"Monday."

"I need to see it."

"The receipt?"

"Yes."

The tech grunted. "All right." He went to the van and unlocked the rear doors. Reaching into a satchel, he came out with a plastic bag. Using tongs, he lifted the document out. "Don't touch it."

"I won't." I leaned in. It was a ten-thousand-mile service checkup. An oil change, new wipers, and tire rotation. I looked at the signature. It was a scribble, but it wasn't Dr. Bigham's name.

Pulling my phone out, I said, "Hold it steady. I want to grab a picture of this."

I DIDN'T REALIZE I was whistling as I came into the house. Mary Ann was transferring clothes from the washing machine to the dryer. "Somebody's in a good mood."

"Let me help you."

"It's okay. I'm almost done."

"You're feeling good?"

She closed the door and hit the button. "The best in over a week."

As I followed her down the hallway, she said, "How was your day?"

"Good. Can't say I'm surprised, but DNA confirmed Ryan fathered the Wright fetus."

She flicked on the TV. "That's terrible. You think he killed her and his own baby?"

"It's looking like that."

The news was on. It was more weather talk. "You think he's the one who also killed the doctor?"

"I'm hoping we find out tomorrow. Ryan and his mouthpiece are coming in. I want to see him explain—"

She pointed to the TV. "Look, that's his lawyer."

It was Leo Feldman. Paunchy and balding, the man was an effective defense lawyer. Remin had wanted to keep the case as quiet as possible, but Feldman was looking to turn it around on us.

"It's a sad day for Collier County when, yet again, one of its citizens is singled out for questioning without cause."

Yet again? "What the hell is—"

"Shush."

Feldman continued, "The sheriff's office has two unfortunate deaths on its hands, and instead of conducting a thorough investigation, they're harassing my client. Mr. Ryan is a hard-working member of the community with nothing more than a parking ticket in his past."

"That's bullshit."

The broadcast switched to the anchor. "In response to our interview with Mr. Feldman, the Collier County Sheriff's Office issued the following statement: 'It is the duty of this office to conduct a thorough investigation of any crime committed in our jurisdiction. Contrary to the belief of certain members of the community, that's exactly what we are in engaged in. As such, we'll continue to interview scores of individuals as we seek to apprehend the person or persons responsible for these heinous murders.'"

Mary Ann said, "Wow. The sheriff isn't backing down."

"He must have grown a backbone in the last couple of hours."

"He's angry about what Feldman is trying to do with his grandstanding."

"I hate it when the press gets involved."

"You can't have it both ways."

"What's that supposed to mean?"

"You go to the press to get the word out when you need help identifying someone, don't you?"

I hated it when she threw things like that in my face. "Yeah, but that's different."

She smiled. "It's not, but I'm going to let it go."

If I was going to win, I wanted it to be a real win, but I remembered what Dr. Bruno had taught me and said, "Do people really think we focus on people without reason?

Someone has killed two women, and Ryan is linked to both of them."

"You have to do what you know how to, Frank. Don't let anything distract you."

"Trust, me. I'm going to stay focused." I said it with more conviction than I felt.

10

———

I CHECKED THE VIDEO FEED. FELDMAN AND RYAN WERE IN the interview room. I smiled when the lawyer used his handkerchief to mop his brow. I'd raised the thermostat to a toasty seventy-nine.

Derrick limped back from the bathroom and said, "You ready?"

"After the way he talked about the department, let him sweat for another fifteen."

Derrick winced when he shook his head. "You don't like this guy, do you?"

"He's actually a pretty good lawyer. But he crossed a line by opening his mouth."

"Wonder if he thinks Ryan is guilty."

"He's a defense lawyer. It doesn't matter if he was caught in the act—it's deny, deny, deny."

"A hundred percent."

"How you feeling?"

"Not the greatest. Doctor thinks it could be some kind of nerve damage from the shooting."

"Strange it's showing up now."

He exhaled. "I've had weird stuff going on every now and then."

"Like what?"

"Pinching and numbness."

"Geez. Why didn't you say anything?"

"They said I had to live with it. If I made a big deal, they wouldn't let me come back to work."

I'd felt guilty he'd gotten shot, and the peace I made with it just got machine-gunned. "I want you to take it easy."

"Stop with that, we have serial killer to nail."

"You have to tell me when you're not up to it. We'll figure out how to cover things. Can you do that?"

"I will. Come on, let's get this going."

I squeezed his shoulder. "I got your back, you know that, right?"

He put his hand on top of mine. "I got yours."

"Amen. Let's have some fun here."

I swung the door open. "Gentlemen . . . Wow, it's warm in here. Let me adjust the thermostat."

Feldman was playing with his phone when I stepped back in. Ryan was scowling and avoided looking at me. I set my folder on the table, and Derrick recited the formalities.

I said, "Thank you for coming in today. Mr. Ryan, how did you know Melissa Wright?"

"I told you before."

"Please answer the question."

"We were in a relationship."

"A sexual one?"

"Yes."

"How did you meet her?"

"At Publix."

"You picked up a little something extra?"

Feldman said, "Detective Luca."

"Sorry, that wasn't necessary. Mr. Ryan, are you married?"

"You know I am."

"How long were you and Ms. Wright together?"

"About a year, maybe longer."

"And was it ongoing?"

"No. It ended."

"When?"

"About a couple of weeks ago."

"Right before her murder?"

"It had nothing to do with what happened to her."

"In our first conversation, you claimed to be unaware that Ms. Wright was pregnant."

"That's right."

"You sure you want to stick with that answer?"

"My client denied knowledge of Ms. Wright's pregnancy."

"Did you and Ms. Wright use birth control?"

"I told you, she was on the pill."

"Do you know who the father of the baby she was carrying was?"

"No idea."

I smiled. "Well, it's you, Mr. Ryan."

"What? That's impossible."

"You know, there's a saying I love: 'Impossible is an opinion.'"

Feldman said, "Is this a theory, or do you have evidence?"

"His DNA matches the fetus."

"My DNA, how'd you get that? I told you I wouldn't give you a sample."

"You gave me a business card. Touch DNA is a wonderful thing."

Ryan's face reddened.

Feldman said, "Fathering a child, even the one in this unfortunate case, doesn't prove anything."

"True, but it does point to motive. Mr. Ryan is a married man having an affair. Ms. Wright wanted more, and a baby was the leverage she used to trap him. Mr. Ryan objected and killed her to keep his relationship and the baby a secret."

"Detective Luca, that makes for a nice story, but you'll need more than an imagination to get into a courtroom."

"We'll get it."

"If that's all you have, we'd like to terminate this interview."

"Not yet, Mr. Feldman. I'd like to ask your client about another murder victim, Dr. Sylvia Bigham."

"Oh, come on. You're going to try and frame me for that?"

"How did you know Dr. Bigham?"

"I sold her a car."

"At MINI of Fort Myers?"

"Yes."

"When was the last time you saw Dr. Bigham?"

"A long while ago, at least six months."

"Are you sure?"

"Yeah, what about it?"

I flipped open the file and picked up a sheet of paper. "This says otherwise."

"What bullshit you going to pull now?"

I smiled. "A service receipt from your employer."

"What? Let me see that?"

He reached for it and I pulled it back.

"May I examine the document?"

I handed it to Feldman. "It's for the service done on Dr. Bigham's car. You'll note the signature; it's your client's."

"Hey, wait a minute. I was just doing her a favor. She was busy. I dropped off her car to make it easy."

"You saw the doctor just a day or so before she was found murdered."

Derrick said, "Detective Luca doesn't believe in coincidences."

"Why did you lie?"

"Hey, I told you the truth. I just did her a favor. Us sales guys do this all the time; it's customer service."

"Do you like to kayak, Mr. Ryan?"

"Kayaking? What—"

"Answer the question."

"Yeah, I go. What? I'm not allowed to have fun?"

"You kayak at Baker Park?"

"Hey, wait a minute, I wasn't there." He turned to Feldman. "They're trying to frame me. You got to do something."

"Detective Luca, using someone's leisure activities is a stretch."

"What's a stretch, Counselor, is your client's explanations as to how he not only knew both women but saw them shortly before they were found murdered."

11

DERRICK WAS WRITING A REQUEST FOR RYAN'S PHONE records while I was putting the finishing touches on a search warrant for the car salesman's home. My desk phone rang: "Homicide, Detective Luca."

"Good morning, Detective. This is Annie Bryant from the *Naples Daily News*."

"Morning, ma'am. What can I do for you?"

"We're covering the serial killer murders. You're leading the investigation, and we'd like to confirm an arrest is going to be made."

"I can't comment on an ongoing inquiry."

"So, it's true. Bobby Ryan is the killer."

"I didn't say that. This office doesn't discuss active cases. Period."

"But you brought him in."

"We talk to a lot of people, in every case."

"Our sources tell us you have overwhelming evidence."

Instead of saying, 'if we did, he'd be behind bars,' I said, "Have a good day, ma'am."

I slammed the receiver down. "Somebody is leaking to the press."

Derrick pointed to the ceiling. "It had to come from upstairs. There's a lot of pressure on Remin."

I hit the print icon and said, "He took the damn job."

"He knows we're close."

I grabbed the warrant request and said, "I'm going to run this up. Remin said Judge Williams was going to sign it."

WE TURNED onto Wiggins Pass and headed east. Derrick rounded the turn onto Mimosa Court, and I said, "Are you kidding me?"

Three vans, emblazoned with the logos of their respective channels, were parked across from Ryan's house.

"They're here before us. Somebody tipped them off."

As Derrick pulled to the curb, my gaze went to the Ryan house. It was a small, one-story block house, painted yellow with blue trim. Frog statues on lily pads lined the walkway.

I got out as four officers poured out of the patrol cars. Starting for the door, I was barraged by a chorus of questions from reporters. "Step back, or we'll have you arrested for obstruction."

Head wagging, a woman was standing there, looking out from a bay window. Twenty feet away, I could see the disgust on her face.

"Derrick, give me a minute to talk to the wife. Tell everybody to hang back until I say."

Finger about to hit the bell, the door swung open. "Mrs. Ryan?"

She pulled her lips in and nodded. "What's going on?"

"I'm Detective Luca. Is your husband, Bobby Ryan, home?"

She scoffed, "No way. He thinks he can cheat on me and sweet-talk it away? I'm not that stupid."

I wanted to congratulate her. "I understand, ma'am. Is there anything you can tell me about his relationship with either Ms. Wright or Dr. Bigham?"

Her eyes widened. "Oh my God, you think Bobby . . . no, that's crazy, he'd never do anything like that."

"Are you sure?"

"He thinks he's slick, but he's not a murderer."

I refrained from saying you never really knew someone. "All right."

"Now, can you get those sleazy reporters to stop stalking me?"

"We'll talk to them." I reached into my breast pocket for the warrant. "Look, I know you had nothing to do with all this, but we're going to have to conduct a search."

"Of my house?"

"I'm real sorry, but we've got to do this."

"I swear, I going to kill him."

I signaled Derrick. "You have a place out back you can wait with an officer until we're done?"

She muttered a "Yes."

As she was led to her lanai, I said to the others, "Everyone has to be respectful. This poor lady didn't do anything. Do your job, but I don't want to see this place trashed in any way. Take your time, and make sure we leave the house the same way we found it."

I assigned rooms to search and checked to make sure the reporters kept their distance. As I turned to head inside, the garage door caught my eye.

Ryan was a car guy. The garage would be a natural place

for him to hide something. I hesitated before heading to the master bedroom; over the years it proved fertile ground in many searches.

The master was the size of a secondary bedroom and had a pinkish hue to it. A frilly bed skirt outlined a double bed I thought too small for two. Mrs. Ryan was going to be able to stretch out.

I went straight to the closet. Only women's clothing. She'd tossed him out. Paging through the hanging garments, a shoebox with the Ecco logo caught my attention. I took it off the shelf. A pair of brown loafers, that looked new, sat in it. Trying to figure why he left them behind, I went to the only nightstand.

Pulling open the drawer, I paused. Neat piles of satin underwear filled the space. Carefully, I emptied and refilled the drawer. The shelf below it held the latest Gillian Flynn novel. I tried to recall *Gone Girl* as I leafed through it.

After checking under the bed and mattress, I went into the bathroom. Nothing. I was going to search the garage next. I stepped into the hallway.

Derrick was outside the kitchen. "Frank! Come here."

"What do you have?"

He pointed to the cabinets. "I was checking the junk drawer."

I peered into a drawer.

"It was at the bottom. He must have forgotten it was there."

The illustration of the Earth was unmistakable, the logo for the Collier County Parks and Recreation Department. I lifted the trifold pamphlet out of the drawer. There were no markings on it.

"Let's bag it. It could be a piece of supporting evidence."

Derrick placed it in a bag. "I still have to go through the pantry."

"The master had nothing. I'm going to the garage."

A two-person yellow kayak hung above a workbench built into a small alcove. Had he lured the doctor to Baker Park with a promise to get on the water? The top of the work surface was littered with tools. I had ten thumbs, but the implements looked old.

Below the bench sat a clear tub with a blue cover. I slid it out and popped the lid. At the top was a box. It was heavy. I took the flowery lid off. It was filled with photos. I rifled through them. They appeared to be family pictures of Ryan as a boy.

I emptied a soldering gun, and a handmade toy boat, before seeing it. It was a long knife. With a serrated edge.

12

I STEPPED INTO THE SHERIFF'S OFFICE. HAND ON THE REMOTE, Remin said, "Take a seat."

The sheriff looked on edge. He checked his watch as I said, "Thank you, sir."

"How'd the search go?"

"Good. We found a knife, with the same edge as the murder weapon. It matches the length as well."

"Any evidence there's blood on it?"

"There might be. We turned it over to the lab for processing."

"I hope we can wrap this up."

"Me too, sir. In the meantime—"

He navigated to channel five: WINK News. "Hang on a second. I need to see what Feldman says."

The banner below the balding lawyer read "Police Closing in on Serial Killer?"

A picture of me at the Ryan's' home filled the screen. The newscaster said, "This morning, the Collier County Sheriff's Office conducted a search of Bobby Ryan's North Naples home."

A picture of Ryan replaced his former residence.

"Sources tell WINK News, thirty-nine-year-old Ryan is the principal suspect in the murders of Melissa Wright and Dr. Bigham. Married, Ryan was having an affair with Ms. Wright and was also believed to be romantically linked to Dr. Bigham."

A picture of Feldman in front of a bunch of microphones filled the screen. "Earlier today, Ryan's attorney spoke to reporters in front of his Naples office."

The lawyer said, "The search conducted at the Ryan home today was the most egregious invasion of privacy in the twenty-five years I've been practicing law. The Collier County sheriff has no evidence my client was guilty of anything more than a romantic encounter. A relationship that was consensual and certainly not against the law.

Desperate to calm a fearful public, the sheriff is pursuing Mr. Ryan with nothing more than circumstantial evidence. We're exploring our options, including filing suit for harassment."

The newscaster said, "We've reached out to Sheriff Remin. His office promised a statement, which we'll bring to you as soon as we receive it."

Remin muted the TV. "What's your gut on this one?"

"The reality is, it's too early to say. Let's see what the lab has—"

"I asked what your belly is telling you."

"I don't know what to think. Ryan was sleeping with Wright, who was carrying his child. His wife was so pissed, she threw him out. The tie with Dr. Bigham is less clear. He—"

"It was strong enough for him to drive her vehicle."

"Could've just been good service."

"I don't buy it. All the dealers I ever bought from, the service department handled the loaners and pickups."

He was looking for something positive to rebut Feldman. "True. If it were me, sir, I'd keep it low key as far as a statement is concerned. We need more time, and we're looking at Ong as well."

THE SMELL of burning cedar intensified as I walked past Z Gallerie. My stomach grumbled. Was it coming from Burntwood Tavern? I circled past two women gawking through a Dunkin Jewelers window.

Poised to grab the handle of the Realtor's door, I spied Ong sitting at a Bar Tulia outdoor table. Fingers around the stem of a martini glass, the Realtor was talking to a server. Another table summoned the waiter, and Ong reached for his glass.

As he put an olive-ladened toothpick in his mouth, I rapped my knuckles on the table. His eyes widened. I slid into a seat. "You lied to me."

"What on earth are you talking about?"

"Don't play stupid. You said you were working the morning Dr. Bigham's body was found."

"I'm always working."

"You claimed to be here, at the Mercato office around nine that morning."

"What day was that?"

"Wednesday."

"I usually cover the floor that day. I must have been busy."

"Where were you?"

"I don't recall."

"You came in around noon and picked up lunch at Bravo."

"What, are you spying on me?"

"Are you going to tell me where you were, or will I have to drag you in?"

He took a deep sip. "I remember now; I was home. I wasn't feeling good and came in late."

"Why did you lie?"

"It was a simple oversight."

He was lying. Again.

"How could anyone forget they were sick and came to work hours after they were supposed to?"

"It happens, okay?"

"Can anyone confirm you were home? All morning?"

He bit his lip. "This is really ridiculous, but Sal Takeya can vouch for me."

"Give me his contact details."

TAKEYA WORKED AS THE MAÎTRE D' at Sails. The high-end restaurant sat at the end of Fifth Avenue. It was supposed to be good, but Derrick's in-laws had taken them to celebrate their fiftieth anniversary and his entrée was eighty dollars. I could take the three of us out for that.

I walked along Third Street, toward Fifth Avenue. A couple of diners were enjoying a late lunch on Sails' terrace. How were the waiters wearing jackets and gloves in the middle of the afternoon?

Recalling Takeya's DMV photo, I saw him. Phone to his ear, Takeya was standing at an outdoor podium. He smiled and held up a finger. After hanging up, he said, "Welcome to Sails. Do you have a reservation?"

I leaned in. "We spoke earlier. I'm Detective Luca."

"One moment, please."

He ducked inside and came out with a woman. "I'll just be a minute, Carol."

I followed Takeya to the next storefront. "What can I do for you, Detective?"

"I'm trying to confirm an alibi. Stephen Ong claims you were with him on Wednesday morning."

He answered too quickly. "Yes. That's correct."

"What were you doing?"

"Excuse me?"

"Answer the question."

"It's none of your business. I'm entitled to privacy, aren't I?"

"Yes, but all I'm trying to do is clear your friend."

A woman in her sixties, carrying shopping bags, stopped in front of us. "Sal! When did you get back?"

"Uh—"

"We came for dinner two nights ago, and you weren't here."

"Was it the same without me?"

She laughed. "Not really. So tell me, didn't you just love the South of France?"

13

Back in the car, my cell rang. "Hey, Derrick. Ong's alibi, his second, just fell apart. We have to press him; he's hiding something."

"We may not need to. The lab just called. The knife had Ryan's DNA on it."

"What about any blood?"

"They said it was clean, possibly bleached."

"What about the type of blade?"

"Lab said it could be the murder weapon."

"We need to grill Ryan. Call Feldman and tell him to get his client in."

"I'm on it."

"Does Remin know?"

"No, first call was to you."

"Thanks. You get to Feldman, and I'll let Remin know."

"You heading in?"

"No, I have to take Mary Ann for a shot."

"Oh yeah, I forgot. Good luck with it."

"Text me when you get through to Feldman."

I PULLED INTO THE GARAGE. Two lizards were by the interior door to the house. Grabbing a broom, I swept them outside. Mary Ann had lived in Florida a long time, but when a brown anole slipped into the house, she acted like it was a rat.

I pecked her cheek. "How you feeling?"

"Good."

"You do your laps?"

"I couldn't. There's a huge frog in the pool. I think it's one of those poisonous ones."

Was I a cop or game warden? I headed to the lanai. "I'll fish it out."

Grabbing the skimmer, I chased the frog. I didn't know what kind it was, but it wasn't a cane toad. People were afraid of cane toads, but they weren't dangerous to humans.

They said dogs were at risk if they brushed against or sniffed one. It wasn't true. The only way a dog could get sick was if it picked one up and shook or squeezed it.

I plated the frog and placed it on the grass, prodding it toward the fence.

"Did you get it?"

"Yep. He's going to Melanie's house."

"Was it a cane?"

"No. Those have big bulging eyes."

"Ick."

"He's gone. Just watch out for the bobcat."

"What?"

"Just kidding. Come on, let's get going."

There was only one empty seat in the doctor's office. Mary Ann sat, and I stood by the door. I did the math; there were nine others in the room, if a third of them were getting shots at two thousand a jab, somebody was raking in the money.

A text pinged. It was Derrick. Feldman and Ryan were coming in the morning. I wrote back, telling him the sheriff ordered surveillance on Ryan. I wanted to tell him Remin suggested going for an arrest warrant if they played games with coming in, but it wasn't a good look for Remin to be so anxious to nail someone for the murders.

Mary Ann's name was called, and we were ushered into an exam room the size of our master closet. A nurse took her temperature and disappeared. After fifteen minutes, I said, "For all the money these shots cost, you'd think they'd wait on you hand and foot."

"You don't have to come, you know."

"I want to."

"It's just an injection."

"I don't care. It's your health, and I want to hear what the doctor says."

The door swung open, and it wasn't the doctor but the physician's assistant. It was the second time in a row we had her.

"How are you feeling, Mrs. Luca?"

"The same."

"Hang in there."

"After this one, if there's no improvement, I'm going to stop getting them."

"Let me consult with the doctor about this, I'm sure she'll want to do a complete evaluation, including drawing spinal fluids."

The PA rubbed Mary Ann's shoulder with alcohol and delivered the shot. "Wait five minutes to be sure there are no adverse reactions, okay?"

"Sure."

Once the door closed, I said, "Why'd you say that about stopping the shots?"

"Come on, Frank. They're not really working."

"How do you know that?"

"'Cause, I'm hardly feeling any better."

"They said it takes time."

"We've been doing this for six months already."

"They said you need at least six months."

"It's not working."

"It could be slowing the progression."

Mary Ann's lip quivered. I had a big mouth. It was the worst-case scenario.

I was saved by a knock on the door. A nurse came in with our bill and a handheld credit card device. I handed over my plastic, annoyed they wouldn't even let you leave the room without paying.

Two steps ahead of Mary Ann, I slowed the pace as we headed to the car. It was hard to assess if my wife was dragging because of emotion or the disease.

She took a couple of seconds to climb in the car. "You feeling all right, Mar?"

"I'm fine."

"Good. I think we should give this another two or three months."

"It's throwing money away."

"No, it's not, and it doesn't matter anyway."

"Of course, it matters. I'm putting our family in hock with all this."

"No, you're not. We're fine; we can handle this."

"Even if we could, and we can't, we're wasting money we don't have."

"We'll be okay."

"No, it can go toward Jessica's education and for us, for our retirement."

"We have the money for college."

"That's for an in-state school. You know she has her heart set on going to Princeton."

"We'll swing it; we have money we can get to."

"What? By cashing in our four-o-ones?"

"Look, if I have to keep working until I'm ninety, I will. I can't sit around doing nothing anyway."

She whispered, "We were supposed to travel . . ."

"We'll get around to it."

She scoffed, "The 'golden years,' what bullshit."

I reached for her hand. "Come on, hon, it's going to be all right; no, make that better than all right."

"I'm sorry."

"You have nothing to be sorry about."

"It's messing up everything."

"No, it's not. You got sick; it's not your fault. We'll deal with it."

She hung her head.

"Look, if this was me, you'd be telling me to stop feeling sorry for myself."

She shrugged.

"Come on, I can hear you." I went into falsetto: "Frank, stop feeling sorry for yourself. What are you, a baby?"

She beat my thigh with her fist and broke into a smile.

14

———

Reviewing the questions I had on Ryan, I turned onto Airport Pulling Road. Today could be a pivotal day. As soon as I pulled into the complex, I hit the brakes. Three news vans were parked in front of the entrance to the sheriff's office.

I turned around and made for the rear door. Was something else going on today, or had they been tipped off Ryan was coming in? Again. Under normal circumstances, between dash and body cams and everyone filming you, we were under constant scrutiny. I understood that aspect of it, but not the press. They made it more difficult to do my job.

The hallway smelled of coffee. I opened the office door; Derrick was tapping on his keyboard.

"Morning. Don't tell me the press is waiting for Ryan."

He shook his head. "Frigging vultures."

"I hope it wasn't Remin tipping them off."

"It probably was. I'm not sure Feldman wants Ryan under the spotlight any more than he is."

I took a sip of the coffee Derrick had waiting for me. "I didn't sign up for the circus."

"Me neither."

"We've got to keep our heads down and see where this leads."

"Bingo."

I opened my inbox. "Damn, sixty emails."

"There's at least ten on sensitivity-and-diversity training."

"I'm getting too old for this."

"How'd it go with Mary Ann's doctor?"

"Standard stuff."

"Good."

I was wrapped up in my own world, never asking how he was feeling. "How about you? How you feeling?"

"So, so. O'Reilly told me to try acupuncture, said it helped his wife."

"You going to give it a try?"

"I think so. It's worth trying."

A shiver went down my spine at the thought of being stuck with scores of needles. An intern stuck her head in the office. "Detective Luca?"

"Yes?"

"Your appointment is here."

"Have them put in interview room two."

"Yes, sir."

She almost saluted before leaving. Derrick said, "Room two? What did you do, raise the AC in there?"

"Who? Me?"

He shook his head. "You're too much."

I checked my watch. It was ten minutes early for a pee. "I'm going to the boys' room."

Sitting on bowl, I coaxed a stream out of the plumbing the doctors made for me. I fingered the scar where they'd cut me to remove my cancer-ridden bladder. It was a close call and I'd been clean. So far.

I shook off the negativity and zipped up. Washing up, I visualized grilling Ryan. It was going to be fun.

Rounding the corner, I slowed my pace. The sheriff was standing outside the room talking to Derrick. Was he going to interfere like he did in the last case? Should I give him an ultimatum if he did? Derrick grimaced as he shifted his weight, and I stepped off the bravado ladder.

Remin turned. "Detective Luca. We ready?"

We? "Yes, sir. Detective Dickson and I are prepared to interview Ryan."

"Good. It will comfort the public to know this department is doing everything possible to bring the killer to justice."

Was Remin going to invite the press to view the interview? "We have an excellent record, sir."

The sheriff scoffed, "The public has a short memory. We need to close this case and fast."

"We'll do our best."

"Update me as soon as you're done."

As Remin walked away, Derrick said, "Talk about laying the pressure on."

"Brush it off. We have a job to do. We can't rush the process."

"You're right."

As I put a hand on the doorknob, Derrick whispered, "Remin dialed up the AC."

I stepped into the room. "Good morning, gentlemen."

Feldman extended his hand and we shook. Ryan had a scowl worthy of a sixteen-year-old punished for the weekend.

I nodded to Ryan. "Mr. Ryan."

"You got me fired with all this bullshit."

"If you're cleared, I'm sure they'll take you back."

"I didn't do anything. You screwed up my entire life. My wife threw me out of the house."

I was going to tell him she had every right to kick his cheating ass out. "Let's get this underway."

After reciting the formalities, I said, "Thank you for coming in to speak with us. Mr. Ryan, we conducted a search of your Mimosa Court home."

"My wife went ballistic."

I threw up a hand. "In the course of executing the warrant"—I opened the folder and picked up a plastic evidence bag—"we discovered this pamphlet in a kitchen drawer."

Feldman said, "May I see that?"

Ryan said, "So what? It's a brochure from the county park system."

"Why was it buried at the bottom of a drawer?"

"How the hell do I know? We probably got it five years ago."

"No, it's not from five years ago. This version was printed sixteen months ago."

"You guys are trying your hardest to frame me. It's—"

Feldman put his hand up, silencing Ryan. "Being in possession of a publication, one I believe with tens of thousands of copies distributed, has no bearing."

"Both Melissa Wright and Dr. Bigham were found dead at parks featured in the brochure."

Feldman smiled. "I refuse to rebut such a ludicrous insinuation."

"Your client owns a kayak. We believe it's possible he lured Dr. Bigham to Baker Park under the pretense of a recreational activity."

"Do you have actual questions for my client?"

Ready to knock the smirk off Feldman's face, I smiled and slid a photo across the table. "We also seized this knife during our search."

Ryan pawed it toward him. "That's a fishing knife my old man had."

"It doesn't matter where you obtained it; we're interested in what you used it for."

Ryan scoffed, "What? You think I used it to stab Melissa?"

It was interesting that we had never released the causes of death in either women. "How do you know if they were stabbed?"

"Why else would you be talking about a knife? It doesn't take a brain surgeon, you know."

"Speaking of doctors, the medical examiner has concluded that the murder weapon, used to kill both women, has the same serrated blade and is the exact length as this one."

Feldman said, "I'm sure there are thousands, if not millions, like it in circulation."

"And one just happens to be hidden in your client's garage?"

"It wasn't hidden."

"We found it at the bottom of a bin, under a workbench. That qualifies as concealed, in my world."

"I didn't hide anything. It was my father's fishing knife. He gave me a whole bunch of tools and things when he moved out of his house. I didn't even want the stuff, but I took it and put it in the garage."

"Did you use the knife at any time?"

"No."

Feldman said, "Your logic escapes me, Detective, but hypothetically speaking, why would my client hold a weapon connected to murder?"

"People do all kinds of irrational things. Perhaps he wanted to use it again, on another woman."

"Other than the similarities in regard to the edge and length, do you have any evidence to support your insinuations?"

"Unfortunately, the blade was cleaned with bleach."

"So, you have nothing."

"Mr. Ryan claimed a moment ago not to have used the knife."

"That's right. I never used it."

"How do you explain the handle has your DNA on it?"

"That's impossible. Oh, wait, maybe it got on it when I went through the box. You see, when I picked it up, I went through it just to see what was in it. That's all I did."

15

———

The murmur from the crowd increased as we escorted Ryan and his lawyer to the exit. I'd given Feldman the option to leave via the rear entrance, but he declined. He whispered to his client just before stepping into the heat of the sun and press.

A chorus of questions rang out from reporters. Feldman raised his hands. "I'd like to make a short statement."

Four microphones thrust forward. "Pursuant to the sheriff's request, Mr. Ryan and I came here voluntarily. We answered their questions, satisfactorily, I might add, and Mr. Ryan looks forward to putting these disturbing allegations to rest. He had nothing to do with the premature deaths of Ms. Wright and Dr. Bigham."

"Is Bobby Ryan going to be arrested?"

"Of course not. There is no evidence—"

"What about the knife?"

"My client has a fishing knife his father gifted to him years ago."

"It matches the murder weapon."

"It may be similar, but it is not the knife used in the

murders of those poor women. I'm sorry, we've got a full schedule."

Ryan kept his head down, and Feldman led him to his car.

I said, "Come on. I have to bring Remin up to speed."

Derrick said, "What did you think about Ryan's knife story?"

"It's plausible. I remember my uncle giving me all kinds of tools. I didn't have the heart to tell him I'd never use them."

"My old man did the same thing. I never had to buy a tool."

"Mary Ann barred me from doing anything more than a simple job."

Derrick laughed, "She did you a favor."

"I'll see you after I talk to Remin."

The door to the sheriff's office was closed. I smiled at his secretary. "He's busy?"

"He's with Parton."

Remin was meeting the head of the department's Media Relations. "I'll come back."

"No. He said to let him know when you came."

She picked up the phone to alert Remin. I grabbed a copy of *American Police Beat* magazine. Looking over the table of contents, the door swung open. Remin said he'd get back to Parton. I leaned back as I shook the PR guy's hand and followed Remin into his office. It reeked of Parton's musky cologne.

He slid behind his desk. "What happened?"

"Ryan said the knife was his father's."

"What do think?"

"There was no blood, but it may have been bleached."

"What else?"

"Said the pamphlet was old. It's barely circumstantial anyway."

"But it supports the narrative on where the bodies were posed. What did he say about his relationships with these women?"

"He stuck to his story, had no idea Wright was pregnant, and was just doing a favor for Dr. Bigham. I pressed him on the car service thing; it doesn't ring true. He originally said he hadn't seen Bigham in a long time, and it turns out he saw her days before she was found dead."

"We need to see if he was in a relationship with Bigham. Or maybe he wanted one and she rebuffed him."

"Could have been trying to get on her good side by doing her a favor, and the payoff never came."

"What about anger issues?"

"We looked, but nothing more than what we all do."

"Press his wife. She should know him best."

"She should, but she missed his affair."

"She could have known and was trying to patch the relationship up."

"True. She threw him out but that was after learning about the pregnancy."

"We need to see what she knows. Why don't you bring her in?"

"I'd rather not interview her here. She's been through a lot and, well—"

"You know, people tend to be more, uh, helpful when we talk here."

He was right, but I felt for Mrs. Ryan. "I'll go see her. If she's holding back, we'll get her in."

"Fair enough. Parton's getting besieged over this serial killer case. He's gotten fourteen interview requests, and one of them is out of Atlanta. He's worried it's going to go national."

"Feldman isn't helping."

"The press can be helpful here, with the focus on Ryan; someone may step forward with information."

"We can make another public appeal."

"Let's give the press a couple of days. They'll be following Ryan so closely, the only place he'll get privacy is the bathroom."

"Even that's debatable these days."

Remin smiled. "He'll be hounded until he confesses or someone else is tagged with it."

"Or until another shiny object catches their attention."

"No doubt attention spans are short." He exhaled heavily. "But when two defenseless women are found murdered, we need to change the narrative. They're making it as if we're sitting on our hands here."

"We're going to get whoever is behind this."

"Can't be soon enough. Make sure I'm informed of all developments."

GETTING OUT OF THE CAR, Jessie came into the garage. "Hey, Dad."

"Hi, Jessie. How are you doing?"

"Okay."

"How's Mom?"

"She's cool. We took a walk when I got home."

"She was good?"

"Yeah, but it was hot; we just went around the block twice."

"Good. Where you going?"

"Going to hit some balls with Carolyn."

"Have fun. I'll see you later."

Sitting on a barstool at the kitchen sink, Mary Ann was

rinsing zucchini. She turned toward me and smiled. "Just a little tired."

"Jessie said you went for a walk."

She nodded. "It knocked me out."

"It was the heat. You should've waited. I would have went with you."

"Jessica suggested it, so, have to take advantage of the offer."

It was good to hear Jessie was pushing to keep her in motion. "I nodded. "Got to squeeze in as much time before she goes off to college."

She frowned. "I'm going to miss her."

I wrapped my arm around her shoulder. "We both will, but we'll go see her, and she'll come back during breaks."

"I know. Anyway, how was your day? What happened with Ryan?"

I filled her in on the interview. She said, "It's been all over the news. The press followed Ryan to a house in East Naples."

"He say anything?"

"No. They swarmed him in front of the place. I almost felt sorry for him the way they attacked him. When he pushed his way inside, they started looking in the windows. He pulled the shades down."

16

————

Derrick wasn't in the office, but a cup of java was sitting in the center of my desk. I shed my sports jacket and took a sip. Derrick hadn't been in much earlier than I.

Powering up my desktop, he walked in. "Morning, Frank."

"Hey, buddy. Thanks for the java."

He flashed a thumbs-up. "What's the agenda?"

"Talking to Mrs. Ryan. She may have insight into her husband's anger issues and prior violence not bad enough to get us involved."

He eased himself into his chair. "She's likely to talk now."

"That's the hope. You feeling all right?"

"Pretty good today."

"Great."

My desk phone rang. I glanced at the time. It was five after nine. "Homicide, Detective Luca."

"Hi, um, I think I have some information about that guy, Ryan."

I straightened up. "Thank you for calling. Would you like this to be confidential?"

"No, it's okay. My name's Mary Keane."

"All right, Ms. Keane. What's on your mind?"

"You see, we live in Jacksonville, but my daughter lives in Naples. Anyway, I was visiting two weeks ago and stayed at the Hyatt House. When I was there, I was parking one day, and I saw a couple arguing. I'm certain it was that man Ryan."

"Who was he arguing with?"

"Melissa Wright."

"Are you sure it was her?"

"Definitely. I've seen her at the hotel a whole bunch of times."

"How certain are you it was Bobby Ryan?"

"I didn't know who it was until I saw the news last night before bed. I was like, oh no, that was him."

"Where did you see them?"

"The parking lot was pretty full, and I went to the right side and passed them. They were standing next to the building."

"How do you know they were fighting?"

"Because of the way people move, and you know, after I got out of my car, I had to walk past them. They were shouting but quieted down when they saw me."

"Okay. It'd be helpful if you could pin down the day and time of what you witnessed."

"I'm pretty sure it was a Monday. I usually drive down on a Thursday to beat the traffic and come back on Wednesdays."

"What exact date?"

"Uh, let me check my calendar, hold on."

I put my hand over the receiver. "Derrick, this could be the break we need."

"Hello, you still there?"

"Yes, ma'am."

"Okay, I'm pretty sure it was Monday, the fourteenth."

"January?"

"Yes."

"What time?"

"Sometime around eleven."

I took her contact information down and hung up. "The caller saw Ryan and Wright arguing at the Hyatt House right before she was found dead."

"Bingo."

"Do me a favor and run down there while I go see Mrs. Ryan. There's got to be some CCTV footage of the two of them."

I gave him the details. Derrick grabbed his jacket. As he left, I picked up the phone to give Remin a heads-up Ryan may have been fighting with Wright days before she was killed.

THE PRESS HAD MOVED on from Ryan's house. I knew they'd be back if Ryan remained the leading suspect. Gasoline fumes hit me as I walked to the door. A neighbor was blowing grass clippings with a blower emitting a cloud of smoke. The sound of leaf blowers and air-conditioners were lousy background music.

Dish towel in hand, Mrs. Ryan opened the door. "Hello, ma'am. I'm Detective Luca."

"Yeah, I remember you."

"I'd like to ask you a couple of questions about your husband."

She frowned. "I guess I have to? Right?"

"Not exactly, but I'd appreciate it if you did, and it may help to end this, uh . . ."

"Nightmare."

I nodded and she stepped aside.

We sat in the kitchen. The sign hanging on the wall couldn't have been more ironic: "I'd Rather Be at the Beach." I said, "Is that new?"

"Kind of. Bobby thought it was stupid, so we never hung it."

Relieved I hadn't missed it during the search, I said, "It works for me."

She smiled. "I can spend all day at the beach, but Bobby never wanted to go."

Was he one of those who hated sand? "I enjoy it but don't go as much as I used to."

"Been there three times since this, uh, all happened. Maybe it's because I'm in a bathing suit or something, but nobody bothers me there. It's my safe haven."

It was all about context. Most people struggled when they saw someone in a different surrounding. "I'm sorry you have to deal with all this."

"It's bad enough he had a baby with another woman, but people are saying he killed her and another woman? It's crazy."

"What can you tell me about your husband's anger issues?"

"Anger issues? Bobby didn't have a problem with anger."

"You're sure about that?"

"Yes. He'd get mad about something every now and then the same way everybody does."

"How about when he fought with someone?"

"You mean, like physically?"

"Yes."

"He never did that."

"Did he have someone do his dirty work for him?"

She scoffed, "Look, after what he did, I'll never, ever, get back with him, but I can't see him killing those women like they're saying he did."

"He carried his knife around with him, right?"

"He didn't have a knife. At least, not that I knew about."

I asked a couple more questions before leaving. She was convincing. I knew love made people protect others when they shouldn't, but she was believable. The bigger question was whether Ryan was telling the truth.

Making a U-turn, Derrick called, "You free?"

"Yeah, just left Ryan's wife. You get the video?"

"Yep, and it's Wright and Ryan. They're arguing, no doubt about it."

The seesaw just went in the other direction. "I'll see you in fifteen."

17

———

DERRICK HAD A LOTTERY WINNER SMILE ON. I TOSSED MY jacket onto a chair as he held a thumb drive up. "You want popcorn for the movie?"

"I'm a Milk Duds kind of guy."

He popped the drive into his desktop. "Can't stand they way they stick to my teeth."

As he navigated through the drive, I said, "You say anything to Remin yet?"

"No. Was waiting for you."

"Thanks."

"Here we go. There's Ryan, he must've called her."

"Zoom in."

It was Ryan. He was pacing along the right side of the hotel.

"Here comes Wright."

Dressed in a gray sports jacket and black pants, Melissa Wright approached her lover. Ryan took a couple of steps forward. He was shaking his head and jawing at her. She slowed her pace.

Derrick said, "Man, I wish we could hear what they're saying."

"Soon enough they'll have cameras with audio pickups."

Ryan banged his fist against the wall. I said, "Maybe she told him about the baby."

"Could be."

They looked toward the parking lot and seemed to calm down a bit. It probably was the witness approaching. Twenty seconds later, Ryan shook his finger in Wright's face. She backed up.

A second later, Wright turned around. "Zoom in."

Lips pulled in and eyes narrowed, she was angry. "Okay, let it roll."

Wright disappeared. Ryan, hands on hips, stared in her direction. He leaned against the wall and wagged his head before going off-screen. Something was going on between them.

"This doesn't help Ryan. Run it again."

We watched the video two more times. "I've got to tell Remin what we have."

"You think it's enough to get an arrest warrant?"

"I don't think so. It's a compelling narrative, but everything is circumstantial." I didn't want to tell him Remin would probably discount what I thought and make the call. "Do me a favor and write up a report on this while I see what they say upstairs."

Trudging up the stairs, I sorted through the resources in my head. One solid, physical piece of evidence was all I needed to get comfortable. If it existed, where was it hiding?

"Sit down, Frank."

Frank? The manipulation had begun. "Thank you, sir."

"How did it go with the wife?"

"She defended him. Said he didn't have anger issues and never got physical in all the years they've known each other."

"She could be protecting him."

"Could be, but Detective Dickson secured the video footage from the tip I mentioned." Remin leaned forward as I continued, "Ryan went to the Hyatt House where Wright worked on Monday, around eleven a.m. He waited outside for her and was clearly agitated."

"So much for the wife saying he didn't lose his temper."

"He appeared upset but not violence prone."

"Any physical contact?"

"None, sir."

"What's your take on it?"

"She may have told him about the pregnancy earlier, or perhaps he demanded she get an abortion and she refused. He might have been trying to change her mind. Who knows?"

"No witnesses in the area?"

"Just the lady who alerted us, but she didn't hear any of the discussion."

"I'd like more before we arrest him, but what I like doesn't matter."

"You're going for a warrant?"

"Haven't made that decision yet. I'm going to run it by the prosecutors."

18

———

MARY ANN CAME ONTO THE LANAI WITH A BOWL OF SALAD. I took it from her and said, "Look at the sky. The purple and orange colors are beautiful."

She grabbed the remote and put the TV on. "It's gorgeous."

I plated the turkey burgers.

"Perfect night to eat outside." I went to shut the TV.

"Mute it but leave it on. There's a school board meeting over a new curriculum."

"What's going on?"

"Some nonsense coming from Washington. They better not adopt it."

"They want to control everything." I poured a glass of red wine. "You want a glass?"

"Nah. I'm afraid to drink."

"The doctor said a glass here and there could help you."

"Maybe next time."

I offered her my glass. "Try it. Bilotti recommended it, and Total Wine had it for twenty bucks."

She took a sip. "It's nice. What is it?"

"A Tuscan from Italy."

"It's good."

"The grapes are Sangiovese, which means the blood of Jupiter."

"Eww. That doesn't make me want to drink it."

"It's just a name. You want a glass?"

"Nah. The Ryan case is all over the news; what happened with his wife?"

I cut into a burger. "She doesn't think he's capable of murder. Said he doesn't have a anger issue. But we obtained surveillance video from where Wright worked. Just a couple of days before she ended up dead, Ryan was arguing with her."

"Oh my God. You think he did it?"

"I'm leaning, but we need more."

Mouth full, Mary Ann pointed to the TV.

At the bottom of the screen was a red "Breaking News" banner. I put the sound on.

Sitting behind a desk, a newscaster said, "We're bringing you another WINK News exclusive. This special report concerns the leading suspect in the Wright and Bigham murders. Today we secured video footage of Bobby Ryan, a person police have interviewed several times in connection with the killings. This was captured by surveillance cameras at the Hyatt House, where Ms. Wright was employed as an assistant manager."

I dropped my fork as the screen behind the newscaster came to life. "That's Mr. Ryan waiting on the side of the hotel. Here comes Ms. Wright. It appears the two were engaged in a heated discussion. This footage is critically important as the exchange took place only two days before Ms. Wright was found dead in the Cocohatchee Creek Preserve."

Pushing my chair away from the table, I said, "How the hell did they get the tape?"

"Somebody leaked it."

"I bet it was Remin."

"You sure?"

I pulled my cell out and dialed Derrick. "The footage of Ryan and Wright is all over the news."

"What? I didn't see that."

I walked toward the back of the pool. "You give the thumb drive to Remin?"

"No."

"What did you do with it?"

"I copied it on to my desktop, tagged it, and brought it down to the evidence room."

"Anyone ask about it?"

"No. What's the problem?"

"We have to know if Remin is playing games with us."

"You're right."

"I feel like driving in to check the evidence log."

"It can wait until the morning. Nothing's going to change."

"You have a password for your PC?"

"Yeah, everybody does."

"All right, we'll deal with it tomorrow. See you in the morning."

Mary Ann said, "What did Derrick say?"

"He turned it over to evidence."

"You really think Remin was behind it?"

"I'm not sure. He needs a solve, and it ain't beyond him to cut corners."

"The news said the sheriff's office didn't respond to a request for a comment on the tape."

"The damage is already done."

"They also claimed a confidential source said an arrest was imminent."

DERRICK WAS AT HIS DESK. "Morning, Frank."

"Morning."

He lowered his voice. "I don't think anyone screwed with my desktop."

"Okay. You get along with Gorman better than I do. Why don't you check the log?"

He stood. "On my way."

I powered up my desktop and went through my emails. We needed to confront Ryan on the video. As soon as the clock hits nine, I was going to call Feldman.

While mentally debating whether to speak to Mrs. Ryan again, Derrick came back in.

"Nobody signed anything out."

"He work the night shift?"

"Don't be so paranoid, Frank."

"You're right. It just irks me to no end."

"I'm going to take a ride to the Hyatt House. See if they released it."

Derrick swung his jacket over a shoulder and left. Checking the prior day's arrests, my cell phone rang. It was Remin. "Morning, sir."

"Morning. We need to bring Ryan in. Lean on him hard."

"We plan to. Just waiting till Feldman gets in."

"Today isn't soon enough."

"I'll do my best without alarming Feldman."

"Keep me posted."

"Will do, sir."

I went back to my emails. It was time to renew my marksmanship qualifications. Where did the time ago? The printer spit out the form I needed as the clock hit nine. I set the warm paper on my desk and dialed Ryan's lawyer.

As soon as I hung up, I fielded the first nutty caller of the day. I told the woman we didn't have the manpower to check her home for ghosts and hung up.

Derrick called in, "Hey, Frank, it was the security guy at Hyatt House. He sold a copy to WINK."

"Geez, his boss know?"

"No, and I didn't say anything. The old-timer said he needed the money for dental work. I warned him the next time I'd report it."

"What's wrong with people?"

"That's a harder question than the meaning of life."

"Just about. You talk to Feldman?"

"Yes. He didn't give me a hard time. Said he'd talk to Ryan and get back to us with a time."

19

———————

I PULLED INTO THE LOT FOR LOWBROW PIZZA. IT WAS A weird name but the pie was good. Getting out, I said, "You want to split a sausage pie?"

Derrick said, "Sounds good, I'm starved."

"If Feldman hasn't reached out by the time we're done eating, I'll call again."

"You think he's dodging us?"

We stepped into the white building. "Not particularly. They're probably conferring on how to rebut the video."

"Man, it smells good."

"They should make a cologne like this."

We split the last slice and left. We opened the car doors, and I pulled out my phone as the heat escaped. "Mr. Feldman. It's Detective Luca."

"Hello, Detective."

"I'd like to know what time you and your client are coming in today."

"I've been unable to reach Mr. Ryan, thus far. As soon as I speak with him, I'll advise, but I must inform you, I have a court appearance at three today. It'll have to be tomorrow."

"I understand, Counselor. Our preference is to do this in the morning."

"That may work. I'll confirm it as soon as possible."

I hung up. "They're not coming in today. He said he didn't get ahold of Ryan yet."

"You think Ryan is on the run?"

It had crossed my mind. "No. Feldman said he had a three o'clock court appearance. He probably didn't have the time today and is using it as an excuse."

"Yeah, lawyers, they lie for a living."

It was an interesting way to put it. "I want to see if we can dig up anything to support Ryan's anger or aggression."

"We looked."

"We need to go further back."

"How far back?"

"High school. People are who they are before that, but high school changes a lot of people."

"For sure."

"And we need to look into his work history. He's been at MINI for a couple of years, but where was he before that? People selling cars seem to move around a lot. Or maybe he came out of a different industry."

"And couldn't get a job because of something he did, and they booted him."

Derrick had a black belt in speculation, which was an asset in a homicide detective. "That's the thinking. Or he felt the need to run from his past somehow, step into a new world."

"We'll ferret it out."

Maybe not at the speed Remin wanted, but we'd come up with the evidence necessary to get a conviction. If we stuck to the basics.

"Why don't you check with the high school he went to?

Talk to his teachers, friends, including girlfriends Ryan had. You develop a list, and I'll go see Mrs. Ryan again."

"I'm on it. I'm pretty sure he went to Palmetto High."

MRS. RYAN LOOKED ready for yoga. I wondered if she always exercised or was trying to remake herself to lessen the sting of her marriage meltdown. "Thanks for seeing me."

"How long is it going to take for this to end?"

The real answer depended on whether her husband was the killer. If he was, she was looking at decades of disturbance. "It's difficult to say, but hopefully not much longer."

"This is like being in a movie or something. Half the time, it doesn't feel real."

The right word was nightmare. "I understand. Um, the last time we spoke, I asked about your husband's anger issues."

She frowned. "The video. Right?"

The phone in my pocket vibrated. "Well, not entirely, but it's evidence he has a temper."

"Everyone gets mad, and I'm certainly not going to defend him, not after what he did to me, but I saw the clip on the news, and they're making it out like he hit her or something."

"He was clearly upset, and the altercation did take place just days before Ms. Wright was found dead."

She exhaled. "I get it."

"I was wondering whether seeing the video jogged your mind about any disagreements he had with others. What comes to mind?"

"Really, nothing. I don't believe it proves anything about him."

I raised my eyebrows and she said, "Okay. Obviously, I

didn't know him like I thought I did. He lied." Her eyes moistened, and I worried she'd start crying. "Bobby broke our trust and everything we had together. How could I have been so stupid?"

"Don't blame yourself, ma'am. I can tell you for a fact, nobody really knows anyone."

"That's terrible."

It was. "Oftentimes, we ignore signs or rationalize them away with people we care about. It's the human condition."

She wagged her head.

"Is there anything, even ten years ago, that you may have discounted, that in hindsight could have been troubling?"

"Trust me, I've been over every detail of our relationship, going back to when I first met Bobby. Did I miss, what now seems obvious, that he was unfaithful to me? No doubt. But as far as what they're saying about him, I really can't say anything; it's not the man I knew."

"No fights, anger, blowups?"

"Nothing more than your normal disappointments. He's a salesman. Rejection is something he deals with everyday; it doesn't upset him."

I climbed back in the car and called Derrick. "Sorry, I was with Mrs. Ryan."

"How'd that go?"

"She's adamant. Doesn't recall any violence, anger, anything that would point to him."

"Damn. Say, we got a possible homicide."

"Where?"

"Intersection of Vanderbilt Beach Road and Livingston. A bicyclist was run down by a car. It looks like the driver was intoxicated."

"Jesus."

"I'm on way."

"I'll meet you there."

20

Lights and siren on, I made it to the scene in ten minutes. Patrol cars blocked the intersection, and officers directed traffic away from the accident. Pulling over, I saw pair of EMT techs standing beside an ambulance.

I adjusted my sunglasses and got out. The hum of traffic was decibels lower than usual. Walking toward the intersection, my eyes focused on three uniformed officers standing over a sheet-covered shape in Livingston's second lane.

Derrick hustled over. "The woman who hit him is in the back of Townley's car."

"She failed a sobriety test?"

"Yeah, but it's not alcohol."

"Who was first on the scene?"

He pointed to a stocky officer. "Mallory. Let's talk to him."

We had to move fast. I hustled over. "Officer Mallory, Frank Luca."

I shook his hand. "I understand you administered a field sobriety test?"

"Yeah, she failed walk and turn."

We asked someone under the influence to walk: heel to toe, nine steps, turn around, and return. "What about the one-leg stand?"

"Couldn't hold it more than a second. She's high on something."

"We need to get a blood and urine specimen before whatever it is leaves her system."

"I called for a certified paramedic. Should be here any minute."

"Good. Did you call Corny, the drug recognition expert?"

"Yeah, he's down in Marco Island, giving a presentation."

"How long till he gets here?"

"Sixty to seventy-five minutes."

"Damn. Did you search her car?"

"No, sir. Figured this might be a vehicular homicide and thought your office would prefer to conduct a search."

"Thanks, you handled it perfectly. Who's the victim?"

"John Holt, sixty-six years old. His driver's license lists an address on Tiburon Drive."

Tiburon was a high-end community anchored by the second Ritz Carlton to be built in Naples.

"What about witnesses?"

"Two people said they saw Holt pedaling south on Livingston. They both said he had the green light and was in the bike lane. The driver who hit him was heading east on Vanderbilt, in the turning lane for South Livingston. According to both witnesses, she never slowed down, and hit him."

"Any skid marks?"

"Yes, but after the point of impact."

"What a frigging disaster."

"I know. You want to talk to the driver? Her name's Helena Jackson."

"All right."

Walking to the patrol car, I said to Derrick, "You bike on these roads, you're taking your life in your hands."

"I know. Cars are going sixty, and half the drivers got phones in their hands."

Holt's bike was a twisted mess. "Poor guy never knew what hit him. Out trying to get exercise, and bam, your life is over."

"I'm all for helmets but you get slammed like that, nothing is going to save you."

The officer pulled open the door, and the twentysomething-year-old driver said, "I didn't see him; he came out of nowhere."

"You've been using. Why don't you tell me what you took."

"No, no, I didn't do nothing. Had one little glass of wine with lunch, you know. I—"

"You failed the sobriety test."

"I was nervous, that's all. I mean, it was right after the accident. I feel so bad." She teared up.

A paramedic unit rolled up. "We're going to take some blood from you. If you're not on anything, you don't have to worry."

"Blood? You can't do that."

"Yes, we can. If we suspect someone is driving under the influence, Florida law allows us to use reasonable force to take your blood as part of a DUI investigation."

"No, no, I won't. I got to go to work."

"You don't have a choice, ma'am."

"But—"

"Trust me, ma'am, if you cooperate, it'll be much easier on you."

Tears rolled down her face. I turned to Mallory. "I'd like to go over her car."

"I've got this."

I knew he did. He was another example of the highly trained officers Collier County had. It used to burn me up when the press tried to smear all of us when the rare officer went astray. But I always remembered my mother saying nobody covered the thousands of airplanes that landed each day without incident.

Gloves on, I circled the driver's silver Nissan. The driver's front side had damage from the impact. The rear taillight was busted. A piece of red glass was hanging from the broken light. I snapped photos of the damage.

In the passenger wheel well was a bag from Burger King. I put the back of my hand to the food wrapping; it was still warm. I checked the glove box: five pens, a pack of tissues, hand cream, and the owner's manual.

Both sun visors had pencils stuck in them. Was this kid some sort of writer? I knelt and looked under the seats: a quarter and a ponytail rubber band were all there was. The side pockets and console had nothing incriminating. Had she taken whatever it was before getting behind the wheel?

I popped the trunk. My eyes focused on a gym bag. I pulled the zipper open and drew out a black apron. I dug into the pocket, coming up with a fistful of pens. She was a server.

Cameras swinging off both shoulders, Gianelli was heading in my direction. I said, "Derrick, call for a tow truck. We'll impound the vehicle and see where it leads us."

Gianelli shook his head. "Do we need more proof riding your bike on a major road is dangerous?"

"It amounts to roulette. This poor guy is the third death this year."

"I gave it up ten years ago. With everybody texting, I don't even like walking on sidewalks anymore."

He had a point. I filled him in on the directions, and as he began documenting the scene, we left to deliver the bad news to an unsuspecting spouse.

21
___

I PULLED INTO OUR GARAGE. OUR BIKES WERE HANGING ON the wall. Before heading inside, I thought about letting the air out of Jessie's tires.

Mary Ann was reading in my recliner. I said, "Hey, how you feeling?"

"Good."

I planted a kiss on her cheek. "Is Jessie riding her bike much?"

"Not that I know of. Why?"

I told her about the bicyclist.

"That's terrible."

"It's too dangerous to be riding anywhere but a park. Even in a gated community, you've got to be careful. Everybody's distracted and going too fast."

"Why doesn't traffic safety put up more traps?"

"They'll do something after this, but nobody gets the message."

"They need to find a way to disable a phone when a car is in motion."

"That'd help, but it wouldn't have helped this guy."

"So sad. So unnecessary."

"I know."

"What happened with Ryan?"

"I called his lawyer an hour ago. His office claimed they haven't been able to make contact with him."

"He's on the run?"

"I hope to hell not. Feldman supposedly wasn't in, but he could be stalling for time."

"Maybe he's trying to convince Ryan to make a deal."

"That'd be nice, but Ryan would never do that; it's not him."

"Aren't you the one who says, 'You never really know somebody'?"

I gave her an eye roll a twelve-year-old would be proud of and said, "I'm going to get changed."

AT MY DESK BY EIGHT, I sipped a second cup of java and went through my emails. I kept looking at my watch, wanting to manually move the hands into the future. The lab techs said they'd have the driver's drug test back as fast as possible, and I needed to speak to Cornelius regarding his field assessment of the driver.

It'd be interesting to get an expert's take on whether she was under the influence or not, but the call I looked forward to was the one to Feldman. What was the lawyer planning? If I had to wait another day to confront Ryan with the tape, it would exhaust the little patience I had.

"Morning, Frank."

"Hey, Derrick, beat your lazy ass in today."

Smiling, he put a cup of coffee on my desk. "One out of a hundred isn't a record to brag about."

I tapped the top of the coffee he bought me. "Going to need this today. Didn't get much sleep."

"Me neither. I had dream I was on my bike and got hit by one of the dump trucks they're replenishing the beaches with."

"I'm sure they have their reasons, but I don't get using trucks. I read there was going to be seven thousand truckloads of sand in the first phase."

"Ton of traffic and pollution."

"I know. Why don't they just pump it from offshore like they used to?"

"It's got something to do with disturbing marine life."

"But creating havoc on our roads and wasting, who knows how much energy, is okay?"

He shrugged. "You should run for mayor."

"Mayor? If I run for anything, it'll be for king or emperor."

"King Luca. It has a ring to it."

I laughed.

"Seriously, what would be the first thing you'd do if you ran everything?"

It was interesting question. I had plenty of opinions on how things should operate, but I drew a blank. "Enough fooling around. You want to check on when the driver is being arraigned?"

Coffee cup in hand, Derrick headed to the door. "Sure. Anything back on the blood?"

"Not yet."

My mind went right to the bicyclist, John Holt. When he'd gotten up that day, he had no idea his life would end in a few hours. His daughter was coming for a visit next week. Now, instead of burying her feet in sand, she was burying her father.

The eyewitnesses said Holt had the right of way. What we needed to ascertain was whether this was a tragic accident, or had Holt become another casualty of the drugs eroding our society.

I jumped at the sound of the desk phone ringing. "Homicide, Detective Luca."

"Frank, it's Sully, from the lab."

"What do you have for me?"

"We found evidence of THC in her blood."

She had smoked or ingested marijuana. "Over the legal limit?"

"Just under it."

"Are you shitting me?"

"Sorry, Frank."

"Any alcohol?"

"None."

What she said about having a glass of wine was a lie. "Is there anything else?"

"That's it. We'll put the details in a report."

I disconnected the call and made another one.

"Dr. Bilotti."

"Hey, Doc, it's Frank. How are you?"

"Is everything all right?"

"Yeah, yeah. Just wanted to talk through something. John Holt, the bicyclist who was killed yesterday."

"I haven't done the autopsy yet."

"That's okay. You see, the driver had THC in her blood but not over the legal limit. She failed the field sobriety test, and I'm trying to figure out what's going on."

"THC can stay in the blood for up to thirty-six hours."

"How can we prove she smoked a joint or ate something infused with pot?"

"That's a challenge. The duration of THC is dependent on

several factors, such as how often someone uses, the strength of the marijuana, a person's metabolism, and even hydration."

Bilotti confirmed what I knew about marijuana and driving: without hard evidence she was under the influence, building a case was near impossible. We had zero tolerance laws for drivers under twenty-one, but anyone older could get away with driving under the influence of pot that drinkers couldn't.

If this kid was high and she killed Holt because she was drug distracted, I had to try to find a way to get justice.

My cell rang. It was the sheriff. I swiped the call away and picked up the desk phone.

"Mr. Feldman, this is Detective Luca."

"Hello, Detective. I was going to call you."

Sure he was. "When are you coming in with Mr. Ryan?"

"I'm still unable to reach my client."

I sprang out of my chair. "Is he on the run?"

"I don't know."

"Come on, Counselor, be straight with me."

"I am. I have no idea where Mr. Ryan is."

22

MIND RACING, I CALLED BACK THE SHERIFF. "SORRY, SIR, I was on the phone with Ryan's attorney."

"When are they coming in?"

"According to Feldman, he's been unable to reach Ryan the last two days."

"Do you think he's fled?"

"It's a possibility. I'm going take a ride to his place and see for myself."

"If he's in the wind, he's had a couple of days head start."

"I realize that, but with all the news coverage, it's going to be difficult for him to avoid capture."

"Call me once you know and we'll issue a statewide APB."

I hung up and called Ryan's wife. "Have you heard from your husband?"

"No."

"How long since the last contact?"

"Four days ago. Why? Is something the matter?"

"Not sure, but his lawyer said he's been unable to contact him."

"Oh my God, if he took off, it means he did it."

"If you hear from him, call me immediately."

As I hung up, Derrick came into the office saying, "The arraignment is going be this afternoon."

"Forget about that. Feldman said Ryan is nowhere to be found."

"What?"

"Let's get moving."

As soon as we turned onto Ryan's street, I exhaled. Sitting in the driveway was a green MINI Cooper. "He's here."

"Feldman is playing games."

"Or he told Ryan to consider a deal and Ryan is dodging him."

"Maybe. It takes a while for reality to sink in."

"Park two houses down."

We got out of the car, and I said, "Sneak around the back, I don't want him to bolt if he sees us."

Derrick peeled off and slipped between Ryan's and the next home. I surveyed the windows; the blinds were down. I stood to the side of the door and hit the bell. Letting ten seconds go by, I rang the bell again and pounded my fist on the door.

I put my ear to the door. No sounds. Looking at his car, I wondered if he'd left it behind to throw us off. A lot of runners left their cars at airports or transportation hubs. Ryan worked in the car business. He was suspended from his job but probably had access to another set of wheels.

Stepping off the landing, I peered into the sliver of space between the window frame and shade. The back of the couch was all I saw. Moving to the next window, I looked into the crack of clearance. Pulling my head back, I blinked.

Leaning in again, I squinted. "Derrick!" I ran to the back

of the house. "Something's off. It looks like there's a pool of blood."

"Where?"

"Come with me." We ran to the front.

"Here, look in here."

Derrick put his eye near the glass. "Where?"

"To the left a little."

"Holy shit! It looks like blood."

"We have to bust in."

"One, two, three." We crashed our shoulders into the door. Derrick screamed. I said, "Let me do it."

I raised my foot and smashed the door near the lock. Crack. I shouldered the door and lost my balance when it broke open. I grabbed Derrick's free hand. He pulled me to my feet. Eyes adjusting to the dark, I drew my pistol.

"Mr. Ryan! Police."

I motioned to the room where I'd seen the blood. We separated, and hugging the walls, crept toward it. Two hands on my gun, I approached the doorway. I swung my firearm into the room. I dropped my arms and rushed to the body.

Derrick said, "Holy shit."

Ryan was sprawled on the floor. A dime-sized bullet hole in his temple had fed the pool of blood beside his head. A pistol, a Glock, lay two feet from his right hand. I didn't need to, but I checked for a pulse.

I shook my head and took a pen out of my pocket. Tapping the blood, I said, "A hundred percent dry. He's been dead at least a day."

"I can't believe he killed himself."

"Facing twenty-five to life, who knows, we might do the same."

"Amen."

"I don't see a note."

"Me neither."

"We need to get Bilotti and forensics here."

He pulled out his cell. "I'll call it in."

Trying to envision Ryan killing himself, I circled the room. Unless he'd staggered, he'd been standing in the center of the room, right next to a cocktail table. A tinge of sadness washed over me. You had to be past desperate to kill yourself. Ryan was either consumed with guilt or afraid of the consequences of his actions.

It wasn't that unusual. I'd run into several cases where someone committed suicide to avoid going to prison. And it was worse behind bars; the suicide rate was four times higher than normal.

I made a quick pass through the rest of the house and made a call. "Sheriff Remin, it's Detective Luca."

"What's going on?"

"Ryan's dead. Looks like a suicide."

"Hmmm. What a surprising end to this mess."

"Sure is, sir."

"Do you need anything at the scene?"

"No, we're fine. Dr. Bilotti is en route, and forensics is sending a team to look for evidence related to the murders."

"Good. The public is going to be relieved this is over."

I'd bet my pension he was planning a press conference. "We all are."

I stood there trying to make sense of the situation. Ryan's wife had to be notified. It was puzzling why it seemed he hadn't left a message for her. In every crime-related suicide I'd seen, a note full of apologies had been left behind.

23

Derrick walked in as I read the statement the sheriff released to the press. I said, "You see what Remin said about Ryan?"

"Not yet."

"It was kind of weird. He couldn't miss the opportunity to pat the department on the back for the investigation."

"I don't know. With all the negative press we get, I get it. They say you've got to take every opportunity to toot your own horn."

I shook my head. "I'm not a fan of self-promoting. It's more powerful when somebody toots about you."

"Half of social media is self-promo."

"I wouldn't know."

"You're missing the cute cat pictures."

My cell rang. It was Bilotti. "Hi, Doc, what's going on?"

"Just finished the Ryan autopsy and figured I'd call you before you reached out."

"Now I know why I love you."

"And all this time I thought it was the wine."

"Well, on second thought." I laughed. "What do you have for me?"

"Based on the stomach contents and corneal examinations, I'd put the time of death between eight and eleven p.m., Tuesday."

Feldman was truthful. "Any substances in his body?"

"None. But we're going to run full blood panels."

"Suicide?"

"It appears to be."

"Appears?"

"The bruising in the temple area could have come from multiple attempts to, uh, summon the courage. The trajectory of the bullet suggests a possible weakening of resolve since there were no drugs or alcohol in his system."

"And he didn't leave a note."

"True, but notes are absent in more than half of all suicides."

"I wasn't aware of that."

"Suicides are difficult cases to assess with certainty, but that's the box I'll check on the death certificate."

I thanked him and hung up. "Bilotti says Ryan pulled the trigger Tuesday, between eight and eleven."

"I can't find a record of him owning the Glock or any firearm."

"His wife said he never had a gun. Said she remembered him saying he never fired one in his life."

"He could've picked it up at a gun show. There was a big one in Fort Myers a week ago."

It was another nonsensical loophole created by government. If you purchased a gun from a private seller, you didn't need to notify anyone. "It feels like there's one up there every couple of weeks."

"Americans have always been fascinated with guns."

"I understand the antiques and true hobbyists, but we should have more control over who's buying. Why is a licensed dealer required to do a background check, yet a private seller, at the same show, doesn't have to check?"

"They'll tell you the gangs don't get their firearms from shows."

"True, but if you're contemplating murder and don't have street contacts, you go to a gun show, find a private seller, and pick up something untraceable."

"We'll never find out."

"They have to have video surveillance of these gun shows."

"I'm sure they do. But I'm betting they won't turn it over without a warrant."

"It might be worth a shot."

"A lot of legwork to find a time frame."

"I know, but something doesn't feel right."

"What are you thinking?"

There was a knock on the door. "You gents busy?"

It was Larry Cornwallis, the county's sole drug recognition expert.

Derrick and I stood. I said, "How you doing, Corny?"

"Everything's going well, and you guys are doing good, I guess. The suicide ends that case."

We shook hands. Derrick said, "What are you doing here?"

"Barnett wanted to go over my testimony on the Roberts' case."

Derrick shook his head. "If you crash through the windows of a restaurant, and it's caught on tape, you shouldn't need an expert to testify."

"Not with five-hundred-dollar-an-hour lawyers running around."

"Amen."

"Look, I stopped in, as I'm about to put the notes from my evaluation of Helena Jackson into a formal report."

I didn't like the way this sounded. "Is there a problem?"

"She may have been impaired when she hit the bicyclist, but I can't testify to that, based upon my observations."

"Why not?"

"Her horizontal gaze was normal even though there was a lack of convergence in her eyes when attempting to focus. That would be consistent with cannabis use."

"So, what's the problem?"

"Dilation of her pupils was barely detectable, and that could be normal for her. And Jackson's pulse rates and blood pressure were slightly elevated but within an acceptable range, given the circumstances."

"I don't know what to say."

"I'm sorry, guys."

Derrick said, "Not as sorry as his wife. This woman slammed into Holt and didn't hit her brakes until after smashing into the poor guy."

I said, "I'm sure you know the blood work was inconclusive as well."

"I'm not surprised. The metabolism rate for cannabis is influenced by many factors."

"What's your gut telling you, Corny?"

"I arrived at the scene just over an hour after impact. Jackson is young and probably metabolizing at a quick rate. She could have still been under the influence when the accident occurred."

Derrick said, "We need zero tolerance for drivers of any age."

"We should have the same standard for using alcohol and drugs before driving. Right now, it's a mess."

Corny said, "Behavioral assessments are too subjective, and defense lawyers are good at tearing them up."

"I read they're working on tests and standards like blood alcohol levels. It'll make things easier."

"They better hurry up before more lives are lost."

Corny smiled. "They're going to put me out of job. I'll see you guys around."

After he left, I said, "I get the emotion, especially if you killed someone. We have to look at this from every angle we can, if it's an innocent accident, Jackson doesn't have a problem, at least criminally. But if she was high, we need to do our jobs."

24

Jessie brought out the olive oil and salad. Eyes glued on the TV, she nearly missed the table setting them down.

I said, "Shut the TV."

"I want to see this."

"We don't watch TV when we're having dinner."

Mary Ann said, "What happened is hard to believe."

Jessie said, "Mr. Simon played the press conference with Bobby Ryan's lawyer."

"He did? Why?"

"Said it was a good subject for our debate class. The lawyer said the suicide amounted to murder by the police."

"That's ridiculous."

Mary Ann glared at me. "What did Mr. Simon say about it?"

"He didn't take a position. He divided up the class, and we had to either make arguments defending the police or not."

I jumped out of my chair. "I'm fed up with everybody blaming us. We didn't do anything but our jobs. If anybody pressured Ryan to do what he did, it was the press."

Mary Ann said, "Take it easy, Frank. The teacher was just using it as a subject to debate."

"Yeah, right. He's another one poisoning the minds of our children."

"I stood up for you, Dad."

"Thanks, honey. Police work is difficult, and something like this is totally out of our control."

"Dad's right. It could have been guilt that made him do what he did."

Jessie said, "I said he might have decided he couldn't face a long prison term."

"Exactly." I grabbed the remote and shut the TV. "Let's eat."

I wanted to see for myself what Feldman said, but I knew going down that rabbit hole would raise my blood pressure. Though Ryan was dead, it wasn't enough for me. I had to know what triggered him to kill.

Going after Wright because she was pregnant was twisted but it qualified as motivation. Why he would kill Dr. Bigham was something I needed to find out. If it was connected to an affair, what drove him to stab her? It didn't make sense if Ryan didn't have major anger issues.

Mary Ann was watching a Hallmark movie, and I was running scenarios that would fit on the True Crime Network. Nothing fit. We had two dead women, and the man suspected of killing them decided to check out.

The picture of Ryan on the floor flooded my head. It was one of the most surprising turns in any case I'd handled. He'd stabbed the women to death. But used a gun on himself. It made sense. Stabbings were generally personal, and a gun was a quick but not easy way to end your life.

What Bilotti said about the wound and trajectory kept surfacing. It was normal to waver when killing yourself. I'd never have that problem because there was no way I could do it.

The show cut to a commercial, and Mary Ann said, "Oh my God. Can you believe that twist?"

"Uh, yeah, it was good."

"What was it?"

"Uh—"

"You're not even watching."

"I'm following along."

"You're obsessing over the Ryan case."

I shrugged. "Just trying to put the pieces together."

"You can't be 'on' twenty-four hours a day. The stress is no good for you."

She was right. It was especially not good for her. "Okay. I'll shut it down." I put a thumb and forefinger to my temple and made a twisting motion.

I faked interest in the love story she was watching, even swallowing a comment when the long separated couple randomly met at a gas station.

Minutes after the movie ended, another romance one started. Before the introduction was over, Mary Ann fell asleep. I grabbed the remote and lowered the volume. Closing my eyes, I lay as far back as the recliner allowed.

My thoughts went right to Ryan. He was good looking and a salesman. I remembered going to see him at MINI of Fort Myers. His smile was wide and manner easy. He probably sold a lot of cars.

I ran over our conversation and bolted upright. Was Ryan left-handed? He'd handed his business card to me with his left hand. The gunshot wound to Ryan's head was on the right side.

It was nine forty. I tiptoed into the den and dialed my phone. "Mrs. Ryan? It's Detective Luca."

"Detective Luca?"

"Yes. I'm sorry to call so late, but I have to ask you something."

"Uh, okay."

"Was your husband left-handed?"

"Yeah, why are you asking?"

"Was he ambidextrous?"

"No. What is going on here?"

"I'm looking into whether your husband actually committed suicide."

"You don't think Bobby killed himself?"

"It's hard to say at this point."

"What do you mean?"

"I have some questions."

"You think somebody killed Bobby?"

"I don't know."

"But you believe there's a chance?"

"It's very early, ma'am."

"You wouldn't call me at this hour if you didn't believe it was so."

She didn't know I wouldn't be able to sleep not knowing. "A question came up, and I didn't want to wait until the morning."

"Why would anybody want to kill Bobby?"

My first thought was a husband of one of the women he was screwing. "I know it's hard but don't jump to conclusions. We have to clarify the situation first."

I hung up and made another call. "I'm sorry to call so late, Sheriff."

"It's all right, Frank. I was just reading."

"I didn't want you to say anything more on the Ryan suicide until we have a chance to clarify whether it was a suicide."

"There's a question about it?"

"Ryan was left-handed, and the shot that killed him entered his right temple."

"That's not much, and Bilotti said it was a suicide."

"Yes, but he couldn't explain the bruising or trajectory other than nervousness."

"If it turns out not be self-inflicted, do you have any suspects?"

"Not at this time, but we'll dig in immediately."

"Keep me informed of any developments."

"Will do, sir."

"And keep this quiet until we know for sure."

25

GLAD I'D REMEMBERED TO PUT ON A T-SHIRT, I STOOD IN THE sun to heat up. Two minutes later, I closed the top button of my shirt and pulled open the door to the medical examiner's office. I was hit with air a polar bear would find comfortable.

I held my breath passing the autopsy suites. The chemical smell turned my stomach. Bilotti's office door was open. I guess you can get used to anything.

I rapped my knuckle on the door. Bilotti put down a document. "Morning, Frank. You want a cup?"

"No thanks. If I was juiced up any more, they'd connect me to the grid."

He smiled. I took a seat, asking. "Is that new?"

Bilotti picked up the framed picture of a vineyard. "It's from our last trip to Tuscany. It's an aerial shot of the Banfi estate."

"Wow. I remember you saying it's owned by an American family."

"Yes, from Long Island. They're responsible for putting Brunello di Montalcino on the map."

"One day, I'm going to get there."

"You will. Say, I apologize for being unable to talk last night. We went to Off the Hook last night. You ever go?"

"No."

"You have to go. They get the top comedians in the country. My face is still hurting."

"Who'd you see?"

"I can't remember the first two, but the headliner was Bobby Collins. He was hilarious and clean."

"The best ones don't have to get in the gutter."

"Very true. What's going on?"

"Ryan is left-handed, and the shot was to his right temple."

"Possible homicide?"

"That's what I'd like to check into. You said there was bruising in the area and the trajectory was toward the front."

He exhaled. "I did. The angle could be explained by the inclination to move your head away from the bullet."

"Okay, but that applies to you or anyone shooting. Do you think the bruises were from someone else? A killer?"

"It's possible. I'd have to examine the pictures again, but I remembered thinking they were inconclusive at the time."

"You don't go banging a gun into your head."

"You have to consider someone with suicidal ideation is in a frantic, desperate state of mind. Out of frustration, he may have hit his head to summon the will to do it."

It was a good point. "I don't know, Doc; maybe it's in my DNA to look at every death with suspicion."

Bilotti chuckled. "I remember you saying, 'Better to be suspicious all the time than to let one killer get away.'"

It didn't sound as good as I thought it did. "It keeps me up at night."

"You have to learn to shut it down when you go to bed."

"When I lay down, my mind says, 'I've been waiting all day to talk to you.'"

He laughed. "You have to work at it."

"I will, but right now, job number one is checking into Ryan."

I WALKED INTO THE SHOWROOM. A father and his young son were hovering over a toy-sized MINI Cooper. It was another example of a company looking to build lifelong customers. The little car had racing stripes running down its hood.

The general manager brought the sales force into his office one by one. The first woman had been there just a couple of months and had nothing to offer. She was in her fifties and didn't appear to be Ryan's type.

John Morris came in next. Shaved head, the forty-year-old had a stocky build. He took a seat and I said, "I appreciate your time. We're looking into the possibility it wasn't suicide."

"Wow. Somebody killed him?"

"We don't know that; we're exploring it. I'm looking for anything unusual concerning Bobby Ryan."

"He was a good guy. We got along, and he could sell, you know."

"Can you think of anyone who wanted to do him harm?"

He scrunched up his face. "Anything?"

I leaned forward. "Yes. Even the smallest thing."

"This is going to sound crazy, but about six months ago, he sold the last Sidewalk."

"What's that?"

"A special edition convertible."

"Got it. What happened?"

"Like I said, we only had one left. They're hot and in short supply. Well, he had two people interested and he sold it to a guy in Bonita. Right after he made the deal, the girl who wanted it came in. He told her it was gone. She got pissed and made a big deal about it."

Though I'd seen people killed over sneakers in New York, I was skeptical, "Did she get physical with him?"

"No, no. She left and the next day this guy comes in, tattoos all over, and asked for Bobby. He tells Bobby to step outside and he gets in his face. He slammed him into the window, and I ran out there and separated them."

"Did he threaten him?"

"Oh yeah, said he'd kill him if he didn't get his daughter the car."

"He was her father?"

"Yeah, and I don't know for sure, but he was supposed to be some drug dealer from Lehigh Acres."

"Did he ever come to the dealership again?"

"Just once. He drove into the parking lot and started beeping the horn like crazy. Bobby didn't go outside, and the guy took off after five minutes."

"Did Ryan ever mention him?"

"He brushed it off, but I think he was scared."

It was something to check into. I asked the general manager to check the files for the driver's license the daughter used for the test drive. I talked with four others, but that was all I had to look into.

I stepped into the sunshine and checked the sticker on a an off-white convertible before getting back into my boring car.

Passing the Coconut Point Mall, my cell rang. I clicked the console to accept the call. "Detective Luca."

"Uh, hi, you were just here, at the dealership, right?"

"Yes. Who is this?"

"Frankie, I work in parts. They told me you were asking about Bobby and who killed him."

"Do you have information?"

"Yeah, I think I know who did it."

26

Derrick looked up from his monitor as I swept into the office. I said, "We have two leads on Ryan's possible killer."

"Whoa."

"One of them is really interesting. Ryan was screwing around with another woman named Gloria. Her husband got wind and confronted Ryan at least three times."

"How long ago?"

"Six months ago. The time line doesn't jive, but the husband is Raymond Bolero."

"Bolero? Don't tell me the Cuban mob family."

"Bingo."

"Wow. Those guys are vicious, but they're a Miami gang."

"They are. Raymond Bolero doesn't seem to be involved in their criminal activities, but his brother and uncle are high on the food chain."

"What's he do?"

"He owns the brewery across from the hospital."

"The Bone Hook?"

"Yeah. Haven't been there since they expanded."

"Me neither, but we'll be fixing that."

"We need background first."

"It could be that Bolero called in a favor, decided he needed the family."

"Or they acted on their own. These mob guys don't like it when somebody disgraces the family."

"That's more likely; it would explain the time lag."

"I'm going to call my Miami buddy, Longo."

"Great idea. He really helped on the Miller case."

I dialed his number, and he answered on the first ring. "Detective Longo."

"Vinny, how are you, my man?"

"Frankie, how's it hanging?"

"Oh, it's hanging."

We both laughed. He said, "How's the kid? Mary Ann?"

"All's well. Jessie's about to head off to college."

"Holy shit, man. Time flies. And how's Mary Ann doing with that MS thing?"

"She doing good."

"Beautiful."

"And you and Cathy?"

"Counting down the days till I get my twenty in. Then it's the good life; get a boat, a cooler full of brews, and hang out."

"Sounds good. I might join you, but I'm going need to be sipping vino."

"Anything you want, Frankie. Anything."

"Hey, I need another favor."

"Anything you need, bro."

I filled him in on the situation and hung up.

Derrick said, "Sounds like he knows the Bolero crew."

"He does, but he's not directly involved. He's going to ask around, see what surfaces."

A ROW OF SHINY, stainless-steel tanks were visible through the windows of the Bone Hook Brewery. I wasn't sure how close wine making was to producing beer. Were they fermentation tanks?

A dozen people were enjoying a late lunch. I smelled barbecue sauce, not beer. Behind the hostess, the wall was covered with hats and T-shirts with the eatery's logo. I asked for Bolero, knowing he was doing well. Financially.

The girl disappeared. I walked to a blue velour couch, passing a wall of chalkboard signs touting beers on tap.

I spied a guy who was munching on a pretzel the size of a pizza, when Raymond Bolero strutted over. His belt buckle was so big, it could probably get HBO. He extended a hand. "How can I help you?"

"I have a couple of questions for you."

"What's this about?"

I lowered my voice, "Bobby Ryan."

He frowned. "What about him?"

"I understand your wife and he had an affair."

He eyes narrowed as he shook his head. "That ended a long time ago."

"Six months isn't a long time."

"What's your point detective? You think I had something to do with what happened to that turd bag?"

"I'm the one asking the questions, Mr. Bolero."

His face reddened. "Go ahead, then."

"When you discovered your wife was dating Ryan, you got angry."

"What was I supposed to do? Of course, I was pissed."

"You were mad enough to confront Ryan."

"Yeah, that's right. I told him to stay the hell away from her."

It took two to tango. "I'm told it became physical."

"It was nothing. Just a little shoving and it was over."

"Someone had to pull you off Ryan."

"It wasn't anything. I was just trying to scare him."

"How many times did you confront Ryan?"

"Just the one time."

He was lying. "Are you sure about that?"

He hesitated. "Okay, it was twice, but that's all there was."

"Where were you last Tuesday night?"

"I was here. Where else would I be?"

"Until what time?"

"We're open until one."

He didn't answer the question. "What time did you leave?"

"I close most nights and don't get out of here until one thirty in the morning."

I'd check into his personal alibi. "Your family has a lot of resources to deal with situations like the Ryan one."

"What are you talking about?"

"Come on, we both know your family runs a criminal enterprise."

"I have nothing to do with that."

It was interesting that he distanced himself from their illegal activities but not the family. "They give you the money for this place?"

"No. I saved my ass off for it. Until a year ago, the bank owned more than I did."

"They help you out, though, right?"

"No. They're in Miami doing whatever they do."

"What do you know about their operations?"

"Nothing, I have enough on my hands running this place."

"How often you go to Miami?"

"Every couple of months. Why?"

"Did you ask your family to punish Ryan for the affair?"

"Oh, come on. You're grasping at straws."

"Answer the question."

"Look, was I pissed off beyond belief? Damn right I was. But much as I hated the bastard, it never would have happened if my wife said no."

He had that right. "But yet, you went after Ryan."

"I threw her out of the house. What else was I supposed to do?"

I felt for him. "Have you patched things up with her?

"No. I mean, how could I?"

It would take a better man than me to forgive her. "I'm sorry."

"This whole thing destroyed my family. My son won't talk to her, and he's mad at me, of all people. It's a frigging mess."

The voice in my head claimed it was more than that. It screamed motivation.

27

DERRICK WAS CHECKING OUT THE OTHER LEAD I'D PICKED UP at the car dealership. The father of the girl who wanted the special car was well known to the Lee County Sheriff's Department. Dupree Johnson had a rap sheet the length of a wedding runner.

He was crooked, but none of his infractions were violent. That meant something, but he could easily have traded drugs for a hit. It was interesting that if Johnson or Bolero hadn't personally killed Ryan, they both knew people who'd do it.

I checked the time. Longo said he'd call me at two. That gave me twenty minutes to relieve my refashioned bladder. Walking to the bathroom, I wondered if the year I'd enjoyed free of medical scares was due to following doctor's orders. Even when inconvenient. The last thing the Luca family needed was another problem.

Sitting on the throne, I thought about how Mary Ann struggled the last time we went to the beach. Sand was a tough surface to walk on and it threw her off. She stayed quiet once we found a spot to put our chairs. I ran as much cover as I could. She feigned not wanting to get wet, but I knew she was uneasy about going in the water.

I finally coaxed her, holding her around the waist like a teenager and it worked. Being in the water was good for her, and she was religious about swimming laps in our pool each day. We had plans to go to the beach to watch tonight's sunset. I'd lost my appreciation, but I knew she treasured it.

Heading back to my office, I reminded myself to make sure I left work on time. My cell rang. "Hey, Vinny, right on time."

"When ain't I on the nose?"

I chuckled, "Dependable as Florida rain on a summer afternoon."

"You know we're coming over, I promise."

He'd been promising for years. "Anytime. We'll have a blast."

"Damn right we will. Just make sure the fridge is filled with beer."

"Consider it done. What did you find out?"

"The Bolero crew has been implicated in take outs. One of their henchmen is going to be charged in a double murder."

"Drug related?"

"No. If you can believe it, it was a fight that broke out in a club the Boleros own in Little Havana."

"Involving a family member?"

"No. It seems two guys at the bar wouldn't move down so these other guys could fit, and words were exchanged, and before you know it, a fight broke out. It was real shitshow. One guy was hit over the head with a bottle and ended up in the hospital, but what ticked off the Boleros was the damage they did to the place. They busted up the place, and two cash registers were emptied."

"Stealing from this gang isn't on the recommended list."

"And how. A week later, two of the guys in the fight were found in a dumpster with bullets in the back of their heads. We're sure Connie Rollin pulled the trigger."

"Any signs they might have taken out Ryan?"

"Nothing concrete, but we're going to lean on a couple of informants."

"Good, good."

"And when we arrest Rollin, I'll dangle a deal if he has info on your victim."

"I appreciate it. How soon you going to bring him in?"

"The DA is waiting on phone records. She's hoping it'll prove he was at the scene."

"How much longer?"

"Warrant was delivered yesterday. Should have it today, and they'll need to triangulate the cell towers."

"All right. I appreciate your help, as usual."

"Anytime. I'll call you as soon as I have something."

As I replayed the call, Derrick came in. I said, "How'd it go?"

"The father has an airtight alibi."

"Like what?"

"He was sitting in Lee's drunk tank. Johnson got picked up for driving under the influence."

I shook my head thinking of the dead bicyclist. "It's incredible how dangerous our roads are."

"We need something to quickly measure the amount of drugs in someone's system."

"I read something last night; they're evaluating a swab test."

"That would be neat. Maybe that girl who hit the bicyclist wouldn't get away with it."

An idea popped into my head. "I wanted to see what kind of camera surveillance the complex she lives in has."

"What are you interested in?"

"Maybe we can catch her driving haphazardly. She lives in Positano. Why don't you make a couple of calls and see what they have?"

"I'll take a ride down there."

"While you're out, you mind checking up on Bolero's alibi?"

"No problem, I'll stop by the Bone Hook, see if we can verify it."

He started for the door. "Thanks. I'm going to go see Remin. He wants to know where we're at. He's looking to put out a statement on Ryan."

Remin's smile threw me off. "Come in."

I settled into a chair. "Thanks, sir."

"How's Mary Ann?"

My guard shot up. "She's doing well. Thanks for asking."

"Good to hear. Health is all that matters."

Instinctively, I put a hand to my gut. After bladder cancer, I didn't need the reminder. "No doubt."

"Are we ready to officially declare it a suicide?"

"I'd like a little more time."

"Why?"

"We're working a lead. Ryan was having an affair with the wife of the man who owns the Bone Hook Brewery."

"What evidence do you have the husband might have killed Ryan?"

"None but—"

"Does he have an alibi for the time period?"

"Yes."

"Then it's a suicide."

"Sir, if I may. The husband is a member of the Bolero family."

"The Miami gang?"

"Yes. He doesn't seem to be involved in their criminal activities, but you know how these people are."

"It's a connection, but as thin as rice paper. I'll give you forty-eight hours. Nothing concrete arises, we declare it a suicide and move on."

28

───────

Derrick came in holding up a thumb drive. "We got her on film backing into a tree."

"Did she seem bombed?"

"Yeah. After she hit the tree, she was on the wrong side of the road. A car swerved to avoid hitting her."

I shook my head. "I hope we can use this."

"Let me show you."

He popped the drive in and navigated to the window of time. "Here she comes."

Jackson was tapping on her phone as she walked to her car. Derrick said, "She looks unsteady."

"It could be she's glued to her phone."

Jackson climbed into her car and backed out, stopping when she hit a palm. A frond fell onto the car. She put it in drive and pulled away, staying too far to the left. "She didn't even get out."

"Watch. Here comes a car."

"Whoa. That was close."

"Guy got lucky."

"He did but not Holt. If they would've had a fender bender, Holt would still be alive."

People liked to say, "If I would've left ten seconds early, nothing would have happened." I learned to think about it another way. How many situations had I avoided by taking an extra second washing my hands?

"Poor guy."

"I want to run this by the prosecutors. They said no to vehicular manslaughter. Maybe we can get them to plea to something."

"You think so?"

"I can't let Holt just be another statistic."

"It a shame."

"What about Bolero? Did his alibi check out?"

"I couldn't get anything. It was all day shifters. I'm going back after work."

"All right. We need something. Remin is only giving us two days."

* * *

I LAID the beach towel over the chair. "Go ahead, sit."

She held on to me and lowered herself down. I said, "This chair is better, right?"

"Yes. I like that it's higher."

Our old chairs were too close to the sand, and getting in and out was challenging. "We were overdue for new ones. How long we had those?"

"About six years. It's so beautiful, going to be a nice sunset."

"Perfect night. The Gulf looks like a lake."

"There's a lot of people here."

"Remember how quiet it was ten years ago? We used come with Jessie, and it felt like being in the Caribbean."

"We haven't been to the beach with her in two years."

"She likes Wiggins Pass, always did. Remember when we'd make our way from the parking lot through the wooded area? We'd pretend we discovered a beach."

Mary Ann reached for my hand. "It's gone so fast. I don't know what I'm going to do when she goes off to college."

"It'll be an adjustment, but she'll come home on breaks, and we'll go see her, if she wants us to."

"The house is going be empty without her."

It was time to change the subject. I pointed to the water. "Look out there. There's not a boat in sight."

"So peaceful."

"You realize this view is the same as it was a thousand years ago?"

"That's true. People, a hundred years ago, sitting right where we are, saw it just as we did."

"A hundred years ago, there was nobody here. There was nothing between Fort Myers and Everglades City."

"I can't imagine it like that."

"Out there, no change." I hiked my thumb over a shoulder. "Back there, tons of change."

She nodded, inhaling deeply. "The vastness of the ocean makes you feel small. It's relaxing, peaceful. It quiets my thoughts."

That's where we differed. I did some of my best thinking at the beach. When I first came down, I used to walk by the water and figure out problems. I knew as soon as we stopped talking, the Ryan case would seep into my head.

It was a fault of mine. I needed to know the details of what happened when someone died unexpectedly. Everyone was fixated on who was responsible for a death. I got it. It was not only the most important thing, it was the essence of my job.

But I had to know the details of the how and why. When they were in doubt, my ability to relax and sleep were compromised.

Remin was adding unnecessary pressure with his deadline. We had an assumption Ryan killed Wright over the pregnancy but nothing on Dr. Bigham other than the speculation Ryan's affair with her soured.

It was hard to live with it, but we didn't operate in a vacuum. Investigations should be their own means to an end. But the press, public, and even our own department, would exert pressure for a conclusion. Most times we were able to hold fast and get the answers we needed to solve a case.

But there were times we couldn't. Times when a family didn't get the answers they deserved. Times a killer got away with it. Were we going to settle for an assumption with Ryan and the two he'd killed?

My stomach growled. "I heard that. Why don't you eat if you're hungry?"

I reached for the Jason's Deli bag. "You want your salad?"

"Okay."

I handed off her dinner and took a bite of my turkey wrap. "I didn't realize how hungry I was."

Mary Ann pointed. "Look how pretty the sky is. That streak of red is amazing."

"Like a painting. The sun is going hit the horizon in five."

"It's beautiful."

My cell rang, and Mary Ann glared at me. "We agreed, no phones."

"I forgot to turn it off."

Mary Ann scoffed, and I snuck a peek. It was Derrick. I swiped it away. The sun had dipped a quarter of the way down and the light had faded. I unwrapped the second half of my sandwich as a text pinged in.

It was Derrick. Bolero had lied about his alibi.

29

Pulling out of the driveway, I hoped taking Mary Ann to see the sunset gave me a pass to step out. She knew the sheriff had laid down a deadline, and there was no way I'd be able to sleep without confronting Bolero.

I moved to the side as an ambulance sped up Immokalee Road, turning into NCH. The parking lot for the Bone Hook was busy. I walked past Komoon, a Thai place Mary Ann liked, into Bolero's establishment.

The band was too loud for my taste, but three women were dancing up a storm. As I waited for Bolero, a waiter carried two plates of ribs past me. Deciding whether it was hickory or pecan they were smoked with, Bolero appeared.

"What can I do for you?"

"You may want to do this somewhere else?"

"Let's step outside."

I followed him out. He made a left and leaned against the building. "What's going on?"

"What's going on is, you lied to me."

He blinked. "What are you talking about?"

"You know damn well what I mean."

"Hey, man, ease up. I don't have any idea."

"You said you were here, working, the night Bobby Ryan died."

"Yeah, so?"

"We checked, and you weren't."

"I was here."

"Not all night. You left at eight. Where'd you go? To pay Ryan a visit?"

He wagged his head. "No, I had nothing to do with that."

"Where were you?"

"This can't get out. Okay?"

"What can't get out?"

"I was with somebody."

"Who? Damn it!"

"She works for me."

"You going to give me her name, or am I going to haul your ass in?"

"Debbie Conover."

"She here tonight?"

"Yeah, but she's, uh, younger, and, uh—"

"How young?"

"Twenty-four."

"Jesus! Can't you find anyone your own age?"

"She's very mature."

"Spare me the bullshit. I want to talk to her."

"Please, this gets out, and it'll be bad for morale and—"

"Can't help you there. You should have thought about that beforehand."

"Can't we keep this quiet?"

"Get her out here, or I'll get her myself."

Bolero trudged to the entrance and disappeared inside. I wanted to slap him to his senses. He was fifty-one. She was a kid. He was using his position to ensnare someone half his age.

A girl, barely older than Jessie, stepped outside with Bolero. He pointed to me and she walked over.

"Miss Conover?"

"Yes, but call me Deb."

"Okay, Deb."

"Ray told me you wanted to talk to me, but what's this all about?"

"It's a long story, but Mr. Bolero said you and he were together last Wednesday night."

"We were hanging out at his house."

"All night?"

"I kinda moved in about a month ago. I mean, I still have my apartment and all but . . ."

"And you're sure he and you were at his home that night."

"I don't remember the days exactly." She smiled. "We've basically, like, been together twenty-four seven, you know."

"I have a daughter a bit younger than you. This, uh, thing you have with Mr. Bolero, well, be careful. He's at a different stage of his life. You understand what I mean?"

"We care about each other. We really do."

"I'm not saying you don't, but the age difference is going catch up with you."

"It's not a problem. Ray has a young spirit; he's got more energy than me."

"That's today, but when you're forty, he's going to be sixty-seven. At forty-five, that makes him seventy-two. Do what you want, young lady, but make sure your eyes are open."

MARY ANN WAS in the middle of another Hallmark movie. I grabbed a bottle of water and settled into my recliner. The show went to a commercial break.

"How'd it go?"

I shook my head. "Bolero lied about his alibi because he didn't want it to get out he's screwing around with an employee."

"Not uncommon."

"The kid is only twenty-four, and he's past fifty."

"A lot of women like older men. Look at me."

"That's not funny, Mary Ann. This girl is not much older than Jessie."

"You have to stop reflecting. How many times do I have to tell you, you can't mirror every case onto you, onto us."

"I know, but what would you do if Jessie was involved with a much older man?"

"As long as she's happy, I'm okay with it."

"How can you say that? You want her to marry some old man? When she's forty, he's collecting social security?"

"You're being ridiculous."

Was I? Why couldn't I expect Jessie to have a path similar to mine? Okay, leave out the divorce. And I wouldn't want her to live anywhere else but Naples.

Mary Ann's family was Spanish and mine from Italy, more similar than you'd think. All I wanted was Jessie to find a partner who had the same background, or at least, values. Was that so wrong? Didn't everybody want that?

Like Mary Ann, what I wanted was for Jessie to be happy. I knew it didn't matter who she was with, but I also knew, choosing someone who was much older or from a completely different background presented more obstacles to overcome.

To me, it was a simple fact I'd learned through experience. A lasting relationship was difficult enough; adding potential problems seemed shortsighted. A text from Derrick chimed in.

I responded. "Sorry. Forgot to call. Bolero was with a girl."

We still needed to confirm it, but I knew it was the real deal. We had one lead, but it was a long shot and would take more time than Remin said we'd get. As Mary Ann's movie dragged on, I considered whether to tell the sheriff to do what he felt he had to.

30

———

I settled into my chair. "I still don't get what the hell Bolero's doing with a girl half his age?"

Derrick said, "Him, I get. It's her that makes no sense."

"Money. He's the boss, so some power thing, and who knows if this kid lost her father early on or he was a crappy dad."

"Or she could've had a good dad, and she gravitates toward older men as security."

He had a point I never considered. "You wouldn't want your kid to get involved with something like that."

"Me and Lynn say as long as she's happy, that's all that counts."

"Until it happens." I laughed, "Then she's happy and you're not."

"We got a long time until I have to worry about that."

I got out of my chair. "I'm going to tell Remin we need more time. I talked to Longo, and it's going be a week or more before they get anything."

I knocked on the sheriff's open door. He was resting his chin in his hand. "Come in."

"Is now a good time?"

He hesitated. "As good as any other."

"Everything all right, sir?"

"Just the town council. They're looking for a five percent reduction across all departments."

"Can't we get an exemption?"

"We probably will, but I was looking for an increase. Our officers deserve more; they put their lives on the line everyday."

He didn't need to sell me. "We appreciate your efforts, sir."

Remin shook his head. "Nobody understands how hard it is working in law enforcement. We have to do our jobs under the glare of the press and public. Everybody has an opinion on what we should be doing."

I wanted to ask him what was really going on. My guess was a couple of newcomers were trying to push their agenda to defund the police. It was another illogical concept, like California's decriminalizing theft under a thousand dollars. How exactly were those policies going to reduce crime?

"Isn't there any way to give the public a ride-along?"

Remin laughed, "Now, that's an idea I can get behind."

"I wanted to let you know the lead we had on the Ryan case went nowhere."

"Do you have anything else?"

"We're still waiting on more intel on Bolero's family. My Miami contact tells me it will be at least a week before anything tangible comes out."

"How confident are you about it?"

"Given the family we're talking about, it's plausible, but at this point, it remains a long shot."

"Is there anything I should know before declaring Ryan a suicide?"

"Nothing more than something feels off."

"I need more than your gut."

He used to be a homicide detective. Gut was another word for instincts. Sometimes they lead you down a rabbit hole, but he knew hunches, filtered through years of experience, generated leads that oiled successful investigations.

"I wish I had more, but it'll take time to confirm what happened."

"The medical examiner said it was a suicide. You keep working it. If it turns out to be otherwise, we have Bilotti as cover."

He wasn't going to throw my friend under the bus. "The medical examiner raised concerns."

"He hasn't altered the death certificate."

"No. He hasn't. I just want to avoid a situation that doesn't put the department in a bad light."

"We can't wait forever. Sometimes you have to make the call based upon what you have."

Taking the stairs back to my office, I knew Remin had the right sentiment. Oftentimes, you had to make decisions without all the facts. Without a homicide to work, my thoughts drifted to wrapping up the vehicular death before dipping into the cold case files.

ANDRE BOSOCK WAS one of the prosecutors working the criminal side for Collier County. He'd played basketball for Florida State, then went to Ava Maria Law before the school moved to Naples.

"How are you, Detective?"

"Good. What's with the detective?"

I looked up and shook his hand. "Old habits are hard to break."

I patted my stomach. "Tell me about it."

"What are you talking about? You look great."

"I'm trying, but me and pasta, we go back a long time."

He smiled. "You have to live a little."

"You look like you can still play ball."

He folded himself into a chair. "It's my metabolism. I eat like a college freshman."

"You're lucky. Speaking of luck, with Holt, the bicyclist, it couldn't get worse."

"It's too dangerous to bike in most of town."

"No doubt, but he should be lying by the pool, not in the cemetery. He was killed, and I don't believe it was accidental."

"That may be true, however, the drugs recognition expert's report doesn't support driving under the influence."

"She failed the sobriety test."

"I'm aware, but cases with drug use and driving are impossible to win in court without testimony from a DRE."

"This is insane."

"I agree. It's frustrating. The legalization of marijuana for medicinal and, in some states, recreational use, and driving under the influence of such, has to be addressed by legislators."

"We have to tag her with something or she'll keep doing it."

"I'm guessing careless driving wouldn't satisfy you."

"Damn right it won't. She was bombed when she got in her car, whacking a tree and almost getting into a head-on in her parking lot, before she killed Holt."

Bosock leaned forward. "What do you have on her actions before the accident?"

"We obtained video of her in her parking lot. Anyone could tell she was impaired. She smacks into a tree and doesn't even get out of her car?"

"You know—"

"I know that's not enough, but can't we use it somehow? Tell her she's in more trouble than she thinks."

"Her attorney would know the law."

"Come on, Andre, this is as wrong as it gets."

"We might be able to tag her with reckless driving. She's exhibited a willful and wanton disregard for the safety of property."

"Can you charge her with a felony?"

"Reckless qualifies as one."

"Jail time?"

"Doubtful, but not out of the question, though it would be in the thirty- to ninety-day window."

I didn't know what was worse for Mrs. Holt: if no charges were brought, it would be an accident. If a short sentence was handed out, it would leave her trying to rationalize the exchange with the loss of her husband.

31

———————

"DERRICK, WHERE'S THE THUMB DRIVE FROM POSITANO?"

He opened a desk drawer. "Right here. What's up?"

"We need to get it to Bosock. He wants to see if he can use it to go for a reckless driving charge."

"That's the best we can get for the Holts?"

"I'm afraid so. It's not right, but the law is what it is today."

"She's just gonna get a fine or thirty in the slammer."

"I know. What do you think is worse for Holt's wife? Calling it an accident or tagging the driver with a reckless charge?"

"That's a tough one."

"Run it upstairs for me. Let them go over it and see what they say."

Derrick pulled the drive out and left the office.

I sat there, disgusted a life had been snuffed out so carelessly. I pulled up the website for Mothers Against Drunk Driving and searched for contact information. They had a presence, and I hoped they'd be able to pressure legislators to enact laws to deal with driving under the influence.

As soon as I hit send, the phone rang. "Homicide, Detective Luca."

"Frank, just got a call. Guy found a body in Logan Woods. It's a male."

"I don't know the neighborhood Logan Woods. Where is it?"

"It's a park, Logan Woods Preserve. It's on the corner of Pine Ridge and Logan Boulevard."

Hearing "Preserve," my stomach turned. "Got it. I'm on my way."

"Good, a unit is rolling. ETA is three minutes."

Pulling my jacket on, Derrick walked back in. "Let's go. We have a body."

"Where?"

I filled him in as we headed to the parking lot.

Turning onto Airport Pulling Road, Derrick said, "Never heard of that park." He pulled out his phone and tapped away.

"Me neither."

"It says the entire park is less than seven acres. Take Logan, it's just north of Pine."

"I think that park backs up to the Vineyards. Does it?"

"Yeah. What are you thinking?"

"Just trying to map out access."

"How old did they say the body was?"

"They didn't. It's almost better the less we have. We see the scene, we don't have any preconceived ideas about it."

"Yeah."

I put my strobes on and slowed. "You see a driveway?"

"No. But there's a patrol car up there. See the back of it?"

"Yeah." I pulled onto the grass, just short of the path the marked unit was on.

As we got out, another marked car pulled up. I scooted in

front of the car as a truck rumbled by. "Derrick, tell him to block all traffic until we can be sure the area is secure."

I headed for a mulched path leading into a wooded area. The air smelled of damp moss. A hundred feet ahead, phone to ear, a uniformed officer was walking in a circle. He was in front of a string of yellow tape crossing the path where it forked. He caught sight of me and hung up.

"You first on the scene?"

"Yes, sir."

"See anything?"

"No."

"Where's the guy who called it in?"

"He left. He had to go to the bathroom, but I have his contact information, and I took a picture of his driver's license."

"Good."

"His name is Len Visick. He's seventy-two."

Would I get a pass from the problems all older men faced since I had refashioned plumbing? "That explains it. He's coming back?"

"Yeah. He lives in the Vineyards."

"Where's the body?"

He lifted the tape. "Take it to the right. It's thirty yards ahead."

Arms crossed over her chest, a uniformed officer stood guard. My eyes zeroed in on a wooden bench. Stopping dead in my tracks, I blinked. The body was in an upright position.

This looked too familiar. As I closed in, the bluer I felt.

"Detective?"

Raising a hand, I said, "Hold on."

I focused on the body's hands. There was something. It looked like the body had four stab wounds to the chest. The previous victims had three. I put gloves on. The corpse was firm and cool. I wasn't an expert, but this guy met his maker way after Ryan died.

Ryan wasn't the killer.

I turned to the officer. "Sorry. Needed to absorb the scene."

"No problem, sir."

"You see anything unusual?"

"No, sir. Been keeping my eyes on the woods."

I nodded as Derrick walked up. "Geez, same MO as Wright and the doctor."

"Yep. It doesn't look like Ryan was the killer."

"It could be a copycat."

He was right, but I knew it wasn't. "I don't think so."

"Looks like four wounds. The others had three."

"True, but this is a male. Whoever did it may have had to stab another time to subdue him."

"He's not that big a guy."

"I'd say five foot ten. One sixty. When your life's on the line, your adrenaline kicks in."

"I wonder who he is; he looks familiar."

"I know what you mean. I've seen him before but can't place him."

"You want to see if we can grab his wallet or ID?"

"No. I don't want to disturb anything till the body and scene are processed."

Derrick bent over, pointing to the corpse's right thigh. "That looks like blood."

I knelt, focusing on a small, red smudge on the outer seam line. "It sure is. It's in a weird spot to come from the chest wounds."

"Maybe when pulling the knife out . . ."

"I don't know. All we can hope is it's not the victim's."

I surveyed the surrounding area. "It's going to be tough

for forensics with all this mulch. It looks like he may have attacked him right here." I pointed to an area where the leaves and pine needles appeared to have been disturbed.

"Yeah, and he was eased onto the bench. There's a lot of blood."

"Maybe another sliced aorta. The killer knows what they're doing."

"But why the repeated stabbings?"

"He or she might have needed to subdue him, like I said, or it could've been personal."

"You think it could be a she?"

"Probably not, but you never know."

"Here comes forensics and Bilotti."

"When he's done, we'll see what's what by his hands. Meanwhile, let's talk to the man who called it in."

32

As I headed out, Dr. Bilotti stepped onto the path. "Frank, what do we have?"

I filled him in. "We didn't disturb the scene or check the victim for ID. Derrick is standing by."

"Good. We'll see if there's anything to help the investigation."

"We're counting on you, Doc."

The first officer walked toward me with a wiry man; I took him to be the guy who found him.

"This is Len Visick. He's the one who called it in."

I shook his hand. It was bony but he had a firm shake. "I can't believe it. I mean, my hands are still shaking."

Visick had a lined face but bright, alert eyes. I pointed to a bench twenty feet away. "Why don't we sit and talk?"

"I'm sorry I had to leave. I know it made me look bad, but when I got to go, I got to go."

He didn't need to know about my problems relieving myself. "I understand, it's fine."

We sat and I said, "Tell me what happened, what you saw."

"Well, I come here two, three times a week. Usually get here around five a.m."

A bird began chirping. "What time today?"

"A couple of minutes before five."

"But you called it in just after nine."

"That's right."

"You were here the entire time?"

"Oh no. I left around six."

"And you came back at what time?"

"Oh, about nine."

"Why do you come so early?"

"I enjoy seeing armadillos. They have a nice colony of nine-banded ones living in here, and since they're nocturnal, you got to get here early."

People's passions never ceased to amaze me, but an armadillo lover was a first. "Where were you from six to nine?"

"Well, I walked to the clubhouse to use the bathroom and to get some breakfast. Since Sandy passed, I eat most of my meals out."

"And why did you come back to the park? Do you usually do that?"

"No, no. I ate and hung around a little, talking and, oh, I read the paper. Then, I went home but couldn't find my key to get in. I figured I dropped it when I took out the food I brought for the armadillos."

Another first. "What did you bring them?"

"Grapes. They really enjoy them."

Armadillos had themselves a butler. "You came back to search for your keys."

"Yeah and I found them."

"And how did you discover the body?"

"I was just walking along, and you know, I knew something wasn't right. I had this feeling. I thought it was because of losing my keys but then I saw him."

"Did you touch him?"

"No. I saw all that blood and panicked."

"When you were at the park earlier, the body wasn't there?"

"I don't think so."

It looked like we had a time line. "You would've noticed him, right?"

"Yes, for sure."

"Then he wasn't there earlier, correct?"

"I don't usually go to the right, where he was. Most of the burrows are to the left; there's a lot more insects for them to feed on."

A chorus of chirping broke out. Were the birds discussing how confusing this man was? "Why'd you go down it the second time?"

He shrugged. "I was looking for my keys, and at my age, I couldn't be certain I hadn't gone down there."

Something was off. "How'd you find your key?"

"After I saw him, I got all panicked. I was looking for my phone, to call nine-one-one, and my key was there. You know that little pocket inside a pocket? It was there all the time."

Witnesses were often unreliable. The way this exchange was going was more than concerning. "Did you see anyone while you were in the park?"

"No."

"No one else was in the park both times you were here?"

"No. It's rare you see anyone."

At five in the morning, that wasn't surprising.

I finished up with him and pulled out my cell phone. "Sir,

I wanted to let you know that Ryan doesn't appear to have been the killer."

"Hmmm."

"We have another corpse with the same MO. Dr. Bilotti is on the scene, and we're hoping to be able to either confirm or deny it for sure."

"It appears your instincts were correct."

"We'll see."

"What resources do you need?"

"We're good at the moment, but we'll need help with making connections, if the killings are related. If they're random—"

"Whatever you need. I'll reassign as many officers as necessary and lean hard to obtain any warrants to further the investigation."

The threat had sunk in. "We appreciate the support, sir. We're good at the moment."

"Don't try to solve this on your own. I know you can, but we don't have time."

I wanted to tell him not to interfere but said, "It's always a team effort, sir."

"If this is the same killer, I want an overwhelming force. This has to end!"

I agreed with that, but whoever was behind this was good. Based on the other crime scenes, the chances they left a clue behind for Bilotti or forensics to find were slim. The last serial killer I'd dealt with was the smartest criminal I'd ever encountered:

Ethan Dwyer had an IQ that put him in Einstein's league. He'd been methodical and had thrown me off his trail several times. After we nailed him, he engineered an escape from prison that still amazed me. Was the person responsible for leaving posed corpses in parks in his class?

As I trudged back to the body, my instincts were ringing an alarm bell I couldn't ignore; this killer was at least as good as.

33

———————

MAGNIFIERS IN HAND, TWO FORENSIC TECHS WERE COMBING the area around the body. Hunched over the body, Bilotti's body straightened up. "Here's his wallet, Frank."

He handed me the slim, faux-leather sleeve he retrieved from the corpse's front pocket. Technology had reduced more than attention spans. "Thanks."

I slid out the contents. An American Express credit card, his driver's license, and three business cards. Derrick leaned in as I fingered the DMV card. "Victor Trent. He's forty-eight. I'm pretty sure that address is in the Moorings."

Placing the license behind the credit card, I pulled out a business card. "Now I know where I've seen him. He has those magazine ads, offering investment advice."

"Oh yeah. I've seen them."

Remembering his ads, I shook my head. "He's got two little kids and a wife."

"They're in all the pictures."

It was a good strategy, presenting himself as a man with a young family to draw trust and money. Every victim has a family, but the thought I'd have to deliver the news to someone with little children was creating bubbles in my stomach.

"Gentlemen, here's the case."

I took it from him and flipped it open. Written on a slip of paper was "One more to go before . . ."

"Before? Before what?"

Derrick said, "He's going to kill again."

"Not if I can help it."

Derrick shouted, "Hey, you!"

A man was running into the woods. Drawing my pistol, I took off. "Stop or I'll shoot!"

The man came to a halt, raising his arms.

"On your knees, and keep your hands up!"

An officer beat me to him and began cuffing him. "Hey, I'm a reporter. Check my credentials."

I patted him down, pulling out his press badge. "What's your name?"

"Matt Grier. I work for the *Daily News*."

It matched his ID. "What are you doing here? This is a crime scene."

"I was on a bike ride. Saw the activity and wanted to check it out. It's crazy, the serial killer struck again."

"Sneaking around is good way to get yourself killed."

"I just wanted to get the scoop. This is huge. He sent a message, like the Zodiac killer. This is—"

"Look, this is an active scene. If you don't want to get arrested for obstruction, you better get out of here."

"Okay, okay."

"Take the cuffs off."

"Would you be up for an interview?"

"No. And I'm warning you not to release any information about a message he or she might have sent."

"But we have a right—"

"That information is confidential. We need to keep a couple of details to ourselves to ensure we apprehend the right people."

"I understand your preferences, but the public has the right to know about threats in the community."

"We have to work together here. We need your help catching those responsible, and there may be a way to use you as the conduit."

"We'll get an exclusive?"

"No, we can't do that, but somebody has to know first, right?"

"We'd need assurances—"

"I'll have the sheriff call your boss and work out the details, but you can't say more about today other than it appears the killer struck again."

He pointed to the body. "Appears?"

"It's up to you, if you want to front run a story that turns out to be incorrect."

"Who's going to confirm it?"

"We will. Like I said, you'll be the first to know. And if anything leaks out about the particulars, I promise I'll find a way to nail you for obstruction."

***

"Did you eat?"

"Does a stale donut count?"

Mary Ann shook her head. "I can make you peas and macaroni."

Pasta e piseli, one of my favorite comfort dishes. "Nah, it's okay."

"It'll take me ten minutes. Go get changed."

"Do you feel all right?"

"Feeling the best in months."

"Really?"

"Yes. A couple of days ago, I felt more stable and it's gotten better."

"Thank God. You think it's the injections?"

"I don't know. Next time we go, we'll see what they say. Meanwhile, fingers crossed."

Heading to the bedroom, I said, "Amen."

MARY ANN SLID A STEAMING bowl before me.

"Smells good."

"You had a rough day. The news has been running the serial killer story nonstop. WINK is doing a special on it."

"Frigging reporter snuck up on us at the scene. If we didn't see him, the poor wife would've found out her husband was dead before we could notify her."

"How did that go?"

I pushed the bowl away. "The whole day was a frigging horror show."

She rubbed my shoulders. "Sorry."

"And that kid who killed the bicyclist isn't going to serve a day. They made a deal, and she got a hundred hours of community service. Big deal."

"Oh, I'm sorry. You had such a rough day."

"It's okay."

She moved the pasta back in front of me. "Eat."

I shoveled a spoonful. "Sheriff's suspending all time off. Going to be running patrols and stationing officers all over town. Going to look like a police state."

"That's good though."

"I don't know if it's going to help. I spoke to Haines at the FBI, and he agrees; it doesn't seem to be random."

"Profiling might help."

"We're going to need all we can get; whoever is doing it is beyond careful."

"Why do people do these kinds of things?"

"If I answer that, can you tell me what Casper was before he became a ghost?"

I HUNG up with Bilotti and hustled down the hallway. The autopsy confirmed the same person was behind all three killings. But there was nothing else. No fibers, hairs, or bodily fluids, except the blood smudge on the seam line of the victim's pants.

The room was packed with uniformed officers before their shifts. Captain Gesso quieted the room, and I stepped to the podium.

"Sheriff Remin asked me to brief you. We believe the same person or persons are responsible for all three murders. Everyone needs to be alert and especially vigilant regarding our many parks and preserves. It's likely the killer is a male, Caucasian, and in his forties or fifties.

"That's not to say it can't be a female. We're going to need help in chasing down connections between the victims, as the theory is these are not random killings. We'd appreciate any volunteers. Speak to Detective Dickson if you can help."

34

———————

I HEADED DOWN MOORING LINE DRIVE, TOWARD THE WATER and made a right onto Bow Line Drive. The Moorings was an expensive neighborhood with its own private beach, but the Trents' home, across the street from Emmanuel Lutheran Church, was in the modest section of the area.

Steeling myself as I approached the door, I hoped the Trent children would be around to lighten the air. About to ring the bell, the throaty rumble of a Ferrari had me turning toward the street. I watched the red sports car accelerate around a curve before I hit the bell.

The door swung open, and Robin Trent offered me a tiny smile. "Come in, Detective Luca."

She was stronger than I expected. I was further buoyed by the sound of kids playing. "Thank you, Mrs. Trent."

I followed her into the main room. Using her foot, she pushed aside a toy car, and we sat on a gray sectional.

"Thank you for seeing me so soon. I know this is difficult. Are you doing okay?"

She frowned. "My mom came to help me with the children." She clasped her hands. "It really hasn't sunk in."

"I'm sorry, ma'am."

She blinked, and I knew I had to start asking questions or the tears would flow. "Is there anyone you can think of who would want to harm your husband?"

"No, it's inconceivable. Victor was a gentle soul. He was always helping people."

"How long have you known your husband?"

"About eight years. We met at work. I used to be an assistant to the manager."

"Did he bump heads with anyone there?"

"No. They loved Victor."

"What about his customers? He was a financial adviser. People can get upset when they lose money."

"His clients adored him. He was like that commercial where the adviser gets invited to a customer's family events."

She was portraying him as godlike. It was going to be a challenge to delicately insinuate she may not have known her husband as well as she thought.

"What about a rival at the firm or the industry?"

"I don't understand what you mean by that. Vic wasn't a competitive person."

"Your husband had a successful career, right?"

"Yes. People trusted him, and he did well for his customers."

"How did he get his clients?"

"I don't know for sure, but he was always meeting people and he'd be recommended, which he really liked."

"He have customers with a lot of money?"

She smiled. "We're in Naples; what's your definition of a lot of money?"

She was right. People who'd made it financially always said, I thought I was doing well until I came to Naples. "I don't really know that world, but let's use a client with ten million to manage. Did he have a lot them?"

"He didn't talk about how much this one or that one had, you know, because of confidentiality, but he had at least ten customers like that. And there was one client, he called him a whale, who had over a hundred million. He lives on Gulf Shore Drive, right on the beach."

"When did he take that new customer on? Recently?"

"Yes, within the last month or so."

"He talk about getting any flak or pressure from whoever he took the client from?"

She gasped. "You think... no, it couldn't be. Why would someone do that?"

At 1 percent per year in fees, it gave someone a million reasons. With that kind of money, the fee may only pay a half of a percent. Still, that was a half a million dollars a year for an adviser. More than enough motivation.

"Mrs. Trent, I know this may seem unusual, and you don't have to answer it, but how much money did your husband make?"

"I don't really know the specifics. Vic was good with numbers; it was his job and he handled our finances."

"Who were his closest friends?"

"Jim Keystone. He and Vic were friends from grammar school."

"They still close?"

"Oh yeah, they had dinner less than a week before . . ."

Her chin quivered. I wanted to ask her about any affairs her husband may have had, but I didn't want to upset her, and his friend would probably know if he had.

AFTER REPEATING THE HOTLINE NUMBER, I made one last plea for the public's help. The camera light went off, and I said, "What do you think? Was it okay?"

"Perfect."

"Great. Make sure it gets out to every channel. Today, if possible."

"Will do."

"Thanks. I have to run."

I took the stairs two at a time and spilled out onto the first floor. I hesitated, talking down my claustrophobic tendencies before stepping in.

Our office was built for two, maybe three. The four officers who'd volunteered were standing in a circle around Derrick's desk.

"Hey, we appreciate your help. I just talked to Gesso. He's going to carve out an area in the bullpen for you to work from. What I'd like you to focus on are the connections between the victims.

"Go back as far as ten years, maybe longer if it warrants it. We know Wright and Dr. Bigham used the same Realtor, Stephen Ong. Derrick and I will dig into Ong, but that's the type of connection we need to discover.

"Not only romantic relationships, but did they belong to the same social club, play pickle ball together, attend the same church. That's the intel that'll lead us to the killer. Any questions?"

They silently shook their heads.

"Good. Derrick has a file on Bigham and Wright. We're still putting together one for Trent, but we'll give you what we have. It may be something will make sense once we throw Trent into the mix."

After they nodded, I said, "Derrick's going to help you settle in after I have a quick word with him. Thanks again."

The volunteers filed out. I said, "Remin wants me at the press conference. I told him you should be there."

"It's okay. We have enough to do."

He was a better man than I. "We sure do. Look, after the PR bullshit, I'm going to see Trent's best friend."

35

Inching east on Immokalee Road, it took all the restraint I could muster to keep from putting my lights and siren on. Why hadn't I taken Logan Boulevard into the most heavily trafficked road in town?

It opened up after passing the interstate exchange. I knew why Walmart, Target and a host of others wanted to be by the ramps for I-75, but why did the city planners allow it? Traffic slowed approaching Collier Boulevard. Eyeing the new shopping and residential community about to open at the intersection, I couldn't imagine how much worse it'd get.

Making a right, I pulled into Bent Creek Preserve. I meandered my way onto Glen Forest Drive where Jim Keystone lived. Prices of anything inhabitable had risen dramatically, and I struggled to estimate the price of the white-and-beige home I parked in front of.

It was a nice home, but there was too much garage for my taste. I took the multicolored driveway to a recessed entry.

Keystone had a mangy beard. "Detective Luca?"

"Yes." I showed him my badge.

"Come on in."

He had a hitch in his step. Bad hip? "Nice home." There were long lake views through a wall of sliders.

"We moved here about four years ago. Lot of families, but the traffic on Immokalee is, well, impossible at times."

"They're supposed to be putting an overpass in at Livingston."

"They're going need a couple more. Somebody should consider tunneling under the roads like Musk said."

I wasn't sure if I'd see it in my lifetime. "That man has a lot of great ideas. Did you know he started Space X before Tesla?"

"Really? Wow. I thought it was the other way around."

"Most people don't know that."

He stopped by the kitchen table. "This okay?"

I preferred the lanai but slid into a seat, nodding. "What do you do for a living?"

"Logistics." He smiled. "It's a fancy word for trans-portation."

"Must be busy."

"It's easier to drive up Immokalee than it is to get goods from Asia here."

"You and Victor Trent were good friends."

He hung his head. "Yeah, I'm gonna miss him. It's hard to understand what the hell happened."

"You have any idea who could have done this?"

"No. He was a sweetheart of a guy. This has shaken everybody. I mean, there's a lunatic killing people randomly. Nobody is safe."

The press was pushing the "random" narrative. Whether it was real or had no bearing, scaring the public sold papers. "We're trying to get a full picture of Mr. Trent."

His face asked a question.

"I realize he was a good friend, husband, and father, but everybody has pimples. You know what I'm saying?"

"Sure. I have my share."

"What you tell me is confidential. Okay?"

"Thanks."

"Did he have any extramarital affairs?"

"Look, Victor was no angel. He screwed around at times before he was married, and as far as I know, he cooled it down."

"No recent affairs?"

"Not to my knowledge."

"Did he have any money problems you know of?"

"He'd complain about how much it cost to buy that house in the Moorings and to keep up the lifestyle he needed to."

"Why'd he feel the need to maintain an appearance?"

"He said people wanted to work with people who were successful."

I understood the reluctance to turn over money to someone who wasn't in your class, but that had nothing to do with competence. "He had some big clients. How'd he get them?"

"Discounting his fees. That was how he was building his book."

"So he wasn't making money?"

"Not really, but he figured money attracted money, and eventually he'd raise his fees."

"Did his wife know?"

"I doubt it. He only told me, like, a month ago. I knew something was bothering him, and after a second bottle of wine, he opened up."

Wine? What kind? "He was feeling pressure?"

"I think so."

"He say anything about what he was going to do?"

"Vic said he had a couple of ideas he was thinking about."

Get-rich-quick schemes? "He share them with you?"

"No."

"Did you get the impression he was going to, uh, stretch the boundaries?"

"You mean, do something illegal?"

"Or ethically gray."

He hesitated. Was there something he knew? "I really don't know."

THE INNER WORKINGS of finance was a black hole to me. Whatever money I had was either in the house or in mutual funds. I ran through the Rolodex of contacts in my head as I drove home. I was starved. I'd catch dinner, check on Mary Ann, and then head back to the office.

The sound of the TV covered my entrance. I called her name and Mary Ann jumped. "You scared me."

"Sorry."

"I didn't think you'd be home with what's going on."

"How you feeling?"

"Good."

"You sure?"

"Yes, Frank. I'd tell you if I wasn't feeling well."

Was the universe evening things out? Could I get a little help with the serial killer?

"Just checking. Did you see the appeal I made on the tube?"

"No." She grabbed the remote and put the TV on.

"What are you making?"

She pointed at me. "You're grilling turkey burgers. They're in the fridge."

"Fresh Market?"

"Yes."

She felt good enough to go out again. "Good, I'll put the grill on."

I headed to the lanai, fired up the barbecue, and flicked on the outdoor TV. It was the weather, again. The minutia of dew points and storms thousands of miles away were lost on me. Were people so bored, this interested them?

Pulling open the slider, I froze when the newscaster mentioned the meltdown at the sheriff's press conference. The screen switched to the video of the sheriff at the press conference.

Hands on both sides of the podium, Remin said, "My office's main responsibility is the safety of the county's citizens. Until this killer is apprehended, we're going to deploy all the resources at our disposal.

"Many of the efforts aren't visible to the public, but I've directed the department to dramatically increase its presence in the community. We're not only going to be out in force in the streets but also in county parks and preserves.

"While this case is of the utmost importance, the public should feel free to go about their lives without fear. This killer poses a threat, but it's not one that should disrupt your routine. Avoid visiting the parks and preserves alone. In the company of two or three friends, we believe you're safe.

"Naturally, keep your eyes and ears on alert, and report anything you believe is unusual. I'll take a question or two."

A tall woman stood. "Carol Wakefield from ABC. Since this is the third killing, and who knows if there are more, why did you wait so long to take action, like increasing the police presence?"

The camera zoomed back to Remin. His eyes had

narrowed. "We respond to all threats; this department is proactive—"

"Excuse me, Sheriff, but it took three murders for you to take action."

"That's not true, ma'am. We've implemented robust measures, many of which are not made public, in pursuit of the person or persons responsible for these crimes."

"Forgive me, Sheriff, but whatever you may have done, three murders in less than a month suggests you're not doing enough."

"We can always improve on our processes, but let me remind you, Collier County has the lowest crime rate of any metropolitan county in the State of Florida."

"That may be true—"

"It's a fact, ma'am."

"If you say so. But with a serial killer on the loose, why haven't you enlisted the help of the state police and FBI?"

Remin pointed to another reporter. As the young man stood, the woman reporter said, "Are you trying to avoid scrutiny of the way the case was handled?"

"Remove her from the room."

"What are you afraid of, Sheriff?"

"Nothing. It's the perpetrator who needs to fear this department. We're coming after you, and you're going to face justice."

Remin stepped off the podium and stormed out.

36

I COULD SMELL MY PARTNER'S COLOGNE FROM THE HALLWAY. It reminded me of the Ralph Lauren Polo my father used to wear. "Good Morning."

"Morning, Frank."

I picked up the coffee Derrick put on my desk. "You see the press conference?"

"Yeah. He lost it."

"It wasn't a meltdown. I'd call it a testy exchange."

"That's good. Maybe there's a spot for you up in PR."

"I hope Remin doesn't start with any knee-jerk policies."

Derrick's desk phone rang. He talked for a minute, wrote something down, and said, "I'll be right there."

He hung up. "We got a lead. That was an Uber driver. He was driving down Logan and saw a car pulled over by the Logan Preserve."

"What time?"

"Two in the morning."

"Could be the killer."

"It gets better."

Here we go with the games Derrick liked to play. "And how does it do that?"

"He said he had one of those cameras recording as he drives."

"He's got video?"

"That's what he said."

"Get on the move. I'm going up to see Sully in the Financial Crimes Unit."

I pushed through a door marked FCU. A bullpen area, with six desks, fronted two private offices. With eight full-time officers, it was a testament to the ceaseless efforts to separate the money in Naples from its residents.

Richard Sullivan was another newcomer, having recently fled Boston's harsh winters. As he finished a call, I couldn't help thinking sitting behind a desk wasn't doing his potbelly any good.

He hung up. "Sorry, Frank."

"No problem, Sully. Everything good?"

"How can it not be? The sun's shining and I'm not wearing gloves."

I laughed. "Look, I'm doing background on the latest victim. He was a financial adviser for Bank of America."

"How can I help?"

"He seemed to be doing well, but it looks like he was living over his head. I have no evidence he did anything wrong, but I'm trying to find out what someone like him could do."

"The big shops like Bank of America, Morgan Stanley, and Goldman, have a ton of checkpoints. It'd be very tough for him to fake or steal from a client. Small, independent places are far more susceptible."

"What could he do? Could he arrange a transfer or wire out of a client's account?"

"That would be almost impossible. He'd have to fake statements and deal with the distribution of the real statement. That would require involving a few others in the scheme, and it still wouldn't take long to uncover."

"Okay, what else?"

"The most likely would be selling someone an inappropriate product. Was this guy a CFP?"

"A what?"

"Certified financial planner. They're rare, but they're held to much higher standards of conduct."

"I don't think so."

"Okay. Selling products that aren't right for a client but pay huge commissions is something bad actors in the business do. They also churn inside a client's account. They trade a lot, generating commissions."

"And that's under the radar?"

"Yes. Until someone complains. The other thing they could do, and it's not as common as it used to be, is to sell someone a penny stock that is pumped up, and when it collapses, the client loses."

"Like those *Boiler Room* movies."

"Exactly. They take a stock trading for, say, fifty cents, and they buy a bunch of it. Then they push it on others as the stock is rising. When they dump their shares, it crashes."

"Anything else?"

"Well, privately held shares in businesses can also be abused in the same way, and then there is outright fraud, where you sell something that may not exist or is fraudulently valued."

My cell rang; it was Remin. I swiped it away. "Give me an example."

"You own a business or shares in it and make it look like

it's doing better than it is. Or with property, you make phony claims about it, and a buyer overpays."

"Thanks, you've given me a couple of things to think over."

"Anytime, Frank."

"I got to go. Remin's looking for me."

Knocking on the door, the sheriff waved me in. "Close the door."

Settling into a chair, I realized Remin wasn't looking in my eyes. Was he about to dump on me? "Is everything all right, sir?"

He tapped a pen on the desk. "I'm sure you saw it."

"I'm not sure what you're referring to."

"The press conference."

I nodded.

"I embarrassed myself and this department."

"She was out of line, sir."

"That doesn't make it right. She made an accusation, and instead of calmly responding, I engaged."

He was right. Stuff happens all the time. You can't control it, but you can manage how you respond. As a law enforcement officer, it was even more important to keep your cool or situations would escalate. "We're human, sir."

"It was unprofessional, and the town council is all over me. The press is hounding members over it, and this has to recede before it becomes the story."

"How can I help, sir?"

"I need you to be the face of the department for this case."

"Me? I'm not good with the press and—"

"You're our lead homicide detective. You're in charge of the investigation, and it's up to you to bring the perpetrator in."

"Yes, and we'll get them, but it'd be a distraction. I need to focus on solving the case."

"You worked homicide up in Jersey, didn't you?"

I knew where he was going. "Yes."

He smiled. "You've told me on many occasions you handled several cases at the same time, right?"

I nodded.

"You have one case now, and dealing with the press won't take much time. You hold a press conference; make it brief, and that's it."

My shoulders sank.

"You'll be fine. I'll schedule it this afternoon."

"Okay, sir."

"Thanks. I owe you one."

I banked the debt, hoping I wouldn't have to cash it in.

37

———

Derrick's smile stretched from ear to ear. "The media darling has arrived. Where's your entourage?"

"Yeah, right. I'm not doing that again."

"Why? You were great." He held up the morning's *Naples Daily News*. The front page headline read "Det. Luca Promises to Nail Preserve Killer." "They love you."

I sipped my coffee. "Stop already."

Derrick read from the paper. "Frank Luca, a homicide detective with movie-star good looks, held a press conference, vowing to hunt down the Preserve Serial Killer."

"Oh geez, are you kidding me?"

"It gets better." He continued reading, "Luca's tone was a refreshing break from the briefing Sheriff Remin delivered. That exchange quickly devolved when he was questioned by a reporter from ABC. Luca defended the sheriff, insisting the department had taken various actions to nab the killer. The veteran was convincing, alluding to several initiatives he believes will bear fruit. Luca projected an aura of confidence sorely needed by a frightened populace."

I shook my head.

Derrick smiled. "You saved the day."

"Yeah, now all we have to do is catch the bastard."

"The lab is trying to enhance the Uber video footage. It wasn't the greatest."

I shook my head. "If the pixels aren't there, you can't make it better. We have to work with what we know."

"Did it have to be a Honda?"

"And white?"

"Half the cars in Florida are white."

"No doubt. Get the DMV to run registrations for white Hondas starting with a K and Z in the plate number. We'll slim it down and start knocking on doors."

"It can't be that big a list."

"You know how to use spreadsheets. Can you run one with the ages of the owners? If we're lucky, we'll knock a few off the list."

"Will do."

"What kind of car did the Uber driver have?"

"I don't know for sure. Why?"

"What was he doing out there at two in the morning?"

"He had a fare. Picked up some college kid from a bar in Gulf Coast Shopping Center who lived off Sycamore Drive."

"We have to run that down. He could be deflecting."

"I'll get on it."

"Not now, the priority has to be the Honda. Tell them we need it immediately. They push back, I'll get Remin to call them."

"Remin? We don't need him, we have good-looking Luca."

I crumpled a piece of paper and tossed it at him. "Don't be a wiseass. I'm going to Trent's office. See what I can find out about him."

Crossing Neapolitan Way, I entered the Park Shore neighborhood. Bank of America operated out of a glass-and-white-stucco, four-story building, built twenty years ago.

Trent had an office on the second floor. The complex manager, Floyd White, was about sixty. He said hello in a folksy drawl. As we shook hands, I pinned him as coming from Tennessee.

"Why don't we step into my office, Detective."

"Good."

My phone vibrated as I followed behind him. "Would ya like a coffee?"

"No, thanks."

He hiked his pants up before sitting. "This is a mighty sad time for us. Victor was a nice boy."

"I'm interested in the relationships he had with his coworkers, clients, and competitors."

"He was a go along, get along type of individual. Sometimes, a directive comes out of Charlotte and it may not make sense. I'd catch flak from the staff but never from Victor."

"Had he lost any clients lately?"

"None that I'm aware of."

"How about any complaints against him, in the last year?"

"I think there may have been one but, that's not unusual in this business. See, when you handle people's money, they get upset over the tiniest things."

"What was it about?"

"As I recall, some gal was unhappy she couldn't get the benefits a friend of hers was enjoying. I explained she didn't have the required assets to qualify for it. You know how folks are: they have fifty thousand in an account, and, well, they want to be treated like the Queen of England." He laughed.

My phone vibrated again. It was Derrick. I swiped it away, and before I put it back, he sent a text: "Call me. We're close on the car."

I stood. "I apologize, but something has come up. I'd appreciate it if you check around on anyone Mr. Trent may have had an issue with."

"Sure."

"Ask around the office as well."

Bypassing the elevator, I took the stairs down two at a time. Pushing through the lobby door, I took my phone out and called Derrick back.

"What do you have?"

"We got the list from DMV and sorted it, eliminating a couple of old-timers."

"How many are there?"

"Take a guess?"

Ugh. "Two."

"Close. There's only three. All males, Caucasian and ranging in ages from thirty to forty-six."

"That matches the profile."

"I know. Looks like we caught a break."

"Keep this quiet. I don't anyone to run on us."

"I didn't tell anybody. Look, this reporter, Jimmy Braun from the *Daily News,* called three times in the last twenty minutes, said he has to talk to you."

"You think he knows about the car?"

"Unless he has a contact at the DMV tipping him off, I don't see how."

"Give me his number, I'll call him on the way back."

The area code was 239, a local number. I started the engine and punched in the number. As it came through the car's speakers, I pulled away. "News desk."

"Jimmy Braun."

"You got him. Who's this?"

"Detective Luca. You called?"

"I sure did. I got a call about a half an hour ago. It was

someone claiming they were the Preserve Killer."

Blood pulsed in my ears. "What did they say?"

"Said to give you a message. Said you're never going to catch him."

I put my strobe lights on and pulled over. "It was male voice?"

"Can't really say. They were using some kind of disguise app."

"Any detectable accent?"

"I don't think so."

"What else they say?"

"That was it. That's all they said."

"That's it?"

"Yeah, they hung up right afterward. The call didn't last more than twenty seconds."

The killer knew what he was doing. "Any background sounds that could give me an idea of where they were calling from?"

"You know, I heard like a horn, you know the kind they use on boats?"

"Yeah. Anything else?"

"I don't know, maybe there were people talking in the background."

"You don't record calls, do you?"

"No. That'd discourage calls like this."

"Okay. You let me know if they call again."

"I will, but we're going to run with this. Would you like to comment?"

I stuffed a no back in my mouth. We needed to draw out whoever it was. The most antagonizing thing I could think of was, "Tell them I don't care what they think. We're going bring them to justice, and it isn't going to take long."

38

A WINK NEWS VAN WAS PARKED IN FRONT OF THE STATION. I parked in the lot for the courts, cut across a lawn, and entered a back door.

Taking my jacket off, I said, "The *Daily News* got a call from someone claiming to be the killer."

Derrick popped out of his chair. "Holy shit."

"They said we're not going to get them."

"That's bullshit. Male or female?"

I told him the caller disguised their voice and hung up quickly. "He said he heard a boat horn in the background and people talking."

"Maybe by a dock or something."

"That's what I thought; it could be the Naples Dock. Sometimes there's a bunch of people streaming out when a party boat docks. We'll have to check if there's video from any of the businesses down there."

"If we can tie in one of these guys who own these Hondas, we'll be on our way."

"Let's dig in. What do you have?"

"I eliminated a couple of elderly drivers and cars older

than 2018. They changed the back of the car, using different taillights. That leaves just three."

"Nice work."

"Here's the DMV records on them."

Derrick spread three sheets on the desk. He pointed to one. The man had a scar running down his forehead, stopping at an eyebrow. "I'm putting my money on Brad Bailey. He has a record. Guess what for?"

"Not paying at a kid's lemonade stand?"

Derrick scoffed, "Aggravated assault."

"Deadly weapon?"

"He's cracked two heads open with the butt of his gun."

It wasn't a stabbing, but it was solid evidence he was violent and unafraid to wield a weapon. "You might have a winner."

I picked up the second sheet. "Mel Frost. Not exactly a Floridian name. Any record?"

"Nothing but a DUI."

He was sloppy. The killer wasn't. "His eyes are weird. Evil looking."

"Creepy."

I swapped the document out for the last one. "Gene McGovern. Anything on him?"

"No record. Just one touch, a road rage incident two years ago, but no charges were brought."

"He's got anger issues but—"

"You want to start with Bailey."

"Yep. Get a bead on where he is. I have to tell Remin about the call and ask for help getting warrants. We need access to Bigham's patients and who Trent handled money for."

"That'd help."

"I'll be back in five."

"I'll meet you in the parking lot."

After seeing the sheriff, I hopped into the passenger seat.

Derrick said, "What did Remin say?"

"Said he'd speak to the prosecutors and draft the warrant requests."

"He think we'll get them?"

"Said it was likely."

"Perfect. What about the message? The sheriff think it's real?"

"He does. Remin said I handled it better than he would've. He liked that I pushed back, said it could make him reach out again."

"Or kill again."

"I know. That's what I'm fearing." I'd been thinking of calling Dr. Bruno to get her take on whether the killer would strike again to show they could kill at will.

"Maybe we should put eyes on these three."

"Good idea, but they'll be on the lookout after we see them."

"Maybe we'll get lucky."

I scoffed, "Luck is nothing but a byproduct of hard work."

"True."

"If we strike out with these three, we're going to have to look at Hondas registered in Lee County."

"Let's hope not. The list would be a hell of a lot longer."

"Pull over."

"What's going on?"

I pulled my phone out. "I want to call Dr. Bruno before we meet any of these guys."

She picked up on the third ring. "Dr. Bruno. It's Frank Luca."

"Hello, Mr. Luca. How are you?"

"Good. Look, I'm working the Preserve Killer case."

"I saw the news."

"Well, whoever it is reached out to the paper, sending a message. Said to tell me we'll never catch them. I responded that I would, trying to draw them out. But now we're interviewing a couple of new leads, and I want to be sure not to provoke them into killing again."

"I see."

"Can you give me any insight?"

"That's difficult to assess without—"

"Let's assume they're some kind of psychopath. Any tips when we talk to them to be sure we don't push them to kill?"

"All I can offer are general rules."

"That's okay."

"You have to keep your emotions in check. If you're frustrated or angry, don't reveal it. And never show you may be intimidated by them."

"Okay. Anything else? What triggers them?"

"It varies, but it's important to note that other than rage, psychopaths tend to exhibit few emotions. The lack of feelings and empathy is a hallmark sign. However, when they do get angry, it can manifest itself in an aggressive rage."

I finished up the call and hung up. "Bottom line is we're on our own. Use your judgment but don't show emotion."

Just after the airport, we turned onto Esty Avenue. Brad Bailey lived near the Salvation Army complex, in a blue home whose paint had faded to gray. Approaching, we heard a TV blaring a sports event.

Bailey had a thick midsection but was solidly built. He'd have no problem subduing any of the victims. I didn't profess to know who was attracted to whom, but I didn't see Dr. Bigham with this hulk of a man.

He didn't invite us in. "What do want?"

"Where were you Tuesday night?"

"Tuesday? Uh, I was out drinking."

"Where?"

"Couple of places."

"Names."

"The Old Naples Pub and Sweetwater's."

That was a lot of territory to cover. "Who was with you?"

"Friends."

"You go to those places regularly?"

"Yeah. What's it to you?"

"How well you know Melissa Wright?"

His right eye twitched. "She used to waitress at Sweet-water's."

He didn't answer the question. "How well did you know her?"

"As much as the next guy. It was a shame what happened to her."

"You know anybody you think could have done it?"

"What are you talking about? It was that Ryan guy."

"Maybe. Are you married?"

"Divorced. Why?"

"You own a MINI Cooper?"

"A MINI? I can't get in those little pieces of shit."

He had a point. "You go to Dr. Bigham, right?"

"I ain't got no doctor. I use the emergency place when I need to."

"What do you do for a living?"

"I'm a mechanic."

"Where?"

"Tuffy's in North Naples."

"What were you doing on Logan Boulevard in the middle of the night on Tuesday?"

"Logan? I don't remember being over there."

"You knew Victor Trent."

His faced clouded. "Trent? Hey, isn't that the last guy the Preserve Killer got?"

I nodded. He wasn't the kind of man I wanted my daughter to come home with, but I didn't think he was the killer either.

39

———————

My spirits rose as we zipped along Airport Pulling Road. "No traffic? Is this an omen?"

Derrick laughed, "The crime gods are giving us a break."

"About damn time. Slow down, it's coming up."

We crossed over a canal into Banyan Woods. Derrick flashed his badge and the guard lifted the gate. "He's on Post Oak Lane."

There was more open space than usual. The development had gone up before much of the growth Naples had experienced. Trash cans lined both sides of the street. Gene McGovern's home backed up to a lake. A pair of palm trees sat like sentinels on either side of the door.

Birds chirped over the road noise as we approached. "Looks like a full-time neighborhood."

"Yeah. Lynn has a friend with two kids that live in here."

Bags under his eyes and standing back, McGovern was wearing a sweater and long pants. It was in the low eighties. The house faced north. I peered over his shoulder, not enough sun beaming in?

Two pictures of bald eagles framed the foyer. We

followed him into a fluorescent-lit kitchen. It could have been the lighting, but McGovern's face looked pasty. Did he venture outside?

Derrick said, "Thanks for seeing us."

"I don't know why the police would want to speak to me."

I said, "We talk with a lot of people. Let's get started. Are you married?"

"No, my wife took off when I got sick."

She'd missed the "in sickness and in health" part. I felt for him. Maybe depression kept him inside. "What do you do for a living?"

"I'm retired."

He was too young for that. "What did you do?"

"Used to trade currencies."

"A lot of pressure?"

"Almost killed me. You can make a lot of money, but you can lose it just as easily."

"I guess you did all right if you don't have to work."

"I don't live high."

"You don't mind me asking, me and the wife are looking for a new financial adviser. Who do you work with?"

"I utilize index funds. Nobody can beat the market year after year."

"I've heard that. So, what do you do with your free time?"

"I volunteer for Rookery Bay. They have an aviary department and it gets me outside."

A vision of him in a tent hat, covered head to toe, popped into my mind. "You ever go to the preserve on Logan?"

"Where's that?"

"At the Vanderbilt Beach Road intersection."

"Oh, right. I've seen it."

"You've never been there?"

"No."

"Your car was seen there last Tuesday."

"Really?"

"We got it on camera."

He asked, "Why would you be checking that?"

"Someone was killed in Logan Preserve."

"Oh yes, I heard about that. Terrible."

Not the reply I expected. "What were you doing all the way over there?"

"I may have driven by it."

"In the middle of the night?"

"I suffer from insomnia. Driving gets my mind off the treadmill; it relaxes me."

"What doctor you go to for that? My wife has trouble sleeping."

"Nothing works. Their solution is doling out sleeping pills."

"You ever hear of a Dr. Bigham?"

"No. I don't believe so."

We finished up with McGovern and hopped back in the car. Derrick said, "What'd you think?"

"He was a little too cavalier. Almost like he forced himself to seem relaxed."

"I didn't get that. He's probably innocent."

"Let's see what we get with Mel Frost."

"Can't get over that name. Maybe the family is from Minnesota."

I laughed, "That would fit. Look, after we're done with Frost, we need to get some photos of these three down to Alice Sweetwater's, see if anybody recognizes them."

Pulling up to Forest Glen's gate, I said, "I've been in here before. Have you?"

Derrick said, "No. But I hear it's a massive community."

"Something like six hundred acres."

Sitting on Collier Boulevard, a long access road provided a nice setback, dumping you into a lush preserve on one side and a long lake on the other. Frost lived in a coach home on Periwinkle Way. It was in the northernmost part of the community, past another roundabout.

An egret stood statue-like to the right of the driveway. I still marveled at its snow-white feathers. It took a couple of ostrich steps away as we approached. Frost's unit was on the second floor, backing up to a preserve.

Derrick had said Frost was rude trying to dodge the visit. When it became apparent it was going to happen, he turned friendly.

Frost pushed open the door. "Come on in. Can I get you anything to drink?"

Declining, we stepped inside. The unmistakable smell of a man living alone filled my nostrils. The only natural light was coming from a pair of sliders with vertical blinds covering most of the glass. It was too dark for my taste.

He pointed to a leather couch as he fell into a recliner. Lowering myself, my eyes focused on two magazines: *Florida Sport Fishing* and the *Angler's Journal*. Frost was a fisherman.

I pointed to the magazines. "You like to fish?"

"Yeah. Anytime I can."

It was a lonely pursuit. "I don't fish much. But I see the allure of it."

"You didn't come here to talk fishing, so, what did you want to ask me?"

His smile was at odds with his face. Eyes didn't talk but his were screaming hate. If I hadn't seen his DMV photo, I'd attribute it to a distaste for the cops. "What do you do for a living?"

"I work for FPL, reading meters."

It was a loner's job. "Good company?"

"They suck, to be honest."

There was a bitter undertone. "They get upset with your DUI?"

His ears flattened. "What do you think? I had to spend five grand on a lawyer to get my job back."

He was lucky they rehired him. "Where's your territory?"

"Don't have one. I float, covering whatever jerk didn't come in."

"You work the Vineyards?"

"Yeah, was there a couple of days ago."

"What time?"

"Like the whole day. They got two thousand doorknobs."

"Your car was seen by the Logan Preserve."

"What, are you trailing me?"

"You know Victor Trent, right?"

"No."

"You sure about that?"

His eyes flashed a wickedness an actor would love to summon. "I told you I don't know him."

"You used to go to Dr. Bigham—"

"No, no. Not her. My guy is Dr. Samuelson. They're in the same group of doctors."

"Oh, we didn't get a breakdown, just a list of patients for the practice. Privacy rules, you know."

He nodded. "It's crazy what happened to her. You think it's one of her patients?"

"We're looking into that possibility."

"I never had her, not even once. I had that other guy, um, Frederik's, or something."

"Dr. Fredrickson."

"Yeah, that's him. He was okay."

We played cat and mouse for a little while longer before I stood. "Thanks for your time, Mr. Frost."

Once we climbed in the car, Derrick said, "Surprised you terminated the interview."

"I didn't want to put him on guard any more than he is."

"We have to check out the security camera footage at the gate. Let's see if he really is out late at night."

"Check with the guards. At that hour, they'd know about his after-hours excursions, if they're real."

"Will do, and what about the Bigham reference? He had to know her."

"We'll check it for sure. But first, let's try to identify who made the call to the paper."

40

DERRICK WAS ON THE PHONE WITH FOREST GLEN WHEN Freddy Garcia came into the office. "Hey Frank. Here's the footage from two places by the Naples Dock."

I took the envelopes from the volunteer. "Thanks."

"I told them to clip it at thirty minutes before and after the call."

"Great. I appreciate that."

"Hope it helps."

I opened one marked The Boathouse on Naples Bay and spilled out a device tagged Entrance/Parking Lot. It'd been awhile since Mary Ann and I had been to the restaurant. If you got the right table, the view would make the meal better.

Shoving the thumb drive into my desktop, Derrick hung up. "Frost is a night owl. They said he goes out four to five times a week in the middle of the night."

"But is he only driving around or not?"

"That's the question. We have to dig in." He came around his desk. "The surveillance footage?"

"Yeah, this is from the Boathouse." There wasn't a soul in the picture.

"That place can be busy. We're lucky it's not lunch hour."

I hit double speed. "I don't get people waiting an hour for a table. Anywhere."

"I guess they go to the bar."

"If I drank for an hour, without eating, I'd be bombed. It'd kill my appetite."

"You can't hang with the big dogs, Frank."

I kept my eyes on the screen. "You're right. But the best part is I don't want to."

"But you and Bilotti go to those wine-tasting things."

"Yeah, but wine's different." I smiled. "At least, that's what I tell myself."

He laughed and I said, "That guy looks familiar." I hit pause and zoomed in.

"I don't think I know him."

I leaned into the screen. "Me neither." I hit play and viewed the rest without coming up with anything. I inserted the next one from the Dock at Crayton Cove.

Derrick asked, "You go there?"

"No."

"They have this Great Dock Burger. I love it. Comes with a homemade sauce that'd make cardboard taste good."

"That's him!" I hit pause. "There's no doubt it's McGovern. He's even got a sweater on."

"Holy shit!"

Slowing it down, we watched McGovern walk up a path lined with pier pilings, into the restaurant.

"Yeah, but the time stamp is twenty minutes before the call."

"Maybe the camera's wrong or the guy at the paper got it wrong."

We stared at the entrance. I said, "Here comes somebody." A staff member appeared and lit a cigarette.

"It's a weird hour to eat."

"My buddy liked to say your stomach can't tell time."

"True. Here he comes."

We watched the back of McGovern. He brushed past the smoker and disappeared off-screen. "He's going to make the call. It lines up."

"We got the bastard."

"It's not enough. We need physical evidence."

"You want to bring him in?"

"No. He'll hunker down if we do. Let's go to his place. See what he says about being in the area. He may trip himself up. If not, we'll ask for a warrant to search his house."

"Let's roll."

I tossed him the keys. "You drive. I want to check in on Mary Ann."

"She still doing good?"

"She says she is."

"You think she's hiding something?"

"Not particularly, but like President Reagan used to say, "Trust but verify.""

He scoffed. "She's going to be fine."

"And what about you? You're moving like a high schooler."

"The new meds really made a difference."

Between Mary Ann's experimental drugs and Derrick's turnaround, I had a front row seat to the progress being made by pharmaceutical companies. Unfortunately, it wasn't cheap. "Are they expensive?"

"It's not bad. My co-pay is forty-five bucks, but I'd pay ten times it if I had to."

I kept my mouth shut. Even though you'd couldn't make a comparison, at ten times, it was still a quarter of what we were paying for Mary Ann's injections. I took my phone out. "Pain ain't fun."

We crept along Airport Pulling Road. Was my luck running out? I saw the sign for Banyan Woods. As we rolled up to the gate, my heart started beating faster. I sorted through our first conversation with McGovern.

A landscaper had parked his truck and trailer in front of McGovern's house. I didn't know what was worse: the deafening sound of blowers or the smell of gas they emitted.

McGovern's eyebrows arched when he opened the door. "What, uh, what can I help you with?"

I played it like Colombo. "We forgot to ask a question yesterday."

His shoulders relaxed. "I don't have much time. I have a doctor's appointment."

I was going to suggest he ask for a B12 shot to give him color. "This won't take long."

McGovern stood to the side and closed the door behind us. He didn't move out of the foyer. "What's your question?"

"You were down by the Naples Dock two days ago."

He shifted his weight. "Yes. And what makes it your business?"

"That's the day someone purporting to be the Preserve Killer called the *Naples Daily News* to say they'd never get caught."

"And?"

I took a shot. "The call was traced to the Naples Dock area."

"So? There's scores of people down there. It's a tourist magnet."

Derrick jumped in: "What were you doing by the Dock at Crayton Cove?"

It was a mistake. He never should have let him know we knew he was there.

"I went to eat. Is there an ordinance I violated?"

"What did you have?"

"My dietary consumption is none of your business."

I wanted to tell him to start eating steak, it might improve his color, when Derrick said, "You must be a fast eater. You were in and out of there in ten minutes."

"If you must know, I went in to make a reservation. Is that okay in your universe?"

"What time did you return?"

"I didn't. There was nothing available before eight and I detest eating late."

We had that in common. "Where did you make the call from?"

His hesitation was revealing. "I didn't make a call."

I was going to tell him I'd get a warrant, but we needed him comfortable that he'd thrown us off his tail. "All right, Mr. McGovern. You've answered our questions satisfactorily. We're sorry to have bothered you."

He nodded and swung the door open. I stepped into the sunshine thinking there was a good chance McGovern was our guy.

41

I closed the murder book, saying, "It feels like we're doing a jigsaw puzzle and can't put the frame together. We need something."

Derrick said, "We'll get it."

A volunteer walked in with a thick manila envelope. I said, "What do you have?"

"Dr. Bigham's patient list."

He handed it off. "It's fatter than I'd hoped."

"You want me to take it back?"

"Volunteering doesn't give you a license to be a wiseass, Ramirez."

Derrick said, "Yeah, that's *my* role around here."

"Everybody's a comedian."

"All right guys, have a good one."

I slid the inch-high report out. "We're going to have to split this up."

"Can't we get a digital version? We can search for particular names in a flash."

"At least it's alphabetized."

Derrick came around his desk. "Great."

Ditching the methodical approach that served me so well, I flipped about three quarters of the way down. Landing on last names beginning with an L, I turned three more pages. Following my forefinger down the last, I said. "McGovern was a patient."

"Wow. When's the last time he saw her?"

"It doesn't say."

"Was she his regular doctor?"

"I guess so. The practice is a family one."

"McGovern lied about going to her."

Theories were the currency of a homicide detective, yet I struggled to find a reason for McGovern to lie. "The only thing that makes sense is he wanted to keep it quiet."

"He figured privacy laws would prevent us from finding out."

"It's a connection we'd been looking for. Now, what links him to the other victims?"

I flipped to the pages where patients names started with an F.

Derrick said, "The volunteers came up with nothing."

"We have to dig deeper, get creative." I scanned the list. "Well, what do you know; Frost was also a patient of Bigham's."

"He said he went to the practice, maybe one time she filled in for his doctor—what was his name?"

"Samuelson." I surprised myself coming up with it so fast. Was the fog from chemo finally lifting?

"That's him. If Frost is on the level, he shouldn't mind asking them to release information that backs his story up."

"True. But it doesn't obviate the connection. He interacted with Bigham at least once. We need to find out whether it was an innocent encounter or if something was triggered."

"How?"

If I knew, I'd tell him. My desk phone rang as I said, "Back to fundamentals."

Derrick stood and nodded. "I got to take a leak."

I answered the call. "Homicide, Detective Luca."

"I know who killed those people."

I moved to the edge of my chair. "What people?"

"The ones the Preserve Killer murdered."

"And how do you know this?"

It was the third person to call in in the past two days who claimed to know the killer. The others were typical: one was a well-meaning woman whose imagination had run away, the other was someone not in full control of their faculties.

"Because the guy lives next door to me."

A slight vibration ran across the base of my skull. "And who might that be?"

"Brad Bailey."

Stiffening, I took his name and address and told him I'd be right over.

Bailey had fallen off the top of the suspect ladder but had a record and knew Melissa Wright. I opened the murder book, flipping to the section on Bailey. Staring at his face, I wondered how he'd gotten the long scar marring his forehead.

A SLEEK PRIVATE jet screamed as it climbed at a forty-five-degree angle. Before it disappeared, another plane came into view. The Naples Airport had gotten busier as the area grew. But wasn't there a limit to how many people could fly private?

Passing the Beach House, I turned on to Esty Avenue. It began drizzling as I parked. Roger Turner lived to the left of Bailey's house.

The front door was open. Turner opened the screen door, motioning to me as he looked toward Bailey's house. I slipped in. The house was compact but neat.

We shook hands. "I'm telling you, it's him."

"What makes you believe that?"

"First off, he's weird. And mean."

"I need specifics regarding your claim he's the Preserve Killer."

"He's out late every night, including the ones when those women were killed."

"That's hardly enough to accuse someone—"

"The night that Trent guy was murdered. I saw him come back. It was like two in the morning. I was outside; I forgot to take the trash to the curb, and he was getting out of his car. He had something wrapped around his hand, like it was bleeding."

My mind went to the drop of blood on Trent's pants. "How did you know it was bleeding?"

"You could tell. He had it raised up, like this." He put his hand up as if taking an oath. "I asked if he was okay and he turned toward me. That's when I saw it."

"Saw what?"

"The knife."

"How large a knife?"

He put his hands about eight inches apart. "About this big."

I took my time asking questions, but Turner never wavered on the details. Seeing someone out late, even with a possible cut and knife was circumstantial. But the fact Bailey had a record leapfrogged him to the top of suspects.

Bailey needed a closer look. Much closer. Pulling my cell out to call Derrick, it began ringing.

It was Dr. Bilotti. The call changed everything.

42

———

THE SHOCK FROM WHAT I HEARD LEFT ME STANDING IN THE rain. I jumped into the car as the rain intensified. "How reliable are the results?"

"About as sure as we can get."

"Really?"

"Yes. The chances it's wrong are one in nineteen billion."

"It doesn't make sense."

"It may not, but the blood on Trent's pant leg was female."

"How long do you think it was there? Could it be from a long time ago?"

"No. We ran it through a Raman spectroscope; it was fresh."

"I can't believe it."

"Believe it."

"Did you upload it to see if it matches anything in the system."

"Yes. I made the request immediately."

"Thanks, Doc."

"I'm sorry this turns your investigation upside down."

"I wish it were upside down. We got nowhere to turn; we're starting from zero."

"Hang in there, Frank."

"I'll try."

"If I can help, let me know."

"You want to tell Remin for me?"

"Whatever you need, my friend."

"Thanks, just kidding."

I fired up the engine and turned the windshield wipers on. Running the investigation through my head, I felt good it wasn't an oversight or pigheadedness that kept me from thinking a woman was responsible.

We followed the leads we had, and even the FBI profilers believed it was a male. We hadn't made a mistake but so what? I needed to figure out where to steer the case before I told the sheriff we'd been off base.

Pulling away, I knew it was time to think outside the box. I drove slowly. The first thing we'd do is check the DMV list for female drivers of white Hondas. Expand it to registrations in Lee County. The beginnings of an action plan felt good. For a moment. Until the call to the paper popped into my head.

They'd thought it was a male voice. Was it a woman, purposely disguising herself as a man? Whoever it was, was formidable, but if they'd hidden their gender, their invincibility approached legendary.

I set aside Ryan's death. Though there were doubts whether it was a suicide, it seemed easier to focus on the others. This had started with women victims. What was common about them? A lover other than Ryan?

Approaching Airport Pulling, the blue feeling I'd had since Bilotti called, darkened. I attributed some of it to having to tell Remin, but the main reason was the growing fear there was more than one killer.

THE SMELL of curry hung in the air. Remin had Indian food for lunch. The spice-induced reddening of his face drained as I declined to take a seat. "Is there a problem?"

"I'm afraid there's been a development, sir."

Remin cast his eyes toward the ceiling. "What now?"

"The blood on Victor Trent's pants was female."

His shoulders sank. "The killer is a woman?"

"It appears so."

"They age it?"

"Yes, it was fresh. It lines up with the time of death."

He slammed a palm onto his desk. "Damn it."

"It's a setback but we're pivoting—"

"What females are you looking at?"

"We're taking another look at the Honda registrations and expanding it to include Lee County."

"This is a disaster. You told me you were zeroing in. What the hell happened?"

"It's an unexpected twist, but we've accumulated a lot of data. We'll go out to the public—"

"How the hell are we going to ask the public for help? We'll look like clowns."

"We never mentioned the gender of the suspect."

"You remember Ryan?"

"I know, but I'm not sure of his role."

"What? Now, you think it was a suicide?"

"I'm not sure, but we can't discount the possibility there are two killers."

"We can't catch one, and now you're inferring there's two?"

"It's feasible, sir. There are four victims. Two male, two female. If we leave Ryan out, we're left with Trent and the women. We've developed connections between—"

"I'm not saying you're wrong, but unless you have something concrete, you're choosing victims to fit a suspect."

It was a valid assessment. "I understand your concern. I'm sorry if I didn't express it properly; the point is, we've got to explore every conceivable scenario."

"The public is demanding a solve. We can't tell them we're starting from zero. Geez, we can't even get the gender correct."

"We'll get them, if it's the last thing I do."

"I commend your commitment, but maybe it's time we ask the FBI for help."

"That's your call, sir. But the FBI profilers were positive it was a male as well. We can do this without them. You've handled cases where the feds were involved. The bureaucracy will weigh the investigation down."

"I don't give a damn about bureaucracy; I want this case solved. All the good will this department has earned is at stake. Do you understand that?"

I nodded. He continued ranting.

I let him vent his frustration as I'd learned from Dr. Bruno. The good feeling I'd had from keeping my cool evaporated before I hit the stairwell. The pressure was on.

Trudging down the stairs, I searched for something to focus our attention on. I pushed the winning lottery ticket out of my head. If there was a DNA match, it would be a total surprise; I didn't catch breaks like that. It was going to take work. A ton of it.

We had the Honda angle, but we still didn't know

enough about each victim. There had to be a connection. I needed to let Mary Ann know I was going to be logging heavy hours at the office. I hit our floor and went straight for the door to the parking lot. I didn't know if it was the heat I needed after Remin or some combo of comfort and encouragement.

It could have been the sun, but Mary Ann's voice sounded sweeter than ever. "Is everything all right?"

"There's another twist in the Preserve case."

"What happened?"

I told her the killer was a woman. "Oh my God. That's unusual."

"I know."

"What are you going to do?"

"The fundamentals. You know ninety percent of this job is about process. We stick to it, and we'll be cuffing someone before you know it."

"I hope you catch a break."

"I used up all my breaks when I met you."

"Aw. That's sweet, Frank."

"I mean it."

"We're both lucky."

"We are. How you feeling?"

"Pretty good."

Between the hesitation and the pretty good, I knew she'd slipped. "Not as good as the last couple of days?"

"It's nothing."

It wasn't. "You in pain?"

"Not really, just feeling like I'm carrying a hundred-pound backpack."

"Did you call—"

"Yes, I told the doctor. She said to give it a few days, see if it improves."

Though I doubted it, I said, "It will. They said it isn't a straight line with the injections."

"Don't worry, I'm fine. You have a killer to catch."

"You tell me if it gets worse, okay?"

"I will."

"Until this is over, it's going to be crazy."

"I know. If I can help, let me know."

"You want to talk to the media for me?"

43

GEORGE GOFF HANDLED PUBLIC RELATIONS FOR THE SHERIFF'S department. Having worked in Washington before coming to paradise, he knew how to talk for thirty minutes without saying anything. Though I found it frustrating, it was a useful skill to deploy when needed.

I'd asked him for advice, and as I walked down the corridor, I kept reminding myself to keep upbeat, focus on the new evidence while alluding to fresh leads.

A bank of cameras lined the rear of a room full of reporters. I'd seen many of them over the years, but it still felt like being on a raft during a hurricane; one slipup, and I'd be fighting to get back on safe ground.

Afraid my smile was too bright, I toned it down, and stepped up to the podium.

"Good afternoon, ladies and gentlemen. In our continuing effort to inform the public, I'd like to update you on the case known as the Preserve Killer.

"We're making progress in apprehending the individual or individuals responsible for the murders. Our forensics unit collected a blood sample from one of the crime scenes. An analysis of that specimen determined that it came from a female."

A murmur rippled through the crowd.

"We're asking the public to factor in the gender change, as they think about the case. If you have any information you believe could help, please call the hotline. Your assistance is critical in bringing this killer to justice. Remember, your call will be kept confidential."

Surveying the faces, I felt it had gone well. So far. I wanted to leave, but Goff had said taking a couple of questions was an effective way to get the media on your side.

"I'd be happy to answer a question or two." Hands shot up. I pointed to a familiar face.

"Thank you. Sandy Baker from WINK News. Detective Luca, up until today, you've believed it was a male, correct?"

"That was the assumption."

"Given the abrupt change from a male to a female suspect, how sure are you that the killer is a woman?"

"We believe, either the killer is female, or a woman was present at, or near, the time of death."

"So, now you're saying there's more than one person doing this?"

"We have no evidence to support it, but we cannot, and will not, discount the possibility." I pointed to an older reporter who'd covered the first case I'd worked in Naples.

"John Griswald, the *Naples Daily News*. Have you or anyone in the sheriff's office heard from the killer again?"

"While we've not had any further contact, it's important to note we have no proof the individual who made the call was involved in any of the murders."

"Do you feel the caller was challenging you, making it personal?"

"Every crime committed in the county is a personal

affront to me. When I'm assigned to a case, especially a homicide, I live, eat, and breathe it. It's the only way I know."

"You've had a long and distinguished career. Is this case the most difficult one you've encountered?"

"Every case presents its challenges. Let me finish up by saying, I'm confident we'll apprehend those responsible."

"How can you say that with at least four known deaths?"

"Because I've been able solve every homicide that's been assigned to me."

"But there are thousands of unsolved murders across the country."

It was actually two hundred thousand. "That's true."

"Is this the case that will ruin your record?"

I'd thought of that, but before I could respond, he followed with, "Is this killer just too good to be caught?"

Was this reporter a mind reader? "No. That's all for today. I have to get back to work." Making for the door, I hummed to prevent hearing the questions being shouted.

THE SHERIFF HAD GIVEN me five officers and the use of a conference room for as long as necessary. They filed into the room, taking seats around an oval table.

Standing, I said, "We've been thrown off track with the blood results. Instead of getting down about it, we need to continue probing. Go deeper and widen the avenues of pursuit.

Detective Dickson has a revised DMV list on the Honda seen at Logan Preserve. There are six women we need to take a look at. If nothing comes of it, we'll work on ones registered in Lee County. With two of us taking three each, running them down shouldn't take long.

Who wants to help with that?"

A pair of hands went up. "Good. Casey and Blake will cover that." Derrick handed off the list, and I said, "There wasn't a direct hit on the blood DNA, but I want to pursue the familial DNA angle. Between the federal and state data banks, we might find a relative allowing us to trace whose blood was on Trent's pant leg. Foley, you have lab experience; can you help?"

"Definitely. I'll even see what the commercial DNA sites have."

"I thought they shut out law enforcement completely."

"Most did, but a few ask customers to opt out, so it's definitely worth checking."

"Anyway, if we can increase the odds, it can make a difference. That leaves Cobalt and Willis. Now, I know we've been looking for connections with the victims. We didn't get much, so, I want to go further back. Check what grammar schools they went to. This is an organized serial killer, one who might be harboring resentment for something that happened in the sixth grade.

"There has to be something linking these victims, and if it turns out there aren't any, we'll know it's random. Highlight anything, even if it applies to just two victims. And make sure to include Ryan."

I looked at each member of the team and said, "Our mission is to nail the SOB who's doing this. I don't have to tell you how important it is to do it quickly. This is our town, and I'll be damned if some lunatic is going to kill at will."

44

———————

I HEARD THE PHONE A FEW FEET OUTSIDE OUR OFFICE. Derrick jogged ahead, lunging for the receiver.

"Homicide. Detective Dickson."

"I need to speak to Detective Luca."

"Who's this?"

"Jimmy Braun from the *Daily News*."

"Hold on."

"Frank it's that reporter from the news, the one who got the call."

One arm still in my jacket, I took the phone. "This is Frank Luca."

"Hi, Detective. The Preserve Killer called again."

"What did they say?"

"That you're not going to catch them, and even if you did, they're not going to jail."

"Anything else?"

"No. It was another quick call."

"How sure are you that it was the same person who called you before?"

"I'm ninety, ninety-five percent positive."

"Could you tell if it was a female?"

"It could've been. It's real tough; again, they're using something to disguise their voice."

"Distortion equipment?"

"Maybe one of those apps."

"Were you able to detect background noises or anything that could help identify where the call was made from?"

"I'm almost certain it was outside."

"What makes you think that?"

"You could hear the wind."

"Okay. Let me ask you, why do you think they're reaching out to you and no one else?"

"I never thought about that. You know, don't look a gift horse in the mouth."

"Think it over. See if anything comes to mind."

"I will."

"Is there anything else you think might be helpful?"

"Not really, but you know, they're confident, not nervous or anything."

"What gave you that impression?"

"The way they spoke. Calm and deliberate."

"Whoever it is better not get too comfortable. We're going to hunt them down, and they'll get the death sentence for this."

"How is the investigation going?"

"Good. We're pursuing several promising leads."

"Can you share anything? We wouldn't use your name; it'd be a well-placed source."

"I'm sorry. I can't discuss an active investigation."

"Is there anything you can tell me off the record?"

I didn't usually speak off the record, and in this case, I couldn't tell him we had no idea who was behind the murders. "Not at this time, Mr. Braun."

After thanking him, I dropped the receiver in its cradle. Derrick said, "They called again?"

"Yeah. They're getting brazen. Braun said they sounded confident."

"Confident? Don't they know Luca's on the case?"

I never felt invincible. In fact, I attributed the doubts swirling in my head to whatever success I'd been able to scrounge together. It wasn't complete insecurity, just a feeling success was never owned, it was rented. "Yeah, right. And don't forget, this is a team effort."

"I know, but you've got the experience, Frank."

"Don't sell yourself short, Derrick. You're a damn good detective. You could replace me tomorrow, and the department wouldn't miss a beat."

"I appreciate that, but we both know it's not true. I need another year or two working beside you."

I wanted to tell him this case was the equivalent of a masters degree in homicide, but I was worried I wouldn't be around to solve it. It was sinking in that if I didn't nail this nutjob soon, Remin would be forced to replace me and call for outside help. "If you can put up with me, I'm happy to pass on whatever I know. But a lot of what makes a good homicide detective is process and instinct."

"No doubt."

"All right, enough blabbing, we've got to get to work. We never really dug past the last year on the victim's social media accounts."

"Who you want me to start with?"

"You take Melissa Wright, and I'll look into Dr. Bigham."

"We should begin with Facebook. Given their age, and since we're going back a couple of years, it makes sense."

I wasn't on Facebook, and outside of staying in contact with people who'd drifted in the sea of life, didn't get it. Mary

Ann would check it once a day, and Jessie used to be on it but had moved on to Instagram.

Since Bigham was a doctor, I expected her posts to be general in nature. Most of what she posted were motivational quotes. It was clear she believed that positive, stress-free thoughts promoted health.

Mary Ann used to remind me to stop being negative. In my business, that was tough. It had been awhile since she said anything to me. Wondering if she'd given up on me, I clicked on Bigham's photos.

The first five lines were either sunsets or pictures taken from a boat. I couldn't recall if there was evidence she had a boat. I jotted a note and scrolled down. A picture of an older couple taken five years ago caught my eye. The resemblance to the woman made me sure it was her parents.

The next several pictures were of a fat tabby cat. The feline must have passed on as well. I clicked on a picture of two women and leaned in. It was Dr. Bigham and a woman with broad shoulders and close-cropped hair. They were kissing, and it was not a hello-type kiss.

I right-clicked it and pasted the image into a word document. Scrolling through more sunsets and beach scenes, I stopped on another photo of the couple. The mystery lady had her head resting on Bigham's shoulder, and the doctor had her arm around the woman's waist. The woman was wearing a top that was more fishnet than fabric.

After saving the photo, I hit print and got up. "Derrick, Bigham may have had a female lover."

"She swung from both sides of the plate?"

I pulled paper off the printer. "I don't know, but look at this."

He nodded. "Oh yeah, these two are more than friends. She looks like an athlete."

"We need to find out who she is."

"You think she could be the killer?"

"Why not? It could be Bigham rejected her for someone else. I'm going to the doctor's office. Get everybody looking for signs Wright may have had a lesbian relationship."

"She could've offed them to keep them away from Bigham or Wright."

"It's possible. After we identify who this woman is, we'll see if Trent or Ryan have connections to her."

"It sounds like a stretch."

"It may be, but, A, nothing is off the table, and, B, there could be two killers."

45

———

THE WAITING ROOM WAS EMPTY AND COLD. SINCE THIS YEAR'S flu was more contagious, medical offices had adopted protocols to slow the spread. In this case, you sat in your car and sent a text you were there. When they were ready for you, they'd call.

It made sense, but some of the rules separating the sick and elderly from their loved ones were awful if not cruel.

I stuck my badge against the sliding window, telling the nurse I wanted to speak to Lisa Bonn: the nurse who had worked the longest with Dr. Bigham. Two minutes later, a short woman in a blue scrub suit and mask came into the waiting room.

"Hi, I'm Lisa."

I stuck my hand out. "Detective Luca. What I have to ask is private in nature. Can we step outside?"

"Sure." I followed her out, and she stripped off her mask.

"Like I said over the phone, I'm here about Dr. Bigham."

"It's still hard to believe she's gone."

"I'm interested in her relationships. Especially, the romantic type."

"I hope I can help."

"Did Dr. Bigham have female lovers?"

Lisa's face reddened, and I had my answer. "She may have."

I took the Facebook pictures out. "Do you know who this woman is?"

She swallowed and nodded. "Yes. It's Diane Milbury."

"She was in a relationship with Dr. Bigham?"

"I-I don't know for sure, but she's been here a couple of times and, uh, well, Dr. Bigham didn't want her coming around the office. You know, Dr. Bigham was very professional. She never mixed her personal life with the practice. I worked with her for nine years and never socialized with her."

"But you know this Diane Milbury?"

"Not know her, just saw her here, and I know that Dr. Bigham didn't appreciate her coming around."

"Did she say anything about her?"

"Not directly, but she was upset after she came here."

"Do you know where she lives or works?"

"No, I'm sorry."

"That's okay. You've been very helpful, ma'am."

As soon as she went back inside, I called Derrick. "Looks like we found this woman. Her name is Diane Milbury. Run her through the system. I'm on my way in."

"Will do. Oh, Remin wants to see you. Shirley called twice."

"He probably wants an update. I'll go straight to see him."

Remin was wearing a red tie and frown. He shook his head as I sat down. "You're worse than me."

"I'm sorry, sir?"

"You told the paper that you'd make sure the Preserve Killer would hang?"

It wasn't a bad idea but it wasn't mine. "No way. I never said that."

"What did you tell them?"

"I never made a statement. They wanted me to but I declined. It was right after the press conference."

"Which the killer saw and called the paper."

"I'm sure they did."

"I'm afraid they're going to strike again. We can't taunt them."

"I'm aware of that, sir. All I said was we were going to hunt the killer down."

"You didn't say they'd hang?"

"No. I'd never say that." I left out the part about getting the death sentence.

"Are you saying they made it up?"

"It may have been taken out of context. I mentioned a serial killer could get the death sentence but never said anything about hanging." At least that was true.

He knew I was spinning things. "This will go away if we catch the bastard."

"It's not 'if,' sir. It's when."

"You have anything new?"

"In fact, we do. There's a new person of interest. It's early, but it's a female and we're about to focus on her."

"Connected to a victim?"

"At least one at this point: Dr. Bigham."

"Good. Get on it."

Hustling down the stairs, I wondered what tomorrow's headline would look like. I should have known better than to express an opinion to a journalist, but he took what I said and soaked it in sensationalism. It was the reason most Americans didn't trust the media. My relationship was more complicated;

they played a role in solving some crimes but also stoked anti-police movements.

Stepping into the office, Derrick punched the air. "We're onto something. Milbury is no angel."

"She has a record?"

"Yep. Assaulting another woman."

"How long ago?"

"Five years ago. But guess what else I found?"

"Just tell me."

"There are two restraining orders against her. And get this, they're both protecting women."

"I wonder if she was in a relationship with them."

"My money is on yes."

"Where she live?"

"In Palm River."

"That's close to where Wright's body was left."

"I think we're onto something."

"What does she do?"

"She's a personal trainer at LA Fitness on Vanderbilt Beach Road."

She had the strength to overpower someone. "See if she's working and we'll pay her a visit."

"Already did. She's training someone and will be done in twenty."

We took Goodlette Frank north. There was always less traffic than Airport Pulling. Arriving five minutes before her session ended, I said, "Why don't you go inside? She may recognize me from the news."

"Sure."

"We need to go easy with her. Maybe she'll give us a DNA sample voluntarily."

"Not if she had anything to do with it."

"A guy can dream, can't he?"

Derrick laughed and opened the car door. "Once I get her outside, come over."

I watched him pull open the gym's door, wondering how the interview with Milbury would go. We needed a break, and though it was unexpected, this could be it.

Eyes on the door, my hopes took a dive when it flung open. Milbury shook off the hand Derrick had on her elbow. I climbed out of the car as she walked to the right.

46

Arms crossed over her chest, Milbury stood a few feet away from Derrick. They had drifted in front of the storefront for the original Crust pizzeria when I hit the sidewalk.

"Ma'am, I'm Detective Luca."

She gave a sneer worthy of a sixteen-year-old. "What do you want?"

"Just have a couple of questions for you."

Milbury was smacking chewing gum. "About what?"

"Dr. Bigham."

I couldn't detect whether that was a surprise to her. "It's none of your business."

"Ma'am, the fact she was murdered makes it my business. We're hoping you'll cooperate, but if you choose not to, we can force you to come to the station."

She scoffed, "Ask your questions, but if they're personal, I ain't answering."

"We know you were in a relationship with Dr. Bigham."

"You got a problem with that?"

"Not at all. My interest lies in what broke you up."

"The same crap that breaks up any relationship."

My first marriage had ended in divorce. I knew what she meant. "I'm going to need you to be specific."

She glared at me. "I told you I'm not getting personal."

The sound of her gum smacking was getting to me. In the millisecond I paused to calm myself, Derrick said, "Detective Luca told you we'd bring you in if you didn't cooperate."

"What do you think this is, Russia or something?"

I said, "Did you argue with each other?"

"Who doesn't?"

She spoke another truth. "Did it ever get physical?"

"I didn't kill Sarah. I loved her. She was the warmest person I'd ever known."

"As a doctor, she didn't like to mix her personal life with her professional one."

"She couldn't accept who she was, always worried what someone thought of her."

"And you're not like that?"

"No way. You live your life that way and you'll never be happy."

She was right. "Would you say Dr. Bigham was happy?"

"When we were alone, she was. It was everything else that interfered."

"Could you elaborate?"

"It's not worth dredging up the past."

Milbury was competing with Buddha. I refrained from saying amen and changed it up. "How well do you know Melissa Wright?"

"Is that the girl who used to work at Alice Sweetwater's?

It was a weird way to reply. She knew she couldn't deny knowing her if there was a connection. "Yes. You two were friends?"

"No. I went there a couple of times."

"Me too. They have pretty good burgers."

She nodded.

Derrick asked, "How did you meet Bobby Ryan?"

The way he framed the question, I knew the department was in good hands. Milbury said, "I leased a car from him a long time ago."

Milbury knew at least three victims. I asked, "You like the MINI Cooper?"

"It was fun to drive but no trunk space."

"How long ago did you have one?"

"Like five years ago."

We'd check DMV. At the moment, a Kia SUV was registered under her name.

"When did the relationship with Dr. Bigham end?"

She took a fresh piece of gum out, put her old one in the wrapper, and dropped it into a trash can. It was a smooth move, allowing her to calculate a time frame. Whether it was a real accounting or one to fit an innocent profile was the question. "I'm not sure; it kind of went on and off for a while."

She didn't answer. "We couldn't help notice that there are two restraining orders against you."

Her eyes narrowed. "Frigging ridiculous."

One maybe, two was a pattern. "Not to the women who felt threatened. Why'd they seek protection?"

"All I did was try to see them, to talk things out."

That was a world-class reframe. "These discussions took place at the end of the relationships."

"Yeah, so what?"

I didn't want to antagonize her; we'd talk to the women and get their side. "Just saying, it's kind of normal when things go sour."

She nodded.

I reached into my breast pocket and pulled out a kit.

"Would you be willing to give us a sample of your DNA?"

"DNA? What for?"

"It's protocol. That's all. Nothing to worry about."

"Yeah, right. So you guys can plant it and blame me for something."

I wished Hollywood would stop propagating the myth that law enforcement planted evidence. "That's unfair, ma'am. I've been a police officer for most of my adult life and never saw a fellow officer place an incriminating piece of evidence."

"I don't care what you say. Besides, my DNA is private."

"I understand, ma'am. We appreciate your time today."

We hopped in the car and Derrick said, "I don't like her. She's hiding something. What do you think?"

"We don't need to go to dinner with her. We just need to find out if she's involved in these murders. The fact she knows three of the victims and wouldn't give us her DNA concerns me."

"Exactly. And she blew off the protective orders like she stepped on somebody's toes."

"We'll talk to the women, but first, let's get the gum she put in the trash can. The lab will grab her DNA off it."

AFTER DROPPING THE GUM OFF, we headed for Spanish Wells. The Bonita Springs community bordered Naples and was where Sheila Lake called home. Lake had asked for a protective order keeping Milbury at least a hundred yards away from her.

Lake lived in a coach home a minute from the Bonita Spring Road entrance. She pulled opened the door wearing skintight exercise clothes. Lake had more curves than a slalom course.

"Hello, Ms. Lake, we spoke earlier."

She looked over our shoulders. "Yes, come in."

"As mentioned, we're interested in Diane Milbury. When did you meet her?"

"Oh, about four years ago. I used to go to LA Fitness and would see her there. After a while, we got to know each, and then, you know, we started dating."

"Why did you seek a protective order against her?"

"Diane was very controlling. She was suffocating me. And she was as jealous as they come. She'd get mad if I talked to anyone at the gym."

Derrick said, "She has a bad temper?"

"Yes, she scared me. I was afraid she'd hurt me."

"Did she get physical?"

She shrugged. "She shoved me, really hard one time. I hurt my shoulder."

"Is that when you went for a restraining order?"

She shook her head. "No. It was when she came after me with a knife."

"What happened?"

"We were in the kitchen, and she got all mad when she found out a guy I knew from my old neighborhood came to see me. It was nothing, just a hello, but she freaked out and pulled a knife out of the block"—she pointed to the counter —"said she'd kill me if she ever found me with him."

47

———————

I HUNG UP THE PHONE. WE NEEDED TO CONFIRM WHETHER Diane Milbury's DNA matched the blood found on the pants of the last victim. "Sheriff said he was going to get the lab to prioritize the gum sample."

Derrick said, "It feels like it's going to be Milbury."

"We get a DNA match, and hopefully, she'll confess to the other murders. Otherwise, we'll have to obtain solid evidence to get more than a conviction for the Trent killing."

"We need a motive for Trent. What do you think, some kind of love triangle?"

Before I could answer, Officer Casey stepped in the office. The volunteer said, "We went through the list of females with white Hondas. Two stood out, Riley Addison and Tina Dreman. We ran quick background checks on them."

He handed me two sheets of paper.

"Addison works at the same Bank of America where Trent worked?"

"Yep. And it gets better, Dreman served a stint in New

York for stabbing someone on a subway platform. I put in a request for the file."

I popped out of my chair. "Good work, Casey. We're going to jump on these two."

Derrick said, "Should we wait until we get the DNA back on Milbury?"

"It's going to be a day or two. We can't wait."

"Okay, you want to start with Dreman? She's been violent."

"No doubt."

Dreman lived in Lago, a new apartment complex at the intersection of Livingston and Radio roads. Her unit was on the bottom floor of a white four-story building. We circled around a busy pool and grill area and knocked on her door.

She tried to close the door when Derrick flashed his badge. He put his foot against the door. "If you don't talk to us now, we'll be back with a subpoena."

"What do you want?"

He hiked a thumb behind him. "You really want to do this out here?"

She exhaled and stepped aside. It was a small place, furnished cheaply. But it had white cabinets and granite in the kitchen, giving it a fresh feel. The dining table was anchored by a wine bottle covered in candle wax.

Dreman didn't offer to sit. Leaning against a counter, she tugged at a string at the hem of her cutoffs. "What do you want?"

Derrick said, "You own a white Honda."

"It's a piece of crap. I should've never traded my MINI in."

Bingo. I said, "I love MINIS. Did you get yours from MINI of Fort Myers?"

"No. I bought it used from Germain."

"I'm thinking of getting one. You get yours serviced at the Fort Myers dealer?"

"Yeah, but they're rip-offs."

"Thanks for warning me. Say, how well you know Victor Trent?"

"Victor Trent? I don't know him."

"Who do you use to manage your money?"

She scoffed, "What money? I can barely afford to live here. They're jacking up rents all over town. I got lucky subleasing this from a friend."

"Where do you work?"

"I'm an assistant manager at Spencer Gifts in the mall."

I was surprised the novelty chain was still in business. "What were you doing in Logan Preserve on Tuesday, February first?"

"The first? Oh, I was visiting my sister in Jacksonville."

"What time did you leave?"

"After work, about six. I stayed overnight."

We'd check her alibi, but it wasn't unusual for a family member to lie to protect a relative. "Can we have your sister's contact information?"

She frowned but told us. I asked, "Tell me about the stabbing you were convicted of."

"It's over. I did my time and paid my debt."

"What happened?"

"I don't have to talk to you and I ain't going to."

There was no use pushing her; we'd get the file. We thanked her and left. Back in the car, Derrick asked, "What did you think?"

"Tough to say. She could've met Ryan at the MINI dealer."

"We need to vet her alibi, but it's her sister."

"Drive around the parking lot. Let's see if we can find her car."

The Honda was parked alongside a fence. I got out, looked inside, and climbed back in the car. "She's got a SunPass toll account. If she used it, we'll get a time line on where she was. Let's go see Addison."

WE DROVE east along Route 41, turning into the Isles of Collier Preserve. I'd never been in the new community and looked forward to checking it out. Dozens of homes were going up. What did this mean for the town's infrastructure? "I wonder how many doorknobs are in here?"

Derrick said, "At least eight hundred."

"Is there no end to the demand?"

Sun glistened off a massive lake. We circled around it, finding our way to Tobago Drive.

Derrick pulled up in front an expansive home with a three-car garage. "Addison is doing pretty damn good. I can't see someone risking all this."

The last several days, my partner had impressed me with how good a detective he'd become. The comment set him back. "Countless people with more than her, pissed it all away by doing something stupid."

A strong tropical breeze swept through as we approached the house. As I hit the bell, Derrick sniffed. "Is that pot?"

"No, it smells like incense."

In white clam digger pants, Riley Addison didn't look like the photo on her driver's license. She looked something like a female Hugh Jackman and had a nice smile. "Can I help you?"

Derrick displayed his badge, explaining we needed to talk to her.

"Sure."

As we followed her in, I tried to decide whether she'd had cosmetic surgery. The home was drenched in light and nicely furnished. I especially liked the whitewashed shiplap walls in the main room. What I didn't like was a musky smell that grew stronger as we settled into chairs opposite a TV larger than a bedsheet.

I spied the aroma source, a diffuser on an end table. I leaned away. "You knew Victor Trent well."

She was either stunned by skipping the small talk or the name of the victim. "He worked in the complex."

Addison was putting distance between them. "We understand he had a reputation for, uh, womanizing."

Her cheeks tinted but she said nothing.

"Did you have a relationship with Mr. Trent?"

She whispered, "It was a one-time thing, a mistake."

"How did this come to be?"

"He took advantage of me. I'd just broken up with someone. I was heartbroken and he, he . . ."

"You got angry he manipulated you?"

"Yes. But more disappointed in myself. I should've never allowed myself. I knew I shouldn't have, but he was so, you know . . ."

I could imagine the vulnerability. Trent may have been a predator but did Addison exact the ultimate revenge for it? "Your car was seen at Logan Preserve in the middle of the night, just hours before Mr. Trent's body was discovered."

"No, it wasn't me. I wasn't there."

"Where were you that night?"

She cleared her throat. Was it legit or a stalling tactic? "I was at a friend's house."

"Until what time?"

"I slept over and came home the next morning to change for work."

"Who is this friend?"

"I'd rather not say. It's, uh, delicate."

"I'm sorry, ma'am, but you'll have to let us know."

She lowered her head. "He's married."

"And you stayed over at his house?"

"Yes, his wife was away."

People liked living dangerously. "I'll need his name and address."

Her face tensed. "Please. If you go there, she'll find out, and . . ."

Extramarital affairs were something I didn't approve of, but that wasn't my job. "Give me his name and number; we'll see him on neutral ground."

Jotting down the number, a sense something was about to break washed over me. The feeling left as quickly as it came.

48

I SHUDDERED WALKING INTO THE CONFERENCE ROOM. "Derrick, raise the thermostat. It's freezing."

"Frank's always cold."

My partner fiddled with the dial, and I stood, addressing the team of officers assigned to the case. "We have a lot of ground to cover. The lab said we'll have the DNA results on Milbury later today, so let's concentrate our efforts on Addison and Dreman."

There was a knock on the door. Casey got up and cracked it open. He was given a manila envelope. He handed it to me. "It's for you."

A buzz ran across the base of my head. Pasted onto the outside were cutouts of letters reading Detective Luca - Urgent. They were underlined.

Holding it up to the light, there was a rectangular shadow. Running a finger across it, it seemed harmless. Opening the clasp, I slid out the contents.

It was a Tarot card. Staring at the message, Derrick came around the table. "This bastard is getting too ballsy."

He reached for the card, and I said, "Don't touch it. I doubt there are any prints, but you never know."

We took pictures of the card as the rest of the team hunched over the table. There were nine swords on the card. I searched Google. "It's in the Suit of Swords; it's called the Nine Swords."

"What the hell does it mean?"

Heat rose from my neck to my eyes. "Helplessness, anxiety, and despair."

Derrick said, "The bastard is taunting us."

He said "us," but I knew it was me. "I don't want this to distract us from our mission. They can send and say all the bullshit they want; we're going bring them to justice."

Casey said, "Damn right we will."

My partner said, "No doubt. You know, this could be Milbury trying to rile us up. Man, we get that DNA match, I'm gonna enjoy hauling her ass in."

The reminder we were waiting on the DNA results boosted my mood. Though hopeful, I said, "We can't sit around waiting for it to come to us; we have to go get it. We need to rule out or focus on Dreman and Addison."

Casey said, "I called for the Dreman case file again. Told them it's become a priority. They said it's being scanned. We should have it before the meeting is over."

"Good. Check her SunPass account. She claims to have been in Jacksonville visiting her sister. Her sister confirmed she was there, but I don't have to tell you about family alibis."

"I'll handle it."

"Blake, I'd like you check into the psychic community. Focus on card readers, ones who use Tarot cards. It could be nothing, but it doesn't feel like it."

Blake said, "Will do. There's a woman in Venice who reads Tarot cards out of her home. She's supposed to be real a nutjob with a record. I don't know if it's worth going up—"

"It doesn't matter; we've got to see her. In fact, make it a priority. Derrick and I are going to check into Addison. Cobalt and Willis, I need you to map any connections Dreman and Addison might have had with the victims."

Blake stood. "Let me get going. Venice is two hours away."

"Good luck. Foley, I know we're waiting on the Milbury results, but how many more databases can we tap?"

"Twenty-three states have come back negative. I'm still waiting on the others, as well as approval to run familial testing."

"All right, why don't you help out on the card readers. while Blake is on the road?"

"Happy to pitch in."

"All right, let's get to work."

Derrick was more confident than I was, and as we walked back to the office, I said, "I'm going to step outside for a minute to warm up."

"You're still cold?"

I nodded. "Then I have to tell Remin about the card."

"See you later."

It wasn't just the air-conditioning I wanted to escape from; I needed to hear Mary Ann's voice. Once in the sunshine, I turned toward the sun to warm up and pulled out my phone.

"Hey, how you doing?"

"Okay. Is everything okay?"

"Yeah, just wanted to say hello."

"Something happened?"

She knew me too well. "It's nothing. I didn't want you to hear it on the news, but we received a Tarot card in the mail."

"Oh my God, that's weird."

"Don't say anything."

"I don't like this, Frank. They're too brazen."

She was right, but I said, "I'd call it sloppy. It'll end up helping to catch them."

"Did they make any threats?"

"No. Just trying to rub our, my, face in the fact we haven't caught them."

"You'll get them. You always do."

"I guess so."

"You guess so? You're the best detective in the world. You always get the solve."

I appreciated the vote of confidence, but there wasn't anyone with an unblemished record. Was this going to be a first for me? "Anyway, I called to see how you were, not talk about the case."

"I'm doing fine. Was just about to swim a couple of laps."

A couple. I knew her almost as well as she knew me. She wasn't feeling as good as she said. We were both fibbing. "Go ahead. I have to tell Remin about the contact."

"Okay. But be careful."

"Don't hold dinner for me."

I soaked in another thirty seconds of vitamin D before heading upstairs. The sheriff was reading a report when I was shown in. He tossed it aside. "What's going on, Frank?"

"It looks like the killer sent a message. We received an envelope containing a Tarot card."

He leaned forward. "What does this mean?"

"As far as I can tell, it looks like a taunt. The card symbolizes hopelessness and despair."

Remin pounded the desk. "Who the hell do they think they are?"

"We'll get them, sir. Contact is good."

"You're right. You think they reached out to the media as well?"

"Not that I can tell."

He fell back into his chair. "We're probably going to have to make a statement."

"I don't know about that. They may be looking for attention. If we don't mention it, they may make another contact."

"Or they'll kill again."

"True, but if they get press coverage, who knows what they'll do next."

"I'll have to think this over. Tell everyone to keep it quiet."

"The lab has it. I doubt there's any prints on it but you never know."

"Let's hope the DNA for Milbury is a match, and we can end this nonsense."

I stood. "All right, sir. We have a lot of leads we're pursuing. I have to get going."

I headed down the stairs, ping-ponging the merits of not making a statement the killer had made contact, when my phone rang. It was the lab.

49

I STOPPED ON THE LANDING. "HELLO?"

"Frank, it's Geary from the lab."

"You have good news for me?"

"Afraid not. The DNA extracted from the gum doesn't match the blood found on the last victim's pants."

Our most credible suspect was off the hook. I leaned against the wall.

"Frank?"

"Are you sure about this?"

"A thousand percent."

"All right. Thanks."

"Sorry, buddy."

"I'll see you around, Geary."

I sat on the stairs. We had a couple of leads being worked, but we were far from a solve. Most homicide investigations were marathons, and though the finish line was in sight, I'd been forced to start all over again.

The sound of footsteps got me up. I exited into the hallway to my office. Forcing myself not to dwell on the non-match, I stepped into the office.

Derrick looked over his monitor. "What did Remin have to say?"

Damn. Remin had to be informed Milbury was no longer a suspect. "He took it pretty good. He's not sure whether we should make a public statement, so, we've got to keep it quiet."

He reached for the phone. "No problem. I'll let the others know."

"Hold on a second."

"What's up?"

"Milbury's DNA didn't match."

"Geez! Can't we catch a break?"

I threw up my hands, and an idea popped into my head. "What if the blood was planted?"

"Oh man. You think it's possible?"

"Why not? This killer is good."

"It'd be consistent with the taunting."

"They could be trying to throw us off."

"We have to be careful."

I nodded. "We had a case just before you got here. Me and Mary Ann worked it. The killer planted evidence pointing to others. It was done well."

"But you nailed him."

"We did."

"What do you want to do?"

"Check whether Milbury recently gave blood or has a friend who works anywhere blood is collected or stored. Even hospitals."

"Everybody knows someone who works in the medical field."

"I know but you'd have to be really close or have something on someone to get them to help you."

"The blood was fresh, so it'd have to have happened within a day."

The time line made the likelihood remote. "Yeah, or they had a vial, which when stored properly would last awhile."

"Have someone check the Quest and LabCorp places. See if they've been missing a vial within the last two weeks."

"I'm on it."

"Let the others know about the Milbury DNA; we need to find something."

"Got it."

"All right, I'm going to tell Remin about the DNA."

MY MIND WAS full of thoughts. They were banging into each other, preventing me from systematically thinking through possibilities. Instead of heading back to the office, I made a left onto Mooring Line Drive.

When it ended, I went left, along the water. The parking lot for Lowdermilk Park was jammed. Pulling alongside the curb, I tossed a placard on the dashboard and made a beeline for the sand.

Carrying my shoes and socks, I walked south. The Gulf was lapping the shoreline. I inhaled deeply. The salt-infused air had a sweet edge to it. My mind began quieting; no wonder people flocked to the beach.

A patrolling pelican arced up and dove into the water, coming up with a meal. Life was simple. How did we humans complicate things so badly? I surveyed the crowd; most people were chatting or reading.

They didn't seem to have a care in the world, yet here I was, burdened with keeping them safe. I circled around two kids building a castle. They had a right to live free from worry that a deranged killer might prey on them.

My vow to protect and serve had seeped into my genes. Whether I wanted to or not, I had to. Every case seemed difficult, but this one would be hard to top. As a pair of sandpipers pecked the sand for a snack, I shook my head. It was time to get fundamental.

There were four corpses. At least three were homicides. The killer or killers were on the loose. It appeared a woman was behind the murders. An intelligent one but someone who had a thing for poking you, for sticking it in your face.

Was a single individual or group responsible for the deaths? Or was a copycat killer muddying the waters? Understanding whether we were chasing one or multiple people was central to the case.

The other basic fact needing clarity was whether the blood on Trent's pants came from the killer or was put there to distract us. If it was the killer's, did they realize they'd left it behind?

If it was the killer's, we'd eventually nail them. The problem was how many more would have to die until we did. The other point nagging for an answer was whether the killer had chosen their victims. If not, hunting a random killer, one as careful as this one, was an exponential challenge.

This killer had chosen to get personal with me. Whether it was fear or training, I leaned toward there being scores to settle. Tarot cards were subject to interpretation but they had meaning. The problem was there was scant evidence of connections between the dead.

I couldn't recall if we'd checked into whether the victims were into the cosmic or psychic worlds, but we would need to double back if we'd hadn't. We also had to go deep with the first two victims. If there was a second killer, they would've emerged afterward.

Passing the Colonial Club, my phone vibrated. "This is Luca."

"Frank, it's Casey."

"What's going on?"

"I got Dreman's SunPass records, and there's no indication she went to Jacksonville or anywhere near a toll booth."

"Her sister's lying."

"I called her. She admitted Dreman asked her to say she was up there. She's also got a conviction for transporting narcotics."

I spun around. "All right. Get eyes on her. I'm on the way back."

50

———————

Derrick called the novelty shop in the Coastal mall.
Dreman was off today. We sped up Livingston, turning on
Davis Boulevard and into Lago's parking lot. I said, "Are you
kidding me? They send a marked car to keep eyes on
Dreman?"

"Must have been shorthanded because of the flu. Heard a
couple of guys called in sick."

"A little common sense is all I'm asking for."

Derrick pointed. "There's her Honda."

I pulled a few spots away. "She could be watching. You
go to the left and I'll go right."

A group of thirty-year-olds were poolside, drinking beer.
It made me think you never knew who your neighbors really
were. I hit the bell and stood to the side.

"It's open, Julio!"

Fearing a setup, I didn't announce ourselves and rang the
bell again. "It's open!"

I pounded the door with the palm of my hand. A voice,
mumbling curses, got louder. Dreman opened the door. If it

were gorillas instead of us, she wouldn't have been any more surprised.

"I-I, uh, thought you were Julio."

"May we come in?"

She regained her footing. "What do you want?"

"Your alibi doesn't check out. You didn't go to Jacksonville the night Victor Trent was murdered."

"Hey, just because I served time don't mean you're gonna pin this on me."

"You want to do this here? Or shall—"

"All right, all right."

She stepped to the side and we entered her apartment. I picked up the acrid smell of marijuana. My hope this woman had the sense not to drive when using was misplaced.

Dreman slammed the door. I said, "You lied about going to see your sister in Jacksonville."

Her sneer reminded me of what we used to do behind a teacher's back in school. "I got the dates mixed up."

"Where were you the night of February first?"

"I'm pretty sure I was in Miami."

"Your SunPass account has no record of you going there."

"So? I didn't use it."

"You expect me to believe you had a pass that saves time and discounts tolls and you didn't use it?"

"It's still a free country, isn't it?"

"It sure is, but you're not free to lie to the police."

Derrick said, "It's called obstruction. Let's bring her in."

My partner's tone of voice didn't alter her smug expression.

I said, "If you were in Miami, I'll need names, places, and times to back it up."

"I just went to party. It's too quiet around here."

"With whom and where?"

"I don't have to tell you anything. I'm done talking."

She was hiding something. "Look, I respect your right to privacy but I have a job to do. If you're not going to cooperate, I'll ask the prosecutors to see what kind of a charge—"

"That's bullshit. You can't pin anything on me for going to Miami."

It made no sense to continue the war of wills. "Tell me what time you went and came back, and I'll check the cameras at the Alligator Alley toll booth."

She brightened. "I left here at eight and came back through the toll plaza around four in the morning."

"You're sure?"

"Yeah."

"If you're lying again, I swear I'll arrest you for obstruction, at a minimum."

The way she scoffed had a similarity to the taunting nature of the person reaching out to the newsroom. Did Dreman send the Tarot card?

We walked silently past the beer drinkers to our car. I pitched the keys to Derrick. As soon as we climbed in, I said, "Make sure we have eyes on her. I'm going to call Remin and ask him to get ahold of the Department of Transportation. We need to see whether Dreman really went to Miami."

"I don't trust her one bit. For someone who served time, she's got this superiority thing going on."

He was right. I dialed the sheriff and said, "Just like whoever is doing the killing."

I hung up. "He said they're all digital, and he'd have the toll booth footage by the end of the day."

"Good. We need to vet the Addison alibi."

I pulled my notebook out. "Let me call him. If he's working, we'll go now."

"FRANK?"

"Yeah, it's me."

Mary Ann met me in the kitchen. "I didn't expect you home so early."

It was just after eight. "I got tired of banging my head against the wall."

She wrapped her arms around me. "I'm glad you're home. I just put the pasta fagioli in the fridge."

"Sounds good."

"Get changed; I'll heat a bowl up."

"Where's Jessie?"

"Football game."

Even though I'd been down here for more than a decade, I still didn't understand the fascination with high school football. I slipped into shorts and a Beatles T-shirt almost as old as me and headed back to the kitchen.

I took a deep breath. "This smells great. You made it?"

"Who else?"

"Just checking." I spooned three times before coming up for air. "It's the best you ever made."

She smiled. "Tough day, huh?"

I nodded. "We can't make headway. We were supposed to get surveillance film to rule out someone who could be the killer, but now, it's tomorrow. The DNA doesn't match another one, and now we've got to wait on the familial possibilities."

"Oh boy."

"And the guy we need to talk to about an alibi for another person of interest was up in Tampa."

"You'll get it done, Frank."

I shrugged and set my spoon down. "I'm starting to think we won't. And it scares the hell out of me."

"That's okay. Nobody has a perfect record. You'll still be the best detective Southwest Florida has ever seen."

Even though I was, I said, "I'm not worried about my reputation; this is our slice of paradise, and I want to keep it that way."

She squeezed my hand. "It's the fear of failing others, of letting them down that bothers you."

It took me a second to realize that was a big part of it. Some of it was ego, but I did care about our community. "I guess so."

"It's going to work out. It always does."

I wasn't sure and realized I hadn't asked her how she was feeling. I kissed her hand. "Enough about me. How are you feeling?"

"I'm good."

I smiled. "What time is the football over?"

"Around nine. Why?"

"You feeling good enough for you know what?"

51

___

I stared at the copy of the Tarot card taped to the
board. The killer had continued to be careful, not a print on it
or the envelope it came in. Derrick walked in holding two
cups of coffee. "You're here early. Couldn't sleep?"

"Slept good. Got lucky last night."

He smiled. "You devil, you."

I sipped the java. "I'd make a deal with Satan to catch this
bastard."

Derrick tapped on his keyboard. "You ever see that movie
where that guy, I think it's Brad Pitt, makes a deal with the
devil?"

"No." I answered my ringing cell phone: "Detective
Luca."

"Hi, this is Paul Madewell. You called yesterday while I
was in Tampa."

"Yes, thanks for calling back. I'd like to talk to you, at
work."

"About what?"

"It's a personal matter, involving a Ms. Addison."

He sighed. "Oh. Okay. I own Altered Elements in Green Tree Center off Immokalee. You know it?"

"No, but I'll find it. Say a half an hour from now?"

"That works."

I hung up and stood. "That's the guy Addison said she was with."

"You're going to see him?"

"Yeah. He owns a store called Altered Elements, in—"

"In Green Tree?"

"Yeah, why?"

"It's one of those mystic, uh, metaphysical places. They sell crystals and healing stones."

"They sell Tarot cards?"

"I don't know, but probably. Before I met Lynn, I dated this girl who used to go there. She said they had healing stones that spoke to you."

"Rocks that talked to you?"

"That's what she said."

"Good thing you met Lynn."

He answered his desk phone. "Tell me about it."

Derrick said, "Thanks," and hung up. "The toll booth footage is coming over now."

"All right, you check that out while I go see this guy at his rock store."

"Stones, Frank. They're called stones."

I laughed and headed out. By the time I hit the parking lot, the joviality had vanished. Even if this store didn't sell Tarot cards, to me, metaphysical stuff and fortune telling were in the same family.

Experience taught me most killers were "really nice," and my mantra that "you never really knew someone" was indisputable. Then there were the psychos who were driven to kill by the voices in their heads.

As I considered the healing power of crystals, it wasn't a far leap to believe someone could believe a higher, universal force was instructing them to murder. Maybe that was why they posed them in the midst of a nature preserve.

But how were the victims chosen? Was there something they did that could be interpreted as against the universe?

Pulling into the parking lot, I couldn't think of any reason a twisted mind could use to justify taking a life.

I opened the door. Music, reminding me of the Bishop Planetarium we'd taken Jessie to, filled the air. A display of purple-colored crystals sat on a counter. The place had a vibe I couldn't pin down. Then again, I'd never been this close to talking stones.

A man in a tie-dye T-shirt approached. "May I help you?"

"I'm here to see Mr. Madewell."

"That's me. Why don't we step outside?"

The strip center had recently been renovated. He motioned toward a bench opposite a fountain.

"You wanted to talk about Riley?"

"Yes. Ms. Addison used you as an alibi."

Horror spread across his face. "Did she do something . . ."

I didn't think he was involved. "We're following protocol. Now, was Ms. Addison with you the night of February first?"

He nodded.

"Where were you?"

He whispered, "At my house."

"You're married, aren't you?"

"My wife wasn't home."

He said it as if it made it okay. "How long was she there?"

"She stayed overnight."

"Do you sell Tarot cards?"

"No. The metaphysical world is far more accurate in seeing the future."

I wanted to ask him if he could foresee me catching the Preserve Killer. "Does Ms. Addison believe in or have an interest in fortune telling?"

He cringed. "Fortune telling is not the right way to portray it. The universe offers countless signs of what's in store for us. For example, your astrological sign comes with a set of predispositions. Of course, you have free will to impact your life, but ignoring the higher energies of the world makes it harder to understand your place in the cosmos."

When you were born sounded important and probably was in a lot of ways, but not as big a deal as where you were born. "Does Ms. Addison have an interest in signs that predict the future?"

"Who among us doesn't? It's a fundamental desire of every inhabitant of the universe."

Since I always hedged my bets, I didn't ask him whether his wife had looked ahead and saw him cheating. "We're aware of Ms. Addison's temper. How often does she lose it?"

"She's gotten better at it with crystal therapy. Amethyst has strong holistic properties. It's transformational in getting people to break bad habits."

Now, there was something wardens around the world could use. "Is there anything you know about Ms. Addison that could point to her harming someone?"

"No, no. She's not like that. Not at all."

Though he had a belief system far from mine, I believed he was telling the truth. The only thing that lingered was using his home for a sexual encounter. It was bold but also the only way to be unimpeachable. If it were a hotel, there'd be receipts and cameras. I tucked the thought into a pocket and left.

I was turning onto Airport Pulling when the phone rang.

Hitting the button on the steering wheel, Derrick's voice came through: "Frank, where are you?"

"On the way in. What's up?"

"I checked the toll booth footage. Dreman left a half hour before she said she did, but I can't find her coming back."

"That's weird."

"I know. Maybe she came back a different way?"

"Why go out of your way? She must have returned earlier or later."

"If it was earlier, she just moved up the suspect ladder."

52

Derrick left a cup of coffee and the *Daily News* on my desk. I took the cover off, sipped, and slid the paper over. I shook my head at the headline. "Preserve Killer Quiet." I read the first paragraph. It was more of the same; the killer was on the loose, and the police hadn't identified a primary suspect.

Pushing the paper away, I stopped and reached for it again. Opening it to the table listing the paper's sections, I flipped to the horoscope page and read mine: You may experience an emotional climax today. Things could come to a head. Don't be surprised if you run into serious opposition. Disperse your energy freely, but don't be concerned if others try to pull you in the opposite direction. Flexibility is a key for you.

Sitting back, I wondered if there wasn't something to the mystical world. The stars were acknowledging the difficulty this case presented. They promised an emotional climax, but there wasn't a clue as to what it would bring. The only advice it offered was to remain flexible.

I had an open mind with the case, bouncing it around like a Roomba vacuum cleaner. Reviewing the lines of inquiry, I couldn't see where I'd been rigid or unwilling to pursue a lead. Considering if the universe was referring to my personal life, I logged on to my desk top.

There were thirty-two emails waiting. I scanned the list, opening one with a link to the previous day's arrests. Fifteen people were pulled in. I scanned the names and choked on my coffee.

It couldn't be. I clicked on the name and a picture came up. It was Jonathan Ong. He was arrested for disorderly conduct. The charge was related to his interference in the arrest of a woman. I clicked on the related case and froze.

The woman Ong had tried to protect was Riley Addison. I checked the time of arrest; it was 1:37 a.m. No wonder I hadn't been notified. Addison had been arrested for assault. She'd stuck the end of an umbrella into the belly of a woman, sending her to the hospital.

She was violent. She had a white Honda like the one seen at the scene of Victor Trent's murder.

I checked the file. She'd been swabbed for DNA. It needed to be checked against the blood from Trent's pant leg. I printed the booking sheet and headed to the lab.

Taking the stairs two at a time, I wondered about Stephan Ong. Had he and Addison been working together? If they were, it would fill more holes than a pothole crew. Before going into the lab, I called Derrick.

"We might have caught a break. Addison was arrested for stabbing a woman with the end of an umbrella."

"Holy shit."

"And guess who was hauled in with her." It was something he would have said to me.

"Don't tell me Milbury."

"No, Stephan Ong."

"The Realtor?"

"Bingo. With the blood coming from a woman, we backed off him. But, you know, we never cleared his alibi."

"What are you thinking? The two of them are working together?"

"Honestly, I don't know what to think." I cringed at using the word "honestly." It was a stupid preface to use, inferring everything else was a lie.

"This is crazy, it's unbelievable."

I wanted to tell him the horoscope said I'd have an emotional climax today but was embarrassed. "It is, but we've got work to do. I need you to go upstairs to the prosecutors. Tell them there're persons of interest in the preserve killing. We need to hold them. I don't want them getting arraigned and released. They need to know they may be involved in multiple homicides."

"I'll explain the situation to them. They aren't going anywhere."

After telling the lab what we needed, I went to see the sheriff. He smiled when I walked in.

"You're closing in, huh?"

"It's not clear yet, but I need your help in clarifying things."

"Whatever you need."

I explained Addison and Ong were arrested outside of the Blue Martini in Mercato.

"What are the odds of that? Two persons of interest, arrested together for assault?"

"It's strange, for sure."

"What time is their arraignment?"

"I don't know. They were brought in around two this morning."

"We have time on the twenty-four-hour clock."

"I'd like to interview each of them. If you could clear it with the arresting officers—"

"Done. What else?"

"Just so you know, Derrick went to notify the prosecutors and ask them to hold them after arraignment."

"That's the judge's call."

"I know but . . ."

"I'll check who's handling it, and make sure they're aware they may be involved in the Preserve Killer case. Anything else?"

"I asked the lab to run the swab they took when booking Addison against the blood found at the last murder scene. It'd be helpful if you could make it a priority."

"I'll see to it."

"Thank you, sir. I'd like to talk to them as soon as possible."

"Give me ten minutes at most. I'll see that their arraignment is pushed as late as possible and let Captain Gesso know you're talking to them."

I PACED the hallway outside the interrogation rooms. Addison and Ong were holed up in separate rooms meeting with their mouthpieces. There wouldn't be an opportunity to talk to them without a lawyer. Not ideal, but I couldn't wait to see what they had to say.

My phone vibrated; it was Derrick. "Hey, what's going on?"

"I got the footage from Lago, and Dreman came back. But it was ten forty."

"Hmmm." I couldn't remember Trent's time of death. "When did Bilotti say Trent died?"

"It's in the range. But you want to hear the weird thing?"

No, I don't. "What are you talking about?"

"When Dreman came back, her trunk was open a crack. It was tied down with a chain and padlocked. She was hauling something important."

"What could it be?"

"You think it was Trent's body?"

"That doesn't fit. The killer's been too cautious. They wouldn't ride around with a body."

"Maybe, but sometimes the best place to hide something is in plain sight."

He was right. "Yeah, but—"

"She could've killed him elsewhere, and when she went to pose him in Logan Preserve, someone might have been there. You know, Ramirez said he chased a couple of lovers out of there a week before the murder."

"But why go home with the body?"

"Driving around with a body is riskier to me."

"Get a couple of officers and get down to Lago. Talk to everyone in the complex. And get the gate records; see if she left later that night."

53

The door to the interview room opened. "Detective Luca? We're ready for you."

It was Fred Moresco, Ong's lawyer. We shook hands and I stepped into the room. Ong looked fresher than me. He stood. The creases running down his pant legs could slice a steak. He nodded and sat down.

I turned the recording devices on, and after reciting the formalities, said, "Mr. Ong, I'd like to hear your version of events."

"It was a misunderstanding."

"My client was merely attempting to make sure no one was hurt."

"Exactly. I tried to calm Riley down and asked her to cooperate, but the officers were hell-bent on making something out of nothing."

"It was more than nothing. It landed a woman in the hospital with a punctured abdomen."

"I'm not minimizing the injury, though it was just a bruise, but she started it."

"My client maintains the woman was the aggressor, and we've begun to identify witnesses to corroborate that."

"What were you and Ms. Addison doing that night?"

"We were enjoying a night on the town."

"Why stay out so late?"

"Riley and I are night owls. We were having a grand time until that bitch, uh, woman ruined it."

"What happened?"

"She was drunk and had her hands all over me. Riley was trying to get her off me."

"How did the fight break out?"

"We were trying to leave and she followed us outside. It happened so fast; I can't say exactly. I was on my phone hailing an Uber and the next thing I know, I saw Riley using the umbrella to keep her away. Then she fell and Riley used the umbrella to keep her from getting up."

"The report indicates that the weapon's end tip was sharpened."

"Hold on, Detective. This was a simple umbrella, not a weapon, and my client has no knowledge of the ferrule, or tip, being sharpened."

Ferrule. I had a new word for Derrick. "Why did you have an umbrella?"

"The forecast had a chance of rain."

According to the weatherman, it could shower every day. "It was your umbrella?"

"No. We met at Riley's. We checked the weather to see if she needed a jacket. We saw it might rain and we took it."

"Ms. Addison has a temper issue."

"No, that's not true. She's just sensitive about certain things. We all are."

Addison seemed to have a lot of male friends. And some were married, creating angry women.

"Your friend is into mystical things, like astrology, crystals, and fortune telling."

He scoffed at fortune telling. It was the second time I'd been rebuffed using the term. "Every being and thing in this universe are connected. Riley understands the connection, the signals we must open ourselves to receive."

I thought of the vibrations I'd get at the base of my head. It was something I attributed to my gut. Were these people saying it came from a higher power? "Does she like to use a Ouija board or Tarot cards?"

He scoffed, "A Ouija board?"

"What about Tarot cards?"

Moresco interrupted, "I fail to see the relevancy in this line of questioning. Mr. Ong was a bystander to the events. He merely attempted to deescalate the scuffle. If you have questions related to last night's incident, we'll address them, but that's it."

"If your client has information regarding Ms. Addison, and it's not limited to last night, we'll speak to the prosecutors, recommending his release, if he shares it with us."

Moresco smiled. "I'm not sure what your alluding to, Detective, but I'm confident the charges against Mr. Ong will be dropped."

I couldn't blame the lawyer; he had no clue his client would be held after arraignment over concerns there was a connection to the serial killings. Unsure if Ong had a role in the murders, I ended the questioning without divulging my motive. I'd take a shot at Addison and go from there.

Gulping the last of a coffee, I tossed the cup in the trash and checked the video feed. Addison was smiling at her attorney as if on a date. After a quick knock, I threw the door open. Gabe Noto smoothed his comb-over and got up. He extended his hand. "Detective Luca."

Noto wasn't in the top tier of criminal lawyers but served his clients well. I'd encountered his stonewalling tactics, which melded into plea negotiations on two occasions. If his client was the Preserve Killer, he was in over his head. Way over. "Counselor." I nodded to his client. "Ms. Addison."

She gave me a bright smile. "Hi. You know, you really look like George Clooney."

She was flirting. Something was off with this woman. Way off. I clicked the device on and recorded the date and time and who was present. "Tell me what happened last night."

"That woman was drunk; she was all over Stephen. She came right up to us and started pawing at him like I wasn't even there."

"Did you know the lady?"

She hesitated. "Not really."

"Explain that."

"I've seen her around. She's a damn gold digger."

She had a lot of company in Naples. "You could have walked away."

Addison shrugged. Ong said they tried to. Either they hadn't worked out their stories, or there were witnesses who'd set the record straight. "Where'd you get the umbrella?"

"I don't know. I had it." Then she added, "Somebody left it at my house."

She knew I was going to ask about sharpening the end. "Who left it?"

"I don't know; it's been in the closet a long time."

It wasn't raining when they left the house. It made no sense to take an umbrella that didn't collapse. We'd find out if she carried it around as a weapon. "Did she go to the Blue Martini often?"

She frowned. "Yeah. She's a real bitch."

Addison continued to act differently than in our previous interview. Was this the real her? "Your boyfriend, uh, Mr. Madewell, said you're into crystals and Tarot cards, that type of stuff."

Addison nodded and was about to speak when Noto said, "We're getting a little far afield, Detective. Where's the relevancy?"

I couldn't reveal the killer had used Tarot cards. "Ms. Addison, you're still employed at Bank of America?"

Another frown. "I am. But because of that bitch, I'm going to have to clear my name or they'll let me go."

"Who's your doctor? Dr. Bigham?"

Something flashed across her face. Noto put his hand on her forearm and said, "That's a private matter, Detective. You know you can't ask about medical information."

"Sorry, Counselor, you're right. It just slipped out."

Was there a connection, or had the question taken her by surprise? We'd never dug into Addison's background. She had a white Honda, worked with Victor Trent, and was sleeping with a guy who owned a metaphysical store. In addition, the way she was acting raised questions.

After asking a couple of meaningless questions, I closed the interview. I hurried to my office, anxious to examine every aspect of Addison's life. It made no sense to wait for the DNA to come back. Turning my phone on, I noticed two texts from Derrick and pocketed my cell.

54

Derrick leaned into his monitor. "Frank, take a look at this. It's Dreman. The plate matches."

I peered at the screen. "That's definitely her and it's only nine fifteen."

"She had more than enough time to kill Trent."

"No doubt. It makes me wonder why she lied."

"As cover."

I had no problem knocking heads with suspects, but the thought of questioning Dreman on the time difference made me wish I was standing in line at the DMV. "Not looking forward to talking to Miss Personality."

"If you looked up the word recalcitrant in the dictionary, there'd be a picture of Dreman."

"You pick up another ten-dollar word?"

"It was today's word of the day. And if I don't use them, I forget them right away."

"I don't know if it fits her, but nasty sure does."

"No doubt."

"Oh, I got a new word for you, ferrule. Ever hear it?"

Casey stepped in. "You busy?"

"I'm going to talk to Dreman again but what do you got?"

"We went back over the first ten years, looking for connections, but now we're combing over the ten before that, and we have a couple of things that might mean something."

"What did you find?"

"One is all medically related. When she was twenty-six, Melissa Wright worked in a place called Universal Phlebotomy. It's a blood-collection place, and Victor Trent had a job, for a short period, in a medical lab."

"And we have Dr. Bigham. What were Wright and Trent doing in these jobs?"

"Both were in clerical positions: Wright registered patients, and Trent handled paperwork for the lab."

"What were the time frames?"

"For Wright it was ten years ago and Trent about nine."

"It's an interesting find. Can we determine whether Bigham used the services of the companies they worked for?"

"I think we might be able to get that without a warrant."

"Good. What else you have?"

"Dr. Bigham was on her college tennis team. She didn't belong to any club that we could find, but her neighbors said she played in her community. Victor Trent was a member of the Naples Bath and Tennis Academy. Wright didn't appear to play, and Ryan played on his high school team but doesn't belong to a club."

Derrick said, "There's a lot of tournaments here. Clubs and communities compete against each other all the time. Paths could have crossed."

"We'd need to identify the teams or competitions they participated in and time frames."

"I was going to do that but wanted to see if you thought it was worthwhile."

"We can't let anything pass. Could've been some competitive thing or embarrassment, cheating, jealousy, who knows?"

Derrick said, "All you have to do is remember the ice skaters Nancy Kerrigan and Tonya Harding. It wasn't murder but it sure was twisted."

"No doubt. Is that it?"

Casey said, "One more thing, Wright and Trent paddle boarded from time to time."

"Any indication Dr. Bigham did?"

"Not that we could find, but she kayaked, and we know Ryan liked to kayak."

"Let's check to see where they may have rented or launched from. I don't know what would set someone off—"

Derrick said, "There was a crazy case up in New York. This couple was kayaking in the Hudson and the guy drowned. They charged the woman because she took the drain plug out. She got two years but cashed in life insurance on him."

I said, "There was a lot more to that one. It was in October and the water was forty degrees; he didn't have a life jacket on, and there were other extenuating circumstances. I'm not saying she wasn't responsible but it wasn't cut and dry."

Derrick said, "Maybe, but I think she set him up. She made him drink alcohol, promising sex, and there was something wrong with his paddle and—"

"It's far from the situation we're dealing with but it's a reminder there's a lot of ways to kill someone. Let's stay on point. Casey, check on everything you dug up, we're going to see Dreman."

WE WERE a minute away from Lago, the apartment complex Dreman called home. Derrick said, "You okay?"

I hadn't said a word the entire drive. "Yeah, just trying to work through the connections Casey developed. None of them seem to fit all the victims."

"It's early."

"I know, but it makes me think there might be two killers."

The gate lifted and Derrick pulled into a spot. "It would explain a lot."

We got out and headed toward the building. The music got louder as we approached the pool area. Derrick said, "I can't stand this rap music."

"You can't put rap and music in the same sentence."

"You're right. I don't get it. It's violent and denigrates women. Why are kids listening to it?"

"Strong bass line is what I'm told."

"I can feel the vibration from here."

"Smells like ribs to me."

The pool deck was crowded. There wasn't a soul under forty and everyone was holding a cup. Didn't anybody work? Someone lowered the music. Was it obvious we were the law?

I double-pressed the bell, and we stepped to either side of the door. Dreman opened the door and scowled. "What do you want?"

"We'd like to have a quick word with you."

"About what?"

"Your alibi."

"I told you—"

Someone who looked like a maintenance man passed by. "Let's do this inside."

She exhaled and stepped aside. "Come in."

I walked down the hallway and she said, "No. Ask your crap right here. I'm not in the mood."

A Ouija board was on the coffee table.

"And we're not in the mood to be lied to. First, you claimed to be in Jacksonville with your sister. We proved you weren't, and you changed your alibi, saying you went to Miami."

"I went to Miami."

"You may have, but you came through the toll booth at Alligator Alley at nine at night."

She glared at me.

"What did you do the rest of the night?"

"None of your business."

"A homicide makes it my business."

She scoffed, "I went to sleep."

Driving back and forth to Miami was tiring. If she hadn't lied, I may have bought it. "I don't think you were, or you would've said that the first time we asked."

"I don't care what the hell you believe."

Derrick said, "If you don't answer, we'll get a subpoena and drag you in."

"Get out. Now."

I hiked my head toward the door and we left. Derrick grumbled under his breath as we got back to the car. Once inside, I said, "Check with the management of this place. They have controlled access. We'll find out if she came home like she said."

"I'm betting no."

I didn't gamble but my gut agreed. "She had a Ouija board."

"Really? Where'd you see that?"

"It was on her coffee table."

"It's coming together. It's a good thing we have eyes on her."

55

___

Stripping my jacket off as I entered the office, I said, "Derrick, we need to do a background colonoscopy on Addison; something is off with her."

Derrick stood. "Dreman left her place at one oh five in the morning."

"What the hell is she up to?"

"A couple of the neighbors say she's unfriendly and gets visitors they described as"—he finger quoted—"scary."

"Scary?"

"Yeah. They said she's strange, and this guy with three dogs, he said Dreman comes and goes in the middle of the night."

"We need the gate records from the days each of the murders was committed."

"No doubt. You know the dog guy said Dreman drives a couple of different cars, and one of them is a van."

"Did you check DMV?"

"Yeah, nothing else registered under her name."

"All right. We'll have to identify any vehicle leaving the complex late at night. Lago must have a list of vehicles registered to renters. If a car isn't on the list, it might be her driving somebody else's."

"When are we going to get the Addison DNA?"

"Remin said he told the lab to prioritize it. I'm going give them another two hours before busting them."

Derrick smiled. "If this was *CSI*, we'd have it in five minutes."

"I wish."

"I'm going to Lago."

"See you later."

I opened the murder book and flipped to the page on Addison. We had next to nothing on her. First off, we needed to talk to her family and neighbors. I'd hand those off, but I wanted to personally talk to her coworkers.

I'd met with the branch manager after Trent's murder, but his loyalty was to Bank of America, and that meant keeping it out of the news. Protocol would force me to notify him, but while wondering how to approach the situation, Willis and Cobalt stepped into the office.

Cobalt said, "You have a minute?"

"Anytime. What's going on?"

"We checked into the tennis-connection angle and discovered there's a ton of bad blood between Trent and Addison. And, get this, Ong and Bigham had a car accident at the entrance to the Naples Bath and Tennis Club."

"What kind of accident?"

"Ong was heading north on Airport, and Bigham pulled out of the club. Witnesses say Bigham was on her phone and pulled right out without stopping. She slammed into a new Mercedes Ong had just bought."

"Did a fight or anything physical happen?"

"No, but Ong was mad as hell."

"Who wouldn't be? But I don't think it means much."

Willis said, "I felt that way, too, but since the car was totaled, I dug a little. Ong had only picked up the car a week before and didn't have GAP coverage."

"So, he was liable for the difference in what he owed versus the depreciated value the insurance company would pay."

Cobalt said, "The minute you drive the car out of the showroom, it drops twenty percent."

"He could've been out twenty grand."

"Look, I've seen people kill over a phone, but Ong is real estate pro; he's got to be making a ton in this market. It doesn't feel like it fits."

"I checked the photos. Bigham made it a pretzel. He could've hurt his back or something."

I said, "Why wouldn't he sue?"

"Maybe he did. We've got to look further."

"Okay, check it, but what else you have on the Trent-Addison rivalry?"

"According to the club's pro, it started during a match. Addison came to the net, and Trent slammed a ball at her, hitting her in the face. She got a detached retina."

"How long ago was this?"

"Eighteen months ago."

"Anything further between them?"

"She didn't play for a long time, but four months ago, she smacked Trent in the head with her racket. He needed six stitches."

"She assaulted him?"

"There weren't any witnesses. Trent said it was intentional. Addison said she was going for a shot at the net and didn't know where Trent was, and when she realized, she couldn't stop in time."

"Why were they playing alone?"

"They weren't at the club. They were downtown, at the courts by Cambier Park."

"Here's the thing: Trent told the pro that Addison arranged the game, giving him the impression it was going to be a doubles match."

"She wanted him alone. Maybe she lured him with a promise of sex after playing."

"We need to check with Trent's wife. She won't like it, but Addison could be one of those obsessive women who couldn't let go and went way too far."

My desk phone rang. I reached for it. "Hold on, guys."

"Homicide, Detective Luca."

"Frank, it's Gesso. It looks like Dreman is on the run."

I jumped out of my seat. "You sure?"

"She loaded a bunch of luggage in her car and took off. We're following her north on Seventy-Five. Right now, she's approaching the Bonita Beach Road exit."

"Stay on her. If Dreman goes to the airport, we need to know where she's flying and get the locals to watch her."

"Will do. I'll let you know."

I hung up. "Dreman might be on the run. She's heading north with a carload of luggage. Gesso is tracking her."

"It's weird taking off in the middle of the day."

"Maybe not. She might figure she'd blend in."

"She has to know we're watching her."

"Probably, but either it's the hiding-in-plain-sight thing or she made a mistake, but this killer has been too cautious for that."

"I don't know."

"Look, we need to keep working these connections. There's a lot of bad blood, and it got physical between Trent and Addison. You know what they say about a scorned woman."

"When we get the DNA back, we'll know."

"It'll help for sure, but we still need a narrative for the courtroom."

My phone rang again; it was Gesso. "She blew past the airport exit. You want to pull her over?"

"No. Let's see where she's heading."

The phone on Derrick's desk rang. I motioned to Willis to answer it and finished up with Gesso.

Willis hung up. "That was the lab. They got several hits on familial links to the DNA from the Trent crime scene."

56

Pulling the booty over my shoe, I ripped it. Tossing it, I grabbed another. Outfitted in protective clothing, I burst into the lab. "Where's Geary?"

A tech lifted his head off a microscope and pointed to the director's office. In his white lab coat, Geary was peering at an image on a wall monitor with a magnifier. "What are you looking at?"

"Fibers collected from the Waffle House robbery. Remin is going after these guys hard to send a message."

"He's right. They've got to know you try something here, we'll come after you. This isn't California, where they let you steal a thousand dollars."

"It's hard to believe what's going on out there and in New York."

"Amen. What do have for me?"

Geary slid behind his desk and I took a chair. "We focused on twenty critical markers in the DNA found on Trent's pant leg. GEDmatch, one of the public databases where Casey obtained access, provided several possibilities."

"Any relation to Dreman or Addison?"

"It's not possible to tell at this time."

Geary opened a folder, picking up a sheet of paper. "What we have are likely relatives."

"Mother, father?"

"Unfortunately not. A match on ten out of the twenty markers would suggest a close relative such as a parent, child, or sibling. What we have are four individuals whose match suggests a cousin, uncle, or aunt."

"Okay. That gives us something to work with. Out of the four, are any of them stronger than the others?"

Geary held out the document. "They're prioritized." He pointed to the first name. "These two have one more match."

He handed me the report. Scanning it, my eyes settled on the first name: Anthony Hatch. A hometown of Rye, New York was listed. Not too far from Jersey. The second name was Gloria Shea from Louisville, Kentucky.

"This my copy?"

"It's all yours."

I stood. "Thanks, Geary. I have to get moving."

Heading up the stairs, I held the document as if it were a newborn. If the DNA results crapped out, this was our lifeline. Familial DNA was an important tool, and I was glad to live in one of twelve states allowing law enforcement to use it.

The first thing I wanted to do was run both names through the national database. It didn't mean anything if they had records. Depravity wasn't inherited, but the circumstances you grew up in had an effect.

Remin needed to know we had a substantial avenue to pursue. I made a quick detour, handing off the familial results to Derrick before bringing the sheriff up to date. Heading up the stairs, my cell rang. It was Gesso. "Where is Dreman?"

"On Route Four going toward Orlando."

Dreman had left with luggage, but a trip to Disney World rivaled a ride on the SpaceX Shuttle as most unlikely. "Keep following her. We need to know if she's meeting anyone and the whys and wherefores."

PEELING OFF MY SPORTS JACKET, I stepped into the office. "Addison's DNA isn't a match."

Derrick peered over his monitor. "You shitting me?"

Our leading suspect, if not the leading one, had been marginalized. "Wish I was. But don't lose focus; we got the familial DNA to work with."

"I know, but neither Hatch nor Shea have records."

"That's okay. It's not them we're after. You have contact info for them?"

"Yeah. Hatch is forty-nine and living in Yonkers. Shea's forty-three and is still in Louisville. Get this, she works at the baseball-bat factory."

"It's good they're still making them there."

"It sure is."

"What about any siblings or kids they have?"

"All I have at this point is marital status. Hatch got divorced about ten years ago, and it looks like Shea is still married. Here're their DMV photos."

Holding an image in each hand, my eyes bounced between the two. I looked for a message, but what? Neither of them were suspects and lived at least a thousand miles away. I rifled through the homicides. "Did any of the victims live near either of them?"

"No. Nowhere near."

"All right. I'll call Hatch and you tackle Shea. Key is finding out about any kids or siblings they have. Remember, they don't have to cooperate, and if it's a kid, they're going to be protective. We need to be tactful."

"No doubt. We should check on first cousins as well. Who knows where half the marker matches came from."

It was another reality check. I'd assumed, or more like, hoped, we were looking for a close relation. "You're right. Let's get going."

Placing the picture of Anthony Hatch by the phone, I punched in his number. "Anthony Hatch?"

"Yeah. What do you want?"

"I'm Detective Luca, with the Collier County Sheriff's Office, down in Florida."

"Sheriff's office? What's this about?"

"I'm not authorized to release information on an active investigation, but we're working a case, and I have a couple of quick questions for you."

"I don't understand why you're calling me."

"There's nothing to be concerned about. This is purely a background inquiry. You're not the subject of the investigation."

"I didn't think so. I didn't do anything."

"That's right. Now, you're forty-nine and divorced, right?"

"Correct."

"What are your sisters' and brothers' names?"

"My sister is Angela, but I don't have any brothers."

"Where does she live? In Florida?"

"No longer. She's in South Carolina."

"Where'd she live in Florida?"

"She was close to my daughter, in Cape Coral. She rented in the same community, but she met a guy from Gaston and moved there."

"Cape Coral is nice. Your daughter still there?"

"Yes, she went to Gulf Coast College and got a job after graduating."

"Nice. My daughter is going to college but doesn't know what she wants to do. What does yours do?"

"She works for a place called Karma and Coconuts."

Was that a joke? "What do they do?"

"A bit of everything. They have art classes and sell local artists' work, and they have a big section of crystals and stones."

"Wow. I'm into the metaphysical stuff as well. What's her name? I'm up there often. I'll ask for her when I stop in and see what they have."

"Karen. I'm not into that, and to be honest, I think it was a waste of tuition. But you know what—she's happy."

"That's all that counts."

"So true."

"Be well, sir. I'm sorry to have disturbed you."

I hung up as he said, "No problem."

Derrick was still on the phone. I put Karen Hatch into the database. She'd been arrested five years ago. The charge was for carrying a concealed weapon.

57

I PULLED UP KAREN HATCH'S BOOKING PHOTO. SHE'D BEEN crying and looked scared. What was she doing with a gun in her purse without a permit? Hatch filled out the orange jumpsuit and was just under six feet tall. She'd have no problem subduing or moving the victims.

But where was the connection? Why them? I checked for vehicles registered under her name. She didn't own a white Honda or MINI Cooper. She drove a red Chevy Tahoe.

Derrick was ending his call. I stood in front of his desk as he hung up. "Hatch has a daughter up in Cape Coral. She works in a place called Karma and Coconuts."

"What kind of name is that?"

"It's a metaphysical place."

"I can't believe how popular that stuff is."

"Yeah. Not only that, but she was arrested on a concealed-carry charge."

"Whoa. She never used it?"

"Not according to the arrest report. She's now our primary focus. What did you get with Shea?"

"She has a sister who lives on Staten Island. But they

haven't talked in years; she went on forever about how Karen took off when the mother had gotten cancer and left her alone to care for her."

"It's never easy. We need to track her down."

"Working on it. I checked with New York's DMV portal but nothing on a Rachel Shea."

"She could be married."

"I checked the name change records while she was blabbing away."

"You're getting too good to have to report to me."

"No way, man."

"Check with New Jersey. It feels like half the people in Jersey came from Staten Island."

"Will do."

"Look into it when we get back. We need to talk to Karen Hatch."

We took the interstate north, taking the exit for Cape Coral. It'd been awhile since I'd been up to the one of the fastest growing cities in the country. "You know, there's over two hundred thousand people living here now."

"It's right on the Gulf of Mexico. Great if you love to boat."

"Cape Coral has more navigable waters than any place on the planet."

"Really?"

"I read that in a Realtor's marketing piece. Homes are cheaper than in Naples but more than Fort Myers."

"It's all about the water."

"Speaking of the water"—I pointed as we passed Sun Splash Family Waterpark—"we took Jessie there, a hundred years ago."

"Worth the trip?"

"Sure. They've got a big lazy river and a lot of water rides. But wait until Emma's about eight."

"After going to Disney before Emma could walk, there's no way I'm making that mistake again."

"Here we are."

"I didn't know what to expect, but it wasn't this."

I pulled in front of a yellow building that had faded to off-white. A blue-and-green hand-painted sign put the emphasis on Karma. "You're going to leave, a believer."

Derrick scoffed, "I guess you never know."

"Amen."

A pulsating noise, interspersed with wind, sounded when we opened the door. It made me think of a sci-fi movie. Derrick looked at me and shrugged. My eyes were drawn to a painting of a yellow dandelion. We used to make wishes on them as kids.

A tall woman, I believed was Karen Hatch, appeared from behind a display. "Welcome. Are you having a great day?"

"Yes. You're Karen Hatch, right?"

She smiled. "Yes. Have we met? Perhaps in another life?"

If she did what we suspected she might have, reincarnation was her only hope of seeing the sky again. "Your dad told me you work here."

"Ah. How is Tony?"

Calling your father by his first name, if you didn't work together, was a no-no in my book. "He seems well. We have a couple of questions for you."

"Sure. But first, you should know that everything is hand-crafted by local artists—"

"It's not related to the store. Let's talk outside."

Her eyebrows knitted. She peered over our shoulders. "I'm confused—but, sure."

Derrick and I put our sunglasses on, and a squinting

Hatch turned her back to the sun. "Ms. Hatch, we're with the Collier County Sheriff's Office."

She leaned back. "Is Tony okay?"

It was the right reaction, but the Preserve Killer was top-notch. "He's fine. You go to Naples frequently?"

"I wouldn't say frequently. Every now and then, when the spirit moves me."

"Who do you know there?"

"A lot of souls. Why all the questions?"

"You do own Tarot cards, right?"

"Several decks. They're, like, an insight to the future."

Had she seen prison in her future? "You use them to send messages?"

"Sometimes, I'll send one to a friend who's down to remind them this life is temporary. It's disheartening how many people forget we're on a journey from one dimension to another."

I had my doubts, but it wouldn't stop me from hoping she knew something I didn't. "You were arrested on a concealed carry, without a permit."

She frowned. "That was before my enlightenment. I was living in fear and foolishly believed I could control events."

Was she taking a shot at law enforcement? "What were you afraid of?"

"Society programs you to live in fear. We're afraid of each other, of the future. We should embrace each day as it unfolds."

Hatch either believed this or was an actor who'd rehearsed lines. "Would you be willing to give a sample of your DNA voluntarily?"

She folded her arms but said nothing. I could see the wheels turning in her head as I said, "We can do it right here; it's a simple swab."

"I don't know . . ."

Derrick finally spoke, "We'll have to bring her in, Frank."

"To a police station?"

"Exactly. And we'll have to take you to Collier."

"Okay, I'll give it."

Derrick swabbed her twice and we left. Back in the car, I said, "Call Lee County, tell him to keep eyes on Hatch. Tell them we'll stay until a car arrives."

"You think she's going to run?"

"I didn't like the way she was behaving. She was too composed for me."

"She's either a phony or was on something."

After he called the locals, we moved the car a block away and watched the store. I was texting Mary Ann when Derrick said, "Hatch just came out of the side door."

Hatch looked in both directions and took her phone out. It was a quick call. She pocketed the cell and went back inside. It could have been nothing, but the body language signaled otherwise.

58

—————

A CRACK OF THUNDER STARTLED ME AS I SLID BEHIND MY desk. The sun was shining but the rain was coming. Derrick was dropping off Hatch's DNA and filing the paperwork evidence required. I checked the note he'd made on Shea. Rachel Shea was the estranged sister.

As an only child, I didn't understand how siblings got to the point where they didn't talk to each other. I plugged Rachel Shea into Jersey's portal and got a hit: Rachel Theresa Shea. Her address was listed in Lavallette.

A tiny town on the Jersey Shore, its population swelled during the summer. I dug for a number and came up with a landline. It rang five times. As I was hanging up, someone picked up.

"Hello?"

"Is this Rachel Shea?"

"No. She's working."

"Where?"

"Who's this?"

"Detective Luca from the Collier County Sheriff's Office."

"Oh no. Did something happen to her condo?"

I jumped out of my seat. "Not exactly. But she does own one down here, right?"

"Yeah, she's had it forever."

"Well, it could be nothing, but there seems to be a possible fraud attempt, and I'd like to speak to her."

"What happened?"

"I really can't say, ma'am. But what's your name and relation to Ms. Shea?"

"Cathy Garibaldi. Rachel's a lifelong friend. I've been staying with her since my hip replacement. I would've had to have gone to a rehab place without her."

"That's nice of her."

"Yeah. I'm leaving today. Rachel is the best, a real angel."

Had Shea found a way to offset her murderous ways? "That's what I've heard. So, what's her cell number?"

I thanked her and sat back. This had to be played well. Lavallette was in Ocean County. It had been awhile since I worked in the neighboring county of Monmouth, but I still had friends. Toying with calling in a favor, Derrick came back in. He was the perfect sounding board.

"We have the hottest lead in a long time."

His eyebrows raised. "What do we have?"

"I tracked down Shea's sister in Jersey; didn't talk to her yet, but guess where she has a second home?" It was true, you started to become like the person you spent time with.

"Naples?"

"Bingo. She has a condo."

"Where?"

"I made like I knew where it was, to get Shea's number. I didn't get a chance to check the tax records."

Derrick sat at his desk. "I got it." As he tapped away, he asked, "Does she have a record?"

"Nothing I could find."

"Tell me again, how does this familial thing makes her a suspect?"

"Her sister was on the list, matching half of the critical markers. That means it wasn't her, but it could be a close relative of hers."

"Okay, but it could be anyone related to her."

"Yes, but having a place down here raised a flag."

"Her and zillions of other northerners."

"No doubt a tsunami of people moved down the last two years."

"She's got a place in Bridgewater Bay on Wind Song Court."

"That's off Livingston, by Orange Blossom."

"Yep. You know, if she goes back and forth, it'll be easy to check if she was here when the murders occurred."

"Exactly. But I don't want to scare her. If she's the one and we call, asking questions, she may take off."

"We can nose around, find out from her neighbors when she's been here, see if it overlaps the murders."

"I was thinking the same thing but we have to be careful. Somebody calls her, and who knows what she'll do."

"What do you want to do?"

"I have contacts up there."

"That's right. You used to work up there."

My cell rang. "Detective Luca, this is Captain Ruiz with the Lee County Sheriff's Department."

"Hi, what's going on?"

"I'm afraid we've lost track of Hatch."

"How did that happen?"

"They followed her home, and the officer figured he had time to go to the bathroom. He'd eaten some bad tacos and got a case of the runs. He said he was away ten minutes tops and she was gone."

Inhaling, I told myself to keep cool. "She leave on foot or—"

"Her car was missing. We've put an APB out. We'll track her down."

"Let me know when you have eyes on her."

I hung up. "Hatch slipped away."

"You kidding me? How'd that happen?"

I told him and said, "Let Lee do its job and we'll check into Shea."

"How you want to do this?"

"Check with Bridgewater. They're gated, so there has to be a record. All these communities want to know the car you have. If she's got a car, we can check the transponder activity."

"I like that."

"But you have to keep it quiet. Tell them we're checking into a ring selling fake registrations and driver's licenses. Say we picked up a couple using Shea's address. Grab two other names from the tax records and use them as cover."

"Sneaky but effective."

"I want to catch the bastard."

"Amen. I'll get two names and head to Bridgewater. This needs to be done in person."

My desk phone rang. "Thanks."

"Luca."

"Frank, it's Gesso. Dreman just pulled into the Days Inn."

"Don't tell me she's taking a vacation."

"She might be, but it looks like she only took an overnight bag out of the car. The other luggage is still in the trunk."

"If you can spare the manpower, I'd like you to keep watching her. See if she meets anyone or goes anywhere."

"We got a lot of guys out, but Remin said you got carte blanche."

JESSIE HAD JUST GOTTEN BACK HOME. She'd been at the University of Miami banking college credits before starting her freshman year. I was proud, but the twenty-three hundred dollars a credit was challenging. I didn't want her to take out student loans. I knew the benefit of having skin in the game, but Jessie had more drive than a car dealership.

I'd drawn down some of our savings to pay for Mary Ann's experimental drugs, but as pissed as I was, I was thankful they were working. Working till I was seventy was a reality I might have to face, though it'd be in private security.

I closed the garage door and walked in. Mary Ann and Jessie were jabbering like middle-schoolers.

"Hey, kiddo. How's my girl?"

"Dad! I thought you were working."

I wrapped my arms around her. "I am, but it's been too long. How was the drive?"

"Easy. Melissa and I split it up."

"It's good to have you home."

She smiled. "I missed the both of you."

Mary Ann had a lottery-winner grin on, and you know what, it was better than the money. "Mom missed you, but me, I kinda liked the house quiet."

"Hey!"

I kissed the top of her head. Her hair smelled of lavender. Mary Ann said, "Why don't we go out tonight?"

As I said, "Sure," my cell rang. It was Derrick. "Shea was in town for the Wright and Bigham murders."

59

———————

After apologizing to my girls, I headed to meet Sheriff Remin. What was the right way to handle this? If I asked the New Jersey authorities to intervene, and it looked like Shea was the Preserve Killer, she could refuse to come to Florida.

We'd be locked in a courtroom trying to extradite her to Florida. I trusted my brothers in uniform but not New Jersey's judicial system. It was a mess ten years ago and had only weakened, offering more rights to criminals than the victims they preyed upon.

Remin was the keynote speaker at an event being held by St. Matthew's House. I drove past Alice Sweetwater's, where the first victim, Melissa Wright, had worked. It strengthened my resolve. Circumstances were difficult, but I hoped, if I kept at it, this case wouldn't ruin my record.

I pulled into the parking lot for Lulu's Kitchen. St Matthew's House had built the facility to help feed its residents. I sent Remin a text, and he stepped outside a minute later. His dark blue jacket and red tie suited the politician that lurked below the surface.

"Sorry, sir."

"No apology needed. Nothing is as important as this case."

"Thank you. I'm looking for guidance on dealing with Rachel Shea. We know she was in her Naples condo during the time of at least two of the murders. My concern is alerting her and getting into an extradition mess."

"If it's her, I'm fine with getting her off the streets. We'll get her down to face justice eventually."

"I know, but I was trying to find a way to get her down here voluntarily."

Remin smiled. "You want it tied up in a bow."

I shrugged. "I guess so. We told her friend there was a DMV fraud ring using addresses in Bridgewater."

"Why don't you go up there? Talk to her, see how she plays it."

"We need her DNA. If it matches the blood on Trent's pants, we have our killer."

"Yes, but we'll need more than that for the prosecutors."

"I realize that. If it's Shea, once we dig in, we'll build supporting evidence."

"Then get up there and see where it leads."

I sat in my car, checking the flights. There was one at six thirty in the morning. It was early, but I wouldn't be able to sleep with this hanging out there. After booking a flight and car, I told Mary Ann I was going to New Jersey for what I hoped was only a day.

60

———

RIDING ALONG ROUTE 35, IT NARROWED TO A LANE IN EACH direction. I switched on the windshield defogger and slowed down. I turned onto Brown Avenue. It was a short block leading to the ocean. Shea's place was more bungalow than house.

I pulled behind the SUV in the gravel driveway. Squeezing out of my car, I nearly knocked over a garbage can at the curb.

Rosary beads hung off the rearview mirror of the black SUV. Peeking inside, nothing caught my eye. As a blast of wind swept through, I tucked my neck into my coat and hit the bell.

Dressed in a pink knit sweater, Shea matched her driver's license photo. I took my badge out and introduced myself. "Come in. It's windy out there."

"Thank you."

"I can't believe you came all the way up here to see me."

A large picture of the Blessed Mother dominated the family room. "We take fraud seriously, ma'am."

"Rachel. Please call me Rachel."

She seemed down to earth. "Okay, Rachel."

"Let's sit in the kitchen."

It had a half-size fridge, small sink, and large picture of Mother Teresa. She swept up a *Christian Monitor* newspaper and put it on the counter. Shea was a church lady.

"We're looking into this DMV ring—"

"Cathy told me. It's disappointing to hear. But I don't have to worry, right? I mean, they're only using my address."

"You don't have anything to be concerned about."

"I don't understand why you'd come all the way up here, in this weather, to talk to me."

It wasn't easy lying with Mother Teresa staring at me. "I have family in the area and it's good to be thorough."

"Oh, good excuse to come up, but the wrong time of year."

I smiled. "It sure is. Do you go to Naples often?"

"As much as I can. At least four months a year, I'd like to go full-time but I can't leave Ocean of Love. I don't want to sound self-important, but without me, I don't see how they can go on."

"What's Ocean of Love?"

"A charity for children with cancer. After my husband passed away, I decided to dedicate my time to helping others."

"Sorry to hear. Do you have any children?"

"None of my own. But I have plenty at Ocean."

"That's nice. So, you work there?"

"Yes, but I donate my salary. I mean, what better use of my money than helping sick children and their families?"

Had I stumbled upon a saint? "Good for you. They're lucky to have you."

"Oh, I don't know. Truth is, I get more out of it than they do." She smiled.

"I bet you do."

"So, how can I help the sheriff's office?"

"This may sound crazy, but do you use Tarot cards?"

"Tarot cards? That's paganism." She scoffed. "You want to change things, put your time into prayer."

She was as practical as they came. My bullshit meter hadn't even come close to sounding. "May I use the bathroom?"

"Sure." She pointed. "It's right there."

I closed the door behind me and gently moved the shower curtain to the side. There was a single bottle of shampoo and a clam shell holding a new pink razor. A lone toothbrush sat in a cup on the vanity. I cracked open the medicine cabinet. It had nothing of interest and neither did the linen closet.

After counting to thirty, I flushed the toilet and washed my hands. I didn't think for a minute this lady was a killer. There was no way I was going to upset her by pointing a finger at her.

I asked a couple of diversionary questions about her Florida neighbors and it seemed to work. Whatever street smarts she had, the weather might have thrown into hibernation. I stepped outside and shook my head; it was flurrying.

Walking to the car, my eyes settled on the trash can. I surveyed the street. Looking back at Shea's home, I pulled on a glove and lifted the top of the garbage can. Hurriedly, I tore a hole in a plastic bag and pawed away. Another pink razor, the same one Mary Ann used. I bagged it and hopped into the car.

Privacy was impossible to get at Newark Airport. I stood in a hallway and called Derrick. After telling him Shea would be the unlikeliest killer of my career, I said, "We need to go down the list of familial contacts. The person we're looking for has got to be related to one of them."

"I started running them down already. One guy, Brent Turley, is interesting. He was born in Tampa and has five kids of his own."

"Not many people have that many these days. What's the age range?"

"Twenty-four to thirty-two. And guess what?"

Waiting for my flight, I didn't get snarky. "What?"

"They're all female."

"Wonder if the woman we're looking for is one of them."

"Odds are, she is."

As I said, "Maybe," my cell rang. "Hey, let me call you back; it's that reporter the killer made contact with."

I swapped calls. "Detective Luca."

"Hello, Detective. Guess who just called?"

"The purported killer?"

"Yes, sir. Said, 'Luca should stop wasting his time. We're the ones getting justice.'"

"They said 'we'?"

"Yes. I wrote down what I heard. It was a quick call."

I heard my flight over the loudspeaker. "They're calling my flight." Walking to the gate, I asked if there was anything telling about who and where the call was made from but was told it was the same MO.

As the plane rolled down the runway, I focused on three pickups from the call: the use of the word we, the suggestion we stop pursuing, and that they were getting justice.

"We" could mean we were dealing with a conspiracy of some kind. Or were they using it in a broad sense, the way people used 'they'? My thoughts drifted to the killer. Making it appear as if there were more people involved, strengthened the fact they were a formidable opponent.

Or it could be that we were closing in, and they were attempting to distract us. That dovetailed with the "stop pursuing" statement. It was a nice thought, but as far as I was aware, we weren't close to solving the case. What could I be missing?

Was it Dreman or Addison? The DNA didn't match, but was the blood placed there as a deflection? We hadn't focused on the possibility someone with access to a blood supply was the killer. The more I thought about it, the stronger the angle became. We had to redouble our efforts to find the link.

Mentioning they were exacting justice could speak of motivation and help to define the killer. Revenge had driven many to kill but what was the perceived offense? We'd looked into the scorned love angle but hadn't been able to uncover anything.

Could it be embarrassment, humiliation, or envy? I remembered a class I'd taken at John Jay College. A psychologist made the case that sadistic people were more likely to seek revenge. That made sense, but I remembered she'd went on at length about the fact there was a cultural dimension to people's predilection for revenge.

Were we looking for a recent immigrant?

61

I STOOD IN FRONT OF A PAIR OF PHOTOS WE'D PINNED TO A corkboard. Derrick and I worked the Turley daughters, and with two of them serving overseas and another living in Asia, we were left with Ann Marie and Joan.

Blonde-haired and the youngest, Ann Marie had settled in New Hampshire after college. I said, "I don't know what it means, but it's more than interesting that she was on Boston College's fencing team. And the Tarot card had swords on it."

"I know. She knows how to handle a weapon. I bet she knows a lot about the torso."

"And where to stab someone to kill."

"Exactly. The victims were stabbed three times. All in the same area."

"I wonder if the number of stab wounds has any significance."

"Maybe there's a connection to fencing but I can't see it being her; she's too young."

"Not really. Most serial killers claim their first victim while in their twenties."

"I'm going see what the internet has on fencing and the number three."

"Go for it." Staring at the older daughter's picture, I tried to get a read on her hazel eyes.

"Holy shit. Listen to this. Fencing is one of three combat sports. There are three people involved: two fencers and a ref. And there are three disciplines in modern fencing: the foil, the epee, and the saber."

"The last things are swords?"

"Yeah."

"But Bilotti said it was the same knife used to make each wound."

"Maybe it's something symbolic."

"Check her travel; see if she was here when the killings took place. I'm going to work on Joan."

"She was here at least one of the nights. The touch report had her in an accident on the interstate, just south of Tampa, the day Dr. Bigham was murdered."

"Why was she here?"

"I couldn't find evidence she owns anything here. But so many people rent, it doesn't mean anything."

"I'm gonna pull the accident report."

Her address was listed as 11435 Palmetto Court, Apt 3B, in Clearwater. "She's a Floridian, lives up in Clearwater."

Other than that, the record of the fender bender was as ordinary as the sun shining in Naples. Joan Turley was heading south, alone, in a silver Toyota, when a carload of male teenagers rear-ended her. I put aside my assumption the vehicle that hit Turley was filled with testosterone-infused distraction and picked up the phone.

"Joan Turley?"

"Yes, who's this?"

I deepened my voice. "Detective Kenner with the Florida Highway Patrol."

"Is something wrong?"

It was a twisted phrase everyone used. "You were in a vehicular accident on Route 75—"

"Yes, with those boys. I'll tell you—"

"That's the reason I'm inquiring, ma'am. You see, the driver was involved in another accident."

"That doesn't surprise me."

"What had been your destination?"

"Marco Island. Ann Marie, she's my little sister, rented a place on the water for two months. I had to get back for an appointment with my oncologist, but I came right back down."

"I hope it went well."

"It did. Even the accident didn't throw me off. I mean, I was mad the jerk hit me, but after cancer, I don't get hung up on the small stuff anymore."

Boy, did I wish I could say that. It worked for a while but I found myself fuming when the person ahead of me chatted with the cashier, and when it came time to pay, she had to dig out her checkbook. "That's a good policy."

"You've got to go with the flow. Scream into your pillow if you have to."

"Right. You still in Marco?"

"Yeah. We have another six days. It's been fun hanging with Ann Marie again."

Maybe her bottled-up anger resulted in murderous bursts. I had a lot of questions for her but couldn't ask them as someone from the Florida Highway Patrol. "Enjoy it. The wife and I are thinking of taking a long weekend. Is the place you're staying in nice?"

"Yeah. It's called the Tradewinds. You should check it out.

If you like the beach, hardly anyone uses it. We go every day."

"Thanks. Hey, let me ask you; the driver of the car, did he appear to be under the influence?"

"Not that I could tell."

"Do you believe it was intentional?"

"That they crashed into me on purpose?"

"You'd be surprised what teenagers do for kicks these days."

"That's crazy."

No, crazy was killing people and posing them. "If I had time, your head would spin with the stuff I've seen."

My own head spun as I hung up. "We got to focus on both Turley sisters."

"What did you get?"

I filled him in. "They could be in it together."

"More than one killer has been floating around this case for a while now. Can you imagine what a ball the press would have with the 'Sister Killers'?"

"We need to go straight for the DNA. We're out of time to do the footwork."

"Okay. What do you need me to do?"

"They're staying at the Tradewinds on Marco. I need you to collect their DNA."

He nodded. "Can't get it on recycling day, but I'll think of something."

"They go to the beach everyday. Bring your bathing suit and get creative."

"I've got my flip-flops in the car."

I smiled. "While you're digging your toes in the sand, I'm going to see Remin. I got an idea."

62

I stood in front of the sheriff's desk. "You said to ask for whatever I needed. Is that offer still on the table?"

Remin's eyes searched my face. I didn't expect a quick yes and didn't get one. "I consider it my duty to support the needs of the entire department. What exactly are you requesting?"

"The key to solving the case is the DNA. We're working the familial hits, and we'll get there, but it'll take time."

Remin leaned forward. "How much more manpower do you need? I can try my best, but this flu is hitting every department."

"It's not manpower, sir. We need to step up the processing of the DNA samples we need compared—"

"The lab is aware of the priority. I can't just shuffle personnel there; lab technicians are highly trained."

"I understand, sir. I'm grateful we have our own operation."

"The taxpayers in Collier prize independence. But we have limits."

"The Florida Department of Law Enforcement has the

resources we need. Can't we ask the Fort Myers complex for dedicated time?"

"You know it doesn't work like that. Everything is first in, first out, and like every lab in the country, there's a lot of firsts ahead of us."

"I understand, but isn't there a way to jump the line? This case is huge and we need a little help."

"If you get a state-level agency involved, you'll be fetching coffee for them. Is that what you want?"

"No, but I want the case solved. All I want is to expedite a couple of samples. We need a solve before we find another body."

"We can call the feds in, but we'll definitely lose control."

"We don't need the feds; we just need to cross-check a couple of samples. We're not asking for the moon."

"Every homicide detective in the state wants their case prioritized."

"I understand but why shouldn't we ask? We have a serial killer on the loose. Isn't there a way to do it, uh, informally?"

He wagged his head. "Nobody is going to risk their career. We have to go through normal channels. But that could lead to having the case pulled."

"I'd appreciate you making the request."

"You're certain about this? Once this gets going, it's going to be hard to stop."

"I'd appreciate the attempt, sir."

He nodded. "Will do. Our lab is doing the best they can. They're working all the extra time they can."

"I know, sir."

"There's nothing left in the overtime budget, but I'll see if I can somehow find funds to move around."

Every sheriff had a slush fund. They'd over-budget in a sector when presenting their annual budget. It was a quiet way to build a pile of cash. It sounded terrible, but it provided a way to finance unanticipated needs.

"I know that's difficult, sir, but I appreciate it."

"Don't count on it."

He knew exactly how much he had at his discretion. The question was whether the small lab staff could work any more overtime than they were.

I TRIED to chase the blue feeling away. Derrick had been inventive, handing out Popsicle Push-Ups to the Turley sisters and collecting the plastic sleeves they left behind. We had their DNA but had to wait. Sisters, as serial killers, seemed like a long shot, but a TV series called the *Killer Siblings*, confirmed the possibility.

In DNA limbo, we'd need to pursue every lead. The focus being people with access to blood. I wished we could ask the public for help. Making a plea regarding a certain occupation always provided results. Most were useless, but diamonds were uncovered.

However, deploying that tool might trigger the killer to act, to show they're in control. It was a chance I couldn't take.

Swiveling my chair around, I grabbed the murder book off the credenza. Melissa Wright was the first victim. If we missed anything, it could have been at the beginning.

Studying a photo of the crime scene, Casey knocked on the door. "Sorry to interrupt, sir, but I may have something."

Shoving the book to the side, I said, "What do you have?"

"Remember the woman Hatch met up with in Orlando?"

"Sure. What about her?"

"Turns out she's her half sister. They have the same mother but different fathers, thus the Cardinal last name."

I looked at the picture he handed me. Mean looking with short black hair, the woman had a scar over her right eyebrow. "She lives in Orlando?"

"No, they just met up there. Cardinal lives in Punta Gorda."

An hour's drive away. "She have a record?"

"Not as an adult. There's something in the juvenile system, but I can't get visibility."

"We'd need more to get a judge to break the seal." My cell phone vibrated.

"It's Remin. Let me talk to him. I'll meet you in the conference room."

"Sir, how are you?"

"I'm afraid I have some bad news."

"What happened?"

"It's a negative on getting lab priority at the FDLE."

Though I had serious doubts, I played it upbeat. "We'll get it done."

Hanging up, I stared at my desk phone. After four rings, I answered, "Detective Luca."

"Frank, it's Geary from the lab."

"What's going on?"

"We got a match for the DNA found on Trent's pant leg."

I jumped out of my seat. "Who is it?"

"Rachel Shea."

The phone tumbled out of my hand. I put a hand on the desk and picked up the phone. "Are you sure it's her?"

"Unless she has an identical twin, it's a billion to one we're wrong."

63

I PUSHED MY CHAIR AWAY FROM THE DESK AND STOOD. I HAD to force myself to stop the flow of thoughts and assemble an action plan.

Rachel Shea was the killer? I'd never been so wrong in my life.

She'd fooled me like I was a rookie. How did I fall for her being too religious to kill? The picture of Mother Theresa popped into my head.

I was in awe of the saint. No one had lived such a selfless life. Shea was just a woman at the Jersey Shore, living in a bungalow by the beach, not the slums of Calcutta. I pounded my fist on the wall.

"You all right?"

It was Derrick. "No! I'm not."

"Take it easy. What's going on? Something with Mary Ann?"

The idea it could be worse made it easier. "Shea's DNA is a match."

"Rachel Shea? The one you saw in Jersey?"

"Yep. I blew it."

He squeezed my shoulder. "You didn't blow it, man. Nothing happened. We got her now."

"It's embarrassing as hell."

"No, it isn't. If you didn't grab her razor, we'd never know."

I rallied. "I was on autopilot. I didn't think it was her."

"You're always harping on the fundamentals. They should make this a case study and add it to the curriculum at the academy."

"Okay, already. I'll inform Remin, but we need to work up what's needed for a criminal complaint and arrest warrant."

"Go, go. I'll get started. Tell the sheriff we got the bastard."

"Okay."

"Hey, man. Cheer up! We got her."

"You're right. I'll be right back."

REMIN SMACKED HIS HANDS TOGETHER. "Fantastic! Great job, Frank. Is anybody watching her?"

"Not yet. I wanted to let you know and make sure—"

"Get eyes on her. You still have contacts up there? If not, I'll make some calls."

"I got it, sir."

"Good. We have to get the paperwork in place."

"Detective Dickson is working on it."

"Good, good. Make sure the warrant has the extradition forecast."

"Will do, sir."

"Oh, this is great news. The public will be relieved this madwoman is off the streets."

"We shouldn't say anything to the press yet, sir."

"Agreed. We'll wait until she's in custody."

"We need to gather evidence to support the DNA."

"The prosecutors will need motive, access, and opportunity, but DNA evidence is powerful. It doesn't lie, Frank."

"I'm concerned it might get thrown out. It was in her trash, and there's no proof the razor was hers."

"Shea will get swabbed again. Besides, we tracked her through the familial search."

"I know . . ."

"What are you worried about? Is there something I should know?"

I couldn't tell him my pride had been run over and that my gut instincts were no better than a ten-year-old living in the suburbs. "I guess it's just exhaustion seeping in."

"After this is over, you take two, make it three weeks off. Clear your head, okay?"

"Thanks, sir."

"Go make that call. We need Shea under surveillance. I don't want her disappearing into the wind before we have a chance to take her into custody."

I stood. "Yes, sir."

Remin rose and extended his hand. "Incredible work, Frank. From one homicide detective to another, you impress me."

My ego didn't respond. If it wasn't trash day, Shea would have slipped away. I made the surveillance call, and as soon as I received a confirmation the Lavallette Police had a car watching her, I headed to tell the team the chase was over.

After a flurry of high fives, I said, "Without your help, we wouldn't have identified Shea. It was a team effort, and I congratulate each and every one of you. We're expecting an arrest as soon as the paperwork is submitted."

A round of applause broke out. I raised my hands. "You

know the lawyers upstairs want it with a bow, so there are holes to fill. Take the rest of the day off. We'll get started tomorrow."

After shaking everyone's hand, I headed for the parking lot. I had none of the usual euphoria when close to a major arrest. This was a win, but it had a high cost; the revelation the gut I relied on for 90 percent of my solves had softened like my belly.

Father Time had taken a piece of me. Again.

———

"FRANK? IS THAT YOU?"

"Yeah."

Mary Ann was in my recliner reading something with vegetables on the cover. I pecked her cheek. "We're not going vegan, are we?"

"No, but there's so much evidence a plant-based diet is better for you."

"You know me, pasta and any veggie will do. How you feeling?"

"Good. What are you doing home?"

After filling her in on Shea, she said, "That's great."

I nodded.

"What's the matter?"

"Nothing."

"Don't tell me nothing. What happened?"

"I was sure it wasn't her. For the first time, my gut failed me and it wasn't even close."

"But you had the instinct to bag the razor. If you didn't, you wouldn't have gotten her DNA."

"Yeah, and if it wasn't trash day, she would've gotten away with it."

"Did you see the garbage can before you went in her house?"

"Yeah, almost knocked it over."

"You know what? I think subconsciously you knew it was there, and it became a backup plan."

It was something most people would tell themselves. It sounded good, but I knew it was bullshit. "Maybe you're right." I didn't like saying things I didn't believe. The reality was, I failed, while everyone thought I'd succeeded.

Getting the win was all that mattered in the day's culture. But one of the few things I remember my dad telling me was the easiest person to lie to was yourself. I was happy we had the killer in our sights, but I had to call it straight.

64

It was another picture-perfect morning, but my disposition hadn't recovered. I took a ride down to Vanderbilt Beach. I stared at the Gulf for an hour to bring my mood around before heading to the office.

I powered up my desktop. Derrick said, "Glad you made it in."

"Don't be a wiseass."

"Hey, Shea's lawyer called for you."

He handed me a yellow Post-it note with a number. His name was Marco Delmar. "He say anything?"

"Just that it's urgent you call him back."

"Sure it's important. His client is going away for eternity."

I punched in the number as Derrick stepped out. "Marco Delmar. Who's calling?"

The New York accent was unmistakable. "Detective Luca, Collier County Sheriff's Office."

"Thank you for calling me back. I have something you need to know."

"And that is?"

"My client is innocent."

"Save it for the courtroom, Counselor."

"Hold on, please. Ms. Shea donated her bone marrow for use in a transplant."

"That was nice of her but I don't understand what it has to do with the case."

"It's very simple; someone has her DNA."

"Excuse me?"

"I'm not a physician but the recipient of the marrow my client gave, is the one you're looking for. It's not Rachel Shea. She's an innocent party who's been drawn into this mess."

"Are you saying because Ms. Shea donated her, uh, bone marrow, she's had nothing to do with the homicides?"

"I urge you to speak to a medical expert. They'll tell you the person who received my client's bone marrow also has her DNA."

"That doesn't mean she didn't do it."

"What it means is another person, the real killer, has to be identified. You find them, and you'll realize my client is innocent."

"It's an interesting angle, Counselor."

"I understand your skepticism, but it's a medical fact, not a ploy."

"She told you this?"

"Yes. But my office vetted it. My client donated at the Moffitt Cancer Center in Tampa, Florida. I'll send over a release to allow them to share what they can to verify it."

"And when did this transplant take place?"

"Three years ago. June 14, 2019, is when she had the operation. I realize this is an unusual situation, but I promise you, you'll be able to corroborate what I'm telling you."

"I'll take a look into this."

"Thank you. It seems bizarre, but medical advances are

presenting unprecedented circumstances. The landscape is changing."

"No promises, Counselor."

Mind racing, I tossed the receiver onto the desk. What the hell was going on? Was this real? It sounded like a Hollywood scenario. I plugged bone marrow transplant into the search bar.

I began scanning. This was above my pay grade. I grabbed my jacket and headed out.

Dr. Bilotti swung the door open. It was the first time I'd seen him in shorts. "Frank."

"I'm sorry, Doc. I know it's your day off but this can't wait."

Bilotti raised his eyebrows. "Come in. What's bothering you?"

"Shea. This Preserve Killer case. Every time I'm near the solve, it get snapped away from me. It's like the killer is a damn ghost."

"Take it easy." He pointed to a pair of club chairs. "You want a glass of wine?"

"No, no. I need you to explain something to me."

Bilotti crossed his legs. He had bony knees. "I hope I can help."

"We have Shea in custody in Jersey. She's claiming she has nothing to do with it. Her lawyer said she donated bone marrow. I checked Google, and it just doesn't make sense to me. Could someone else have her DNA?"

"If she had a bone marrow transplant, it's very possible, even likely, the recipient would carry the donor's DNA."

"Is it like a blood transfusion?"

"No. Transfusions of blood temporarily changes the DNA profile of blood. Blood cells need to be continually replaced, and those new cells are produced by bone marrow stem cells.

If a person receives a transplant of someone's bone marrow stem cells, new blood cells created would carry the donor's DNA."

I stood up. "So, what you're saying is, her DNA is in another person?"

"It can be."

"This is crazy. Like freaking Frankenstein."

Bilotti laughed, "Sorry. It's actually quite common to use bone marrow stem cells to treat leukemia and lymphoma."

"Don't tell me I'm going to be running into more cases where DNA doesn't count."

"It'll always count, but rarely, it can be a complicating factor. In most cases, doctors remove the patient's own stem cells, freezing them while the patient undergoes chemo-therapy before reinserting them."

"They'd keep their DNA?"

"Yes."

I collapsed onto the couch. "Still, this is nuts. I'm starting from scratch."

"Not necessarily. You might be able to trace the recipient, who might be the killer."

"You think we can get that information in today's world?"

Bilotti shrugged. "With privacy laws, it'll be tough, and oftentimes, it's a blind donation."

"Just my luck."

"You ready for that wine now?"

"One glass only."

I followed Bilotti into the kitchen. He slid a light-colored bottle out of a wine fridge. "This is perfect. It's an Albariño from Spain. Light and refreshing."

As he inserted the corkscrew, I asked, "Can it be a male with Shea's female DNA?"

"Absolutely."

I shook my head. "We can't even rule out a gender."

"Sorry, Frank." He handed me a glass. "See if you can taste the lime and grapefruit in this beauty."

I took a sip, but it was impossible to taste anything but the bile spraying the back of my throat.

65

———

Derrick answered the phone. Putting it on hold, he said, "Frank, it's Dr. Cartwright from the Moffitt Cancer Center."

I swept up the receiver. "Dr. Cartwright, this is Detective Luca. Thanks for calling back."

"That's quite all right, Detective. I'm the one who should apologize for keeping you waiting until legal signed off."

"I understand. What can you tell me?"

"Rachel Shea offered her bone marrow, and I performed the transplant in June of 2019."

"Who got her bone marrow?"

"Up to two individuals received her stem cells, but I'm afraid I can't be more specific."

"I get the privacy laws, Doc, but we're talking about a serial killer."

"Even if I wanted to, I couldn't tell you. It was completely anonymous."

"You mean to tell me, you operated on someone and didn't know their names?"

"It may seem preposterous, but it happens all the time. Donors and recipients have the right to participate anonymously, and in this case they did."

"We're talking about life and death here. You have to help. I promise it'll be kept confidential."

"I'm familiar with life-and-death situations, Detective."

"Sorry, sir. Can't we find a work-around?"

"Breaking the vow of anonymity would undermine our mission. We can't risk damaging our integrity. It would lead to fewer donors and helping less people."

"I find it hard to believe that cooperating to identify a serial killer would hurt your operation. But I'll ask a judge to decide on releasing the information if you force me to."

"The center will defend its rights, including challenging a court order, if you're successful in obtaining one."

"We'll do what's necessary to protect the public. I'm sure it will generate a lot of publicity, which you wouldn't appreciate."

"I've stated the center's position and am out of time."

I hung up wondering if Cartwright had a law degree. "They won't help and said they'd fight us if we go for a court order."

"But there's a serial killer out there."

"The medical community is supposed to be saving lives, not putting them at risk by hiding behind guidelines. Where's the flexibility in a case like this?"

"We going to go for a court order anyway, right?"

"Definitely. I'm going to dump it in Remin's lap. Let him craft the request. I think we'll get it, but if they push back like Cartwright said they would, there's no telling where it will go or how long it will take."

"I can't believe we've got to fight for this."

I shook my head. "Amen. But we can't wait around for the courts to decide. Right now it's Shea, but let's review everybody, male and female, who popped on the radar. Check with Dr. Bigham's office; find out if they treated people with leukemia or lymphoma. And tell the team to get cracking as well."

I started with Melissa Wright. Reading between the lines, I tried to look for clues she might have been sick.

Searching for cancer was off-putting. It had found me without any help. Was looking for it going to infuriate the karma gods? It was a stupid thought. But why tempt whatever metaphysical powers there were?

We never asked about Wright's medical history, but she seemed healthy. I checked the autopsy. Bilotti noted she was in good health. I moved on to Ryan. He'd been screwing Wright. The MINI-Cooper salesman also knew Dr. Bigham, and his suicide still didn't feel right.

Derrick hung up. "Bigham's office doesn't handle cancer. They said if they found something unusual, they'd refer them to a hematologist."

"Did you get the contact info for referrals?"

"Yeah, but I can't see anyone giving us a list of people."

"Probably not, but reach out and find out what oncologist the blood doctor would refer."

"Okay."

Picking up the phone, I said, "The more names, the higher the chance we'll make a connection."

"Got it."

She answered on the first ring. "Mrs. Ryan?"

"Yes. Who's this?"

"Detective Luca."

"Oh. Hi."

"I have a question about your husband's health."

"His health?"

It was a stupid thing to say. "I was wondering if he had any serious blood problems, like leukemia." Before she had a chance to answer, I realized calling her was ridiculous. Ryan was dead when Trent's body was discovered.

"He did. If I remember correctly, he was about ten or twelve. Why are you asking?"

The time line didn't fit. "We're following up on every lead. By any chance, did he have a bone marrow transplant?"

"I don't think so. He was very sick and went through a lot, but he didn't like to talk about it."

"I understand. Thanks. I'll let you know if we need anything further."

You never knew if someone had been stricken with cancer and been through the inevitable battle for survival. Ryan was a womanizer and had cheated on his wife, but I'm sure he suffered physically and mentally. My mind wandered to parents of sick children.

Between my cancer and Mary Ann's MS, there was no doubt we'd been dealt a couple of bad hands. But I was thankful Jessie was healthy.

I flipped the page, and a picture of Stephen Ong stared at me. There was something about this guy. I couldn't figure out what it was. He was fastidious, always well dressed with an apartment nicer than a model home.

Ong lied about his alibi and hung around with Addison. She needed another look as well. We'd never checked Ong's DNA and got off his trail when the blood put the focus on a female.

I read through the interviews and background information we'd developed. Ong had worked for a Realtor in Mercato for three years. We needed someone who knew Ong around the time of the transplant.

The only friend of his we had, Sal Takeya, was used by Ong to fabricate an alibi. He was a natural to start with. If he couldn't help, one name always led to another. I picked up the phone, hoping the chain of names would be a short one.

66

***

Waiting for Ong's friend to call back, I picked up the ringing phone, spoke for a minute and slammed it down. What were the odds the cameras at Bridgewater Bay had been inoperable for the past month? The easiest way to track Shea's movements was off the table. Was the universe against me? Against solving this case?

I took a deep breath, assuring myself we'd already pieced most of it together. We'd confirmed she was in town when each of the murders occurred. One neighbor believed Shea rented a white car but couldn't identify the make, other than believing it was Japanese. We'd need a warrant to get the rental car details.

If it was Hertz, I had a friend who might be able to help, but it was asking a lot. The phone rang and I reached for it.

"Hi, Detective. You left a message for me?"

"Thanks for calling me back, Mr. Takeya."

"No problem. Why the call?"

"Stephen Ong. Did he have cancer about eight years ago?"

"Stephen? I don't know. He never said anything, but we only met five years ago."

"Do you know anyone who knows Mr. Ong well?"

"He has a sister in Ohio. I'm pretty sure her name is Betty, but they don't talk anymore."

"Where in Ohio?"

"Cleveland? I remember him saying the family lived where the Rock and Roll Hall of Fame is."

"That's helpful. Do you know if he went to a hematologist or oncologist?"

"No, but why these kind of questions?"

"Just tying up loose ends."

"Is he in some kind of trouble?"

"No, no. Someone with the same name came up in a fraud investigation, and I'm just checking on every possible lead."

"Oh."

"Thanks for your time. I'll reach out to his sister. If you remember anything, please call me."

"You know, Stephen did mention taking a year off . . ."

"When was this?"

"It's funny. He mentioned being stuck in the house watching commercials Trump and Clinton were running."

"It was around 2016?"

"I guess so."

"Did he mention why he took off?"

"No. He only said it was a bad chapter in his life and didn't want to talk about it."

Ong wasn't the age or in a high-powered position that needed a sabbatical to charge his batteries. The only reason that made sense was health.

It could have been his mental health, and thus, he was reluctant to discuss it. But it could have been cancer as well.

When I had gotten bladder cancer, I felt nobody understood what I was going through and kept it to myself.

Tracking down Ong's sister, I smiled. Finally, a break. There might be scores of people named Ong in New York City or San Francisco, but in Cleveland, there were three and only one named Susan.

I left a message and picked up the murder book, flipping to the section on Addison. Her DNA didn't match the blood on Trent's pants but that was only one victim. She had a white Honda, had been arrested on an assault charge, and had a curious relationship with Ong.

The possibility of two killers remained. Rolling around the chance it could be Ong and Addison, I picked up the phone.

"Casey, it's Luca."

"Hi. What's going on?"

"You're looking into who had access to a blood source."

"Yeah, we are."

"Do me a favor, and for the time being, focus on whether Addison or Ong could get their hands on any."

Hanging up, I began doubting focusing on the blood when the desk phone rang. "Homicide, Detective Luca."

"Frank, it's Mindy Morton."

She was a paralegal working for the prosecutors. "Hi, Mindy. What can I do for you?"

"Nothing, Johnson wanted me to advise you the extradition on Shea is being challenged."

"Are you kidding me?"

"No. The motion filed by her attorney cites the fact this is a capital offense."

"They won't send her because we still have the death penalty?"

"We believe it's a ploy to delay."

"What are we going to do?"

"We responded already."

"How long is this going to take?"

"It's difficult to predict; however, we expect a resolution soon."

"Push as hard as you can. I need to interrogate her."

Why would any state want to protect a possible serial killer? If Shea was the killer, the crimes were committed in Florida and would be subject to our laws. I got up and stepped into the parking lot. The sunshine helped center me.

Closing my eyes, I turned my face toward the warmth. I counted to twenty, as Dr. Bruno had suggested. It reset my thoughts on what my responsibilities were.

My job was twofold: catching the murderer and providing the prosecutors with incriminating evidence. I had to focus on fulfilling my obligation. As hard as it was to accept, what happened afterward was out of my control.

I soaked up another minute of sun and headed in. Steps from my office, I heard my name being called: it was Casey.

"I need a minute, sir."

"Come in."

His eyes were on his shoes. "I'm sorry, but there's been an oversight."

"What kind?"

"Well, cross-checking Dr. Bigham's patient list, we realized Riley Addison was a patient."

"How the hell did we miss that?"

"We should have caught it, but the doctor's office had the name reversed. It was shown as Addison Riley."

"This proves she interacted with Bigham. It could change everything."

"I know, sir. I wish we'd realized it sooner."

Piling on wouldn't help. "The important thing is, you did.

Now we move forward. I'm going to get Derrick to take a ride to their offices. You never know what we might learn about the relationship."

"Sounds like a plan."

"Oh, and look into whether there's evidence Addison had any lesbian relationships."

Casey took off, and I processed the news. Addison had dimmed as a suspect due to her lack of connections. As my phone rang, I wondered how the discovery of a simple transposition would effect the case.

67

———

I REMOVED BOTH PICTURES OF THE TURLEY TWINS. THEIR DNA didn't match. Instead of throwing them out, I put them at the bottom of the whiteboard. "Just in case. I don't want to lose sight of these two."

Derrick said, "And we eliminated Dreman. She was smarter than I thought, fencing goods in Orlando."

I pulled the pin holding Riley Addison's photo and moved it toward the top of the whiteboard. "It doesn't take a rocket scientist to know it's riskier selling stolen goods close to home."

"Amen. But if she was running them in from Miami, it was a pretty good plan."

"Gesso said he was tracing the fenced property with Miami. We'll see what develops. But since Addison and Ong were released, I want eyes on them."

Derrick rose out of his seat. "I'll go see about that."

"The more I think about this, the more convinced I am that, A, the blood connection is key, and, B, it's very possible there are two killers."

"The two-killer angle would explain the lack of connections and motive."

"Not finding any proof that Shea knew Trent would make it a random killing. Either Shea is a world-class psychopath, or a killer has her DNA."

"I'll be right back."

I surveyed each of the photos, lingering on Ong and Addison. They were an odd couple, but were they murderers? What was in Ong's past that kept him out of sight for a year? We couldn't find evidence he had a record. Was it an illness requiring a transplant?

Addison was a conundrum, working in the same office as Trent and having an affair with him. She was a good liar, and by working for Bank of America and partying into the night, seemed to live the double life that a killer needed to blend in.

What did the assault arrest mean? Was she losing control?

My eyes drifted lower, onto Hatch. Most of what we had in this case was circumstantial but it was even thinner on Hatch. There was the metaphysical thing, and her father and Addison had an ongoing affair. There was the concealed-carry conviction and something made her run. We had an APB out on her but hadn't nabbed her yet.

Looking at McGovern, I wondered why the killer had gone quiet. Thankfully, we hadn't had another body. We also hadn't heard from them. Why? Was it because Ong and Addison were in our sights? Or that Shea was behind bars? Or the others were on guard?

Considering possibilities, I studied McGovern's pasty face. We'd had eyes on him but he hadn't left his house in a week. Was it because he was scared we were closing in?

Derrick came back in and stated, "Gesso said with the flu going around, they don't have the manpower to cover anybody else."

"That's ridiculous. I'm going to Remin. He promised we'd get what we need."

DERRICK LOOKED up as I came back into the office. "Uh-oh."

"Sheriff said twenty-two officers called in sick today."

"I knew it was going around but this is crazy."

"Last thing we need is to get this."

"Me and Lynn got the flu shot. Did you?"

"No, I never get it.

"Really?"

"It's only like forty percent effective. And Mary Ann is afraid of putting anything else in her."

"I get that. But you really—"

"Enough, already!" I flopped into my chair. "Sorry, just frustrated."

"It's okay. You know, I can cover Ong if you want."

"I hate to lose you, but I think we have to keep eyes on him."

"That leaves Addison."

As my phone rang, I said, "Tell Gesso to move the coverage on McGovern to Addison."

I picked up the call. A woman with a cold said, "Hi, this is Susan Ong. Did you leave a message for me?"

"Yes. Thanks for getting back to me."

"No problem. Why did you call?"

"It's about your brother, Stephen."

"Oh no. Don't tell me something happened to him."

"No, he's fine."

"Good. Stephen and me kind of drifted apart. I haven't talked to him in years."

"I'm not authorized to say too much, but we're conducting

a wide-ranging investigation, and it involves fake identities and the like."

"They stole his identity?"

"No, but, uh, I really can't disclose, but it's safe to say they had information and were probing."

"It's crazy what's going on these days."

That was on the money. "So, we're looking for, um, independent verification of details that a hacker wouldn't know."

"That makes sense."

"Now, Stephen had a period exceeding a year, we believe, where he didn't work, about four years ago."

"Yeah, he had a breakdown and it wasn't good. I even visited him in that god-awful place he was locked up in."

"What place was that?"

"A psychiatric one in Toledo."

"Right, right. He was there for a year?"

"Just about. After he kept making threats, they said he was danger to himself and others and remanded him there. I saw him right after he went in, and I gotta say, I didn't think he'd ever be released, but thankfully, he turned it around."

"He recovered completely?"

"I spoke with him when he got out, and he was back to his old, dismissive self."

"Dismissive of what happened to him?"

"No. Of everybody and everything. It's not nice to say but he's very arrogant."

"I see. Who did he threaten?"

"His boss, a coworker, and a customer."

"Where did he work?"

"One of those mobile blood banks that got taken over by Quest."

"In Cleveland?"

"Yes."

"Thank you. You've been very helpful. It's important we keep this investigation quiet. We can't have Stephen know about it. If the hackers find out, they'd vanish knowing we're on their trail. It would also be obstruction."

"No worries."

Which phrase did I dislike more: *No problem* or *No worries*? "Thank you, ma'am."

I briefed Derrick on the call. "Get on Ong. I'll get Gesso to switch the McGovern coverage to Addison."

68

As we filed into the house, I said, "I'm really proud of you."

Mary Ann said, "We both are."

Jessie said, "Thanks. I'm glad you both were there."

"Wouldn't miss it for the world, kiddo." It wasn't easy ducking out when your partner was sitting in a car, watching Ong. Heading to the bedroom, I envisioned Derrick cradling a thermos of coffee.

Mary Ann put on another Hallmark movie. I didn't complain; my mind was on the Preserve Killer. Running through the suspects reinforced the idea there might be two killers. My stomach churned; did we have both as suspects?

Ong and Addison were a couple. But were they the Bonnie and Clyde of the Collier Park system? I got up. "You want anything?"

"No, I'm good."

I grabbed a bottle of water and sat down. A wedding scene was playing out. It brought me back to our small ceremony. When the husband recited, "In sickness and in health," my smile disappeared. McGovern had said his wife took off when he got sick.

A text pinged in from Derrick. "Just checking in. It's quiet at Ong's." I felt a weight on my chest. I replied, "Just home from the ceremony."

"It went good?"

"Yeah. We're proud of her."

"Good you were able to go."

"I'm about to head over to keep on eye on McGovern."

"Why?"

I couldn't say that I was feeling guilty. "The murders took place at night. He has to be watched."

He didn't fight me on it. I got off the sofa. "That was Derrick. With this flu going around, we don't have the manpower we need. I'm going to take a ride and pitch in."

"It's eight o'clock."

"It's okay. Don't wait up for me."

I SHUT my lights off and rolled to a stop two houses away from McGovern's. The pressure in my chest eased. Sliding lower in my seat, I sent a text to Derrick to let him know I was in position and tuned the radio to a jazz station.

I didn't listen to much music, but when I was a rookie in New York, my first partner was a big fan of Stan Getz, and he'd put on bossa nova music during a stakeout. It was impossible to tell why it made the time pass quickly.

Bobbing my head to a swing tune, a pair of headlights slowly made its way down the street. It was 9:38 p.m. It pulled in front of McGovern's house. It was late for company. Unless he had an accomplice.

A man in his twenties popped out of the car. He had two

white bags. They were too small for takeout. He went to the door, rang the bell, and handed the packages to McGovern.

The delivery man got back in the car and drove by. There was a placard on the dashboard. It had a red W: Bingo. He was delivering prescriptions from Walgreens. McGovern was sick.

After an hour, I called Mary Ann to say good night and assure her I was all right. Keeping my eyes on McGovern's house, I called Derrick. I needed to go over whether or not to talk to Ong. Everything we had showed that Ong became a real estate agent after getting released. We couldn't find evidence he recently worked for a blood collection firm or laboratory.

It made sense to check out if a friend, including Addison, had any way to access blood. Though I thought I might be able to squeeze something valuable out of Ong, I'd wait.

At three in the morning, I sent a text to Derrick telling him to go home. We needed sleep. I drove home, doubting the decision to wait to talk to Ong, and mulling over how to keep eyes on each suspect.

LIPS GLUED to a mug of coffee, I trudged into the office. Derrick said, "Good morning."

He was fifteen years younger but didn't he need sleep? "Morning."

"How you feeling?"

"Me? Great."

He raised his eyebrows. "Good. I called Gesso to see what the roll-call numbers look like."

"From what I've been seeing, this bug knocks you on your ass for five to seven days."

"I know."

I looked over the previous day's arrests. "This meth crap is filling our jails."

"I read a DEA report a couple of days ago. It said fifty percent of the meth produced in the world is consumed in America."

"That's a hell of a thing to be first in."

"Meth seems worse than the opioid problem. I don't know how we're going to turn this around."

"It's a crisis. They're experimenting with psychedelic drugs to treat addicts at places like John Hopkins, and the results are promising."

"We need to think outside the box if we're going get a handle on it."

I said yes, that might work for drug addiction, but not for hunting killers. What we needed to do was dig deeper, connect the dots, even though some were barely legible. You had to be open to all possibilities and use fundamentals to investigate them.

Derrick picked up the phone. It was Gesso. He gave me a thumbs-up and thanked him. "Gesso said he can cover Addison and Ong."

"Good. Let's go back over everything we have. We could use a refresher. Maybe something will click. And whatever background the team developed was looked at as it came in."

"True. Looking at everything at once may help."

"Why don't you begin with Addison and Ryan. I'll start with McGovern and Ong."

I took a sip of coffee and flipped open the murder book to the McGovern section. Casey and his team obtained twenty pictures of McGovern going back ten years.

There was only one of him outside. He was with a woman. She looked familiar.

I flipped the picture over. It was his ex-wife, Diane. Though the picture had been removed from Facebook, we recovered it. I was sure I'd seen her somewhere and made a mental note to check where she worked.

I read the summary of our interviews with him. The episode at the Naples Dock where we thought he may have been the caller to the newspaper seemed odd. I looked at a picture of his pasty face.

We had him in an area where boats were at the time the call was made. Originally, it seemed incriminating, but was the call really made by the water? We had nothing defining where it originated from. I was suspicious of coincidences, but this appeared to be nothing more.

I skimmed through the remaining material on McGovern. He drove a white Honda and claimed to be an insomniac. He bothered me but was near the bottom of the suspect ladder for a reason.

Flipping to the section on Ong, the fact he lied about his alibi, not once but twice, hit me like a bucket of cold water. I said, "I know we said to wait but I want to talk to Ong."

"Really?"

"Yeah. Sitting back doesn't feel right."

"You want me to come?"

I grabbed my jacket. "No. If there are two of us, he'll retreat."

69

Construction was in full bloom at another building, near Goodlette. Naples Square was part of the effort to enlarge the downtown area. It was expensive to live near Fifth Avenue, and you couldn't get into this development for under two million.

Approaching Ong's apartment, I glanced at the car watching his place. I rang the bell. Ong opened the door, shaking his head. "You have to go through my lawyer."

Something was off. His eyes were glassy and his shirt untucked. "I'm not here about what happened at the Blue Martini."

He started to close the door. "It doesn't matter."

"I spoke to your sister."

He scrunched his face. "My sister?"

"Yes. Susan in Cleveland. She had a lot to say."

"She's has a difficult relationship with the truth."

"What she told me about you making death threats against your boss, a coworker, and a customer checked out."

"That was a misunderstanding."

"It must have been a big one to get you remanded to an intuition."

His face darkened.

"Tell me about working at the mobile blood bank."

He slammed the door. "Leave me alone."

He knew we were onto him. I walked to the sales office. A woman in a painted-on skirt popped out of her chair. "Welcome to Naples Square, where you love where you live."

I smiled. "It's early stages, but I'd like to see your floor plans."

"It'd be my pleasure. Are you interested in a two bedroom, three? Or larger?"

"At least a two bedroom. I'd like to see any with a second entrance. Our daughter is in her twenties, and we'd like to give her the freedom to come and go as she pleases."

"We don't currently offer that option. However, all our residences have been designed to address the privacy needs of owners with comfortable separation from guests."

Ong didn't have another way to exit and disappear from. "I'm sorry, but I think it's best if I come with my wife."

I headed back to the office with two things in mind: making sure we had eyes on Ong and to press the team on the connection between Ong or Addison and access to a blood supply.

Was I giving the blood on Trent's pant leg too much weight? Was it a diversion? I slumped in the seat at the returning thought I was chasing two killers.

Someone planting the blood on Trent ran through my mind again. Then the possibility we were dealing with a second murderer. Each theory filled holes in the cases. I pictured Trent; excepting his philandering, he seemed to be a likable man. But plenty of likable people rubbed others the wrong way.

It was hard for me to think of Trent without his children coming to mind. At the funeral, they clearly had no idea their father was gone forever. I swallowed down the lump forming in my throat and tried to shake the images of the wake from my mind but failed.

Trent's wife was hunched over, sobbing uncontrollably. I remembered bumping into a woman as I escaped to the bathroom. I squinted my eyes. Was she the same woman as McGovern's wife?

I pulled into a Publix parking lot and made a call. "Casey, it's Luca."

"What's going on?"

"You guys dug up a bunch of photos on McGovern."

"Yeah?"

"There was one that was on Facebook of him and his ex-wife."

"Yeah, I remember that one."

"Do me a favor and send it to me, ASAP."

"Will do."

"Hurry. It's important."

My enthusiasm waned as I recalled we had no evidence McGovern and Trent knew each other. I tried to remember the woman at the wake. My interaction was nothing more than an "Excuse me." I remembered she hadn't smiled but that was all. My memory wasn't what it once was.

A text pinged in. It was the photo. I studied it, zooming in. Trying to recall any similarities in hairstyles, I pocketed the phone and put the car in gear.

Route 41 was backed up at the Pine Ridge intersection. I made a right past Waterside Shops and a left onto Crayton Road. Park Shore was one of the neighborhoods I liked, but I had too many cases involving its residents.

I turned right onto Mooring Line Road and made my way

to the Trent's' home. A Kia SUV was parked in the driveway. She had company. I hoped it wasn't male.

Mrs. Trent opened the door. She blinked. "Detective Luca."

"Hello, Mrs. Trent. I'm sorry to bother you, but I'd like to show you a picture of someone. I'm hoping you can identify her."

"If I can help, I will."

I pulled up the image and handed her the phone. It was like I gave her a bag of dog poop. She gave it right back. "That's Brenda McGovern."

"How do you know her?"

She lowered her head and voice. "Vic had an affair with her."

I felt for her, but the relationship needed probing. "When was that?"

"Around eight years ago."

"How long did it last?"

She pulled her lips in. "He said it was over in a month, but I knew it was going on for a pretty long time."

"Did you ever meet her husband, Gene McGovern?"

"I don't think so. Why?"

"I can't say more than we're exploring every possible connection."

I left the house running scenarios through my head. The affair was years ago. Ethan Dwyer came to mind. He'd waited years to get revenge. Could McGovern have gone after Trent for ruining his marriage?

But why the others? It was back to the theory of there being two killers. Had McGovern taken the opportunity that a serial killer presented, by making it look like the same person committed all the murders?

My cell rang as I turned onto Neapolitan Way. It was Casey. "You have a minute?"

"Sure. What's going on?"

"Willis just followed Ong to a medical building."

"Is it a place for cancer?"

"There's three signs on the building. One for pulmonology, nephrology, and one for oncology. I'm pretty sure that's cancer."

It sure was. "Can you find out which office he went in?"

"I'll see what I can do."

"Make sure he doesn't see you."

70

MY CELL RANG; IT WAS GESSO. "WHAT'S GOING ON, SARGE?"

"Just got off the phone with Bemis at the Immokalee Jail. He's got word a prisoner wants to talk. Guy named Orlando Johnson said he has information on who killed Melissa Wright. He wants to talk."

"What did this Johnson do?"

"Armed robbery of the Publix by Ave Maria."

I tried to recall his face from the people arrested two days ago. "He was high. Wasn't he?"

"Yeah, on meth."

"That crap is taking a toll."

"Sure is."

"I'll go see him."

"Good luck with this guy."

People behind bars would say or do anything to get out or reduce their time. I'd had my share of prisoners giving information so thin you could read the newspaper through it. What made this one interesting was the timing.

Johnson had just been arrested. Whatever he had to say wasn't coming from a cellmate looking to burnish his street credentials. A guard, thirty pounds overweight, escorted me to a yellow cinder-block room.

Orlando Johnson was sitting on a metal picnic table. He bobbed his head. His leg bounced like a jackhammer as I introduced myself. Looking at his face, I figured he was entering withdrawal hell.

The bench was cold. "Mr. Johnson, I understand you have information that might interest us."

"Yeah, I got the goods, man."

"I'm all ears."

"But you gotta get me out of here if I tell you."

"You've been charged with armed robbery. That's a felony. I don't have a magic wand."

"But, it's the Preserve Killer, man."

"If it's credible and leads to an arrest, we'll inform the prosecutors who'll factor into your case."

"But, I need a guarantee, man. I got gold and it's worth something."

"Until we know exactly how valuable the information is, you're going to have to trust me."

His shoulders sank. "That's not fair, man."

"In your eyes it may not be. But I promise you, if it's solid info, you'll benefit from it. Tell me what you know."

He scoffed, "I better not get screwed."

"You won't. Start talking or I'm leaving."

Johnson scratched his forearm. "You see, this chick, got ahold of me."

"Who?"

"Riley, uh, Addison."

I leaned in. "Okay, so Addison contacted you."

"Yeah, that's right."

"What did she say?"

"Like, she asked me to kill Melissa."

"Melissa Wright?"

"Yeah."

"Riley Addison asked you to kill Melissa Wright?"

"Uh-huh. She said she'd give me five thousand to off her."

"What did you say?"

"I don't do shit like that. I'm no angel or nothing, but killing, I don't do that."

"When did she ask you to do this?"

"Oh man, it was like just a week or two max before the chick ended up dead. I was, like, I can't believe she did it."

"Where did she ask you?"

"In the parking lot at Alice Sweetwater's."

"Was anyone with you when she asked you?"

"No, just me and her."

"What did you tell her?"

"I said I don't do that kind of business."

"Did you give her someone that did?"

His eyes darted around. "I, uh, I don't know people like that."

"Come on, Orlando. You think I'm stupid?"

"No, I don't think nothing."

"Who'd you tell her to go to?"

"Nobody. I swear, man."

He swore. I had to believe him. "Who'd you refer her to?"

"Nobody. Maybe I said, like, she needs to go to Miami for that shit, but that was it."

"How well you know Riley Addison?"

"I don't know, pretty good, I guess. We used to, you know, hook up, back in the day."

"You used to date her?"

He nodded. "Kinda."

Addison knew him. If she asked him to do a contract

killing, she believed he'd do it or knew someone who would. "Who'd kill Wright for five grand?"

He scoffed, "Half the sausages in this joint."

"Who'd you recommend Addison get to do the job?"

"Nobody, man. You gotta believe me. I don't want that shit hanging on my head."

I was betting in exchange for money to feed his habit, Johnson made a referral. After ten minutes of stonewalling, I left. Something was there. We needed to dive into Johnson's background and see who the candidates were.

DERRICK WAS in front of the whiteboard when I walked into the office. "Casey is on Johnson. Looks like this guy is affiliated with the Saucy Boyz gang."

"They've made a lot of hits, but they're all drug related."

"That we know of. For five thousand, they'd kill their mother."

"Sick bastards. I have to go upstairs, see what kind of leeway they're willing to give Johnson if he sings."

"Okay."

"If this was a contract kill, we probably have two killers on our hands."

"I thought the same thing. I told Casey to have the team look for connections with any of the other victims."

I headed for the door. "Good, but I don't think there are any."

"Hang on a second. I talked to McGovern's wife. She's a manager at that new place, Del Mar on Fifth. Said she doesn't get off till eleven at the earliest."

"Where does she live?"

"Forest Lakes. Off Pine Ridge."

"That's better than going downtown. Give me her number. I'll meet her at her place after work."

"I'll put it on your desk."

"Be right back."

"Oh, one more thing. Willis confirmed Ong went to an oncologist."

"How'd he do that?"

"You know Willis, said he sweet-talked the receptionist."

"Stay on Ong."

I hustled up the stairs feeling like a juggler. Popping out of the stairwell, I thought about asking the sheriff for help. The garden hose of suspects had morphed into a fire hose.

71

Derrick shut down his computer. "That's it for me."

I looked at the clock. "It's almost seven. I got to get going too."

"Good luck tonight with McGovern's wife."

"It's way past my bedtime. I was hoping something would break."

"Leave it for another day. You can catch her before she goes in tomorrow."

I closed the murder book. "Good idea. I'll see if I zonk out on the couch or not."

Derrick laughed as I peeled off a sticky note stuck on the murder book. "I never called this lady back."

"She called today, again. I told her you'd get to her tomorrow."

"Good night."

THE AREA CODE WAS 732. It was a Jersey number, but that didn't mean much as I'd taken my Jersey number with me when I moved.

"Claire Shott?"

"Yes. Who's calling?"

"Detective Luca, Collier County. You called?"

She lowered her voice. "Yes. Two times."

"What can I do for you, ma'am?"

"I want you to look into my friend Natalie. She went missing three years—"

"I'm sorry, ma'am, but I don't handle—"

"Rachel Shea killed her."

"Excuse me?"

"Natalie came down from Albany and was staying with Rachel when she just disappeared. I know Rachel killed her."

I stiffened. "What's Natalie's full name? And how do you and Ms. Shea know her?"

"It's Natalie West. She and Rachel went to college together. I lived on the same block. We used to hang out together."

"Did you file a missing person report?"

"I went to the Lavallette Police, but they said she was an adult and lived in another state, so, they couldn't do anything."

"Did you advise the New York Police?"

"I couldn't go to Albany so I called, but they said there was nothing to indicate anything bad had happened to her. So when Rachel was arrested, I knew it was her."

"Why do you believe Ms. Shea harmed Natalie West?"

"She's a very mean person. Everybody thinks she some kind of angel but she's not."

"Do you know anything concrete concerning Ms. Shea that would point to her being violent?"

"She killed her mother for the money. How do you think she bought the place by the beach and her condo in Florida?"

"That's a serious charge."

"It's true. She had just moved in with Rachel. I went there the day before she died. She was fine, walking around, so how'd she end up dead the next day? Everybody knew something bad happened, and all Rachel would say was that is was her time to go."

"What's her mother's name?"

"Emily Shea. She was a nice lady, so full of life."

"Why do you think her daughter had something to do with her death?"

"She cremated the body right away. No service or anything."

The cremation and lack of religious ceremony didn't fit with who Shea seemed to be. It was a red flag. "Do you know how Emily Shea died?"

"Rachel probably overdosed her like she did to Kenny."

"Kenny?"

"He was Rachel's boyfriend. He overdosed on heroin but it was her. I know. I lived next door to him. He'd smoke marijuana but that was it. He never did the hard stuff. She killed him. I'm telling you."

That made three people around Rachel Shea who, according to Claire Shoot, died mysteriously. I took down Kenny's full name and promised to check into the allegations. It was something I could start looking into at home.

MARY ANN GOT off the couch. "I'm going to read in bed. You want the TV on?"

"Nah, I'm going do some work in the den until I have to go."

"Please be careful."

I went into the den and searched for Emily Shea's death certificate. As I pulled it up, it still amazed me how quickly we could find something in the digital age.

Emily Shea was sixty-two when she died. The cause of death was listed as natural. That didn't make sense. Wasn't she too young to die of old age?

Waiting for McGovern's ex-wife to text me she was home, I went down rabbit holes looking for information on Kenny Green. After confirming he died of a heroin overdose, I looked for possible arrests or treatment for drug use. Heroin was for serious users. And addicts inevitably ran afoul of the law.

Hard as I looked, I found nothing on Kenny. It was ten after eleven, and McGovern's ex hadn't sent me a text. I sent her a message to remind her and started searching for Natalie West.

There were twenty-six women in New York's database. I went through each one, settling on a woman with an Albany address. I pulled up her DMV record and paused. Her license had expired. Where was this woman?

My cell rang. It was Casey. "Sorry to bother you, but McGovern is on the move."

It was just past eleven thirty. "Where's he headed?"

"Moving toward Route 41."

"Stay on him. I'm on my way."

I jogged to the garage and hopped in my car. Exiting the neighborhood, Casey called again. "Looks like a false alarm, McGovern pulled into a Walgreens."

My neck muscles relaxed. "All right. Keep eyes on him."

"Will do."

McGovern's ex still hadn't reached out. I called her. She was on her way home, claiming to have forgotten our appointment. I made a U-turn and headed north. As I drove to see McGovern, I thought over informally releasing the new information on Shea to the New Jersey authorities. It might be enough to force them to stop impeding her extradition.

72

Driving on Pine Ridge near midnight was a pleasure. Considering how to track down Natalie West, my cell rang. "What's up, Casey?"

"I'm responding to an armed robbery and had to break surveillance on McGovern."

The call for assistance had come over the radio. "The Waffle House?"

"Yeah."

"Be careful."

"Sorry."

"It's okay. McGovern's probably on his way home."

"Yeah, he was headed that way."

It was pointless. If he wasn't going home, I'd never find him. My thoughts moved back to Shea. Everyone likes to say this or that would make a good movie, but nothing would top the Shea story if she were the killer.

Stopped at the light for Shirley Street, I realized I should have asked the contacts I had in Monmouth County to vet Shea. Was the goody two-shoes cloak she wore real, or was she the world's best con artist?

I turned onto the access road and followed it to a collection of condos named Mira Vista. Slowing, I checked the number on the building.

A white Honda was parked in the driveway of her unit. Pulling to the curb, I noticed a growing sliver of light at the bottom of the garage door.

Eyes trained on the rising door, two pairs of legs emerged. I lowered myself to avoid detection.

A pair of headlights came down the street, and the couple scooted out of my line of vision.

As the behemoth van passed, the couple came back into view. I squinted. It hit me; it was Gene McGovern, and the Honda they were approaching was his.

McGovern was forcing his ex-wife toward the vehicle.

A glint of light flashed off something. A knife. I unsnapped my holster. I drew my gun and jumped out.

Two hands on the roof, I aimed my pistol. "Freeze! Police!"

Raising his knife, McGovern pulled his ex in front of him. "Get out of here or I'll kill her!"

His wife whimpered, "No, no. Help me."

Gun trained on the couple, I came around the car. "Let her go. We can work this out."

"Get back or I swear, I'll kill her right here."

"Take it easy. Nobody is going to get hurt."

I gasped as he plunged the knife into her shoulder. She crumpled to the ground. "Put it down or I'll shoot!"

"Go ahead. Shoot me. I don't care."

Finger pressing the trigger, I said, "I'm not gonna make it easy on you."

I called for help, and McGovern made for the door handle. "Don't even try it! I'll shoot your knee caps off."

He scoffed, "It doesn't matter."

"You don't know what pain is."

He lowered his head. "That's where you're wrong."

"Throw the knife down or I'll blow your frigging knees off."

McGovern hesitated.

"Put it down. Now!"

McGovern tossed his weapon aside. I rushed him. "On your knees!"

Cuffing him, the sound of sirens intensified. I knelt next to his ex-wife. "You'll be all right."

Her blouse was darkened with blood. It didn't appear to be a fatal wound, but she was gasping and weak. Hoping it was just a punctured lung, I put pressure on the wound as a patrol swung onto the street.

I'd seen plenty of criminals weep when arrested, but McGovern's sobbing made me uncomfortable. He was put into the back of a patrol car.

Standing in the driveway as the car left, I wondered whether another killer was still on the loose.

73

I LOOKED AT THE VIDEO FEED BEFORE ENTERING THE ROOM. Perry Gorman had his hand on McGovern's shoulder. Gorman had switched sides after ten years of putting people in Lee County jails.

Derrick said, "You ever go up against him?"

"No. I've met him at a couple of functions but this is the first. Let's see what McGovern has to say." I knocked and we entered.

McGovern struggled to get to his feet. Gorman said, "Stay, stay." He extended a hand. "Hello, Detectives."

As he shook Derrick's hand, I nodded to McGovern. Anyone spending a night in jail never looks good, but McGovern's pasty look had gone gray.

We settled into chairs and Derrick recited the formalities. Before I could speak, Gorman threw up a hand. "We're hoping the county will take into account my client's willingness to cooperate."

"If he provides a full account and confession and we're able to avoid a trial, I'm sure the prosecutors will factor that in."

"My client is terminally ill, and we'd like an assurance he'd avoid incarceration."

Gorman had balls the size of a basketball. "Why don't we hear what Mr. McGovern has to say, Counselor?"

He hesitated before patting his client's forearm. "All right. Go ahead, Gene. Tell them what happened."

McGovern sniffled. "I did it. I had to. They ruined my life."

I said, "Did what?"

"I, uh, killed them."

"Who?"

"All of them."

"Melissa Wright?"

He nodded. "She was a bumbling idiot."

"Dr. Bigham?"

"Yep, she was the worst, an incompetent fool."

"Bobby Ryan?"

"No, I had nothing to do with that."

If it was a suicide, the press was responsible, but there were no laws holding them accountable. "What about Victor Trent?"

He scoffed. "Those ads. A family man? What bullshit. Bastard ruined my marriage."

"How'd you kill them?"

"Stabbed them with a knife."

"How many times?"

"Three is all it took. Though it might have been four once."

"How'd you get them to go with you to the parks?"

"I used my gun."

"The one we found in the car?"

"Yes."

"But you didn't use it on your ex-wife."

He hung his head. "I was going to do myself in after her."

"You were going to commit suicide?"

"Yeah. I'm dying anyway. Figured I'd save myself pain and misery."

"Why'd you do it?"

McGovern wagged his head and lowered his voice. "They deserved it. Made me go through hell."

I POPPED a pod in the coffee machine and stretched my back. It had been a late night, and rather than wake Mary Ann, I slept in the recliner. Between the chair and what McGovern revealed, I snoozed for just three hours before taking a shower in the pool bath.

Mary Ann padded into the kitchen. "What time did you get home?"

"Around two."

"You look exhausted."

"I'm okay."

"Why didn't you come to bed?"

I poured a splash of milk in my coffee. "I got a couple of hours. I'll be all right."

"What happened?"

I shook my head. "McGovern confessed to killing everyone but Ryan. I guess it was suicide."

"Oh my God. What a monster."

"It was crazy. I almost felt for the guy."

"What do you mean?"

I sat and took a sip of java. "McGovern had leukemia and nobody caught it. He felt sick, and the doctor ordered blood work. Melissa Wright worked at the place registering patients and screwed up the paperwork."

"Oh my God."

"After a couple of months, he was getting worse, and somebody referred him to Dr. Bigham. She ran tests but said he had a type of leukemia that wasn't a major issue, and they'd just keep an eye on it. It turned out she had misinterpreted the tests and the cancer progressed."

"Two mistakes? That's unbelievable."

"That's what I thought, but Bilotti said mistakes can happen at the beginning with registration, like Wright did. And that labs make errors and so do doctors by either missing something or misinterpreting it."

"That's terrible. He got really sick?"

I nodded. "He finally was diagnosed correctly and got a bone marrow transplant. It helped for a while but it came back."

"I get why he was mad, but you don't go killing people when they make a mistake."

"McGovern said he wanted to wake people up, and that's why he posed them."

"He sure did."

"Bilotti said there's evidence people who undergo bone marrow transplants experience mental disturbances."

"It has to make you depressed."

"And Bilotti said very anxious."

"I can imagine."

"I'm not making excuses, but I get why McGovern lost it. He caught bad breaks and it cost him his life. His lawyer said he has less than a year to live."

74

———

I BREEZED INTO THE OFFICE. "IF I HAVE TO DO ANOTHER interview, I'm going to lose it."

Derrick said, "I can see the headline tomorrow, 'Good Looking Luca—"

"Cut it out, will you."

"Enjoy it while it lasts."

"Enjoy it? It's exhausting. I'm going to enjoy the sand. We're going to go to Key West for a couple of days. Mary Ann's friend is letting us use her place."

"Nice."

"Can't wait. I want to look into Shea. What that lady said doesn't fit, but I'm not going on vacation until that and Addison are resolved."

"Don't worry about Addison. While you were doing your PR, we went through the footage from Alice Sweetwater's. We couldn't find Johnson there."

"He knew she worked there and Addison was in the news."

"Yep. And the last time Johnson was arrested, he claimed to have dirt on a drug ring, but there was nothing to it."

I shook my head. "One down. Let's check into Shea, so I can go away with a clear head."

MARY ANN ASKED me to pick up milk on the way home. Publix had an array of milks and it was needed. Mary Ann drank almond, Jessie preferred soy, and I liked skim milk. I loaded the bottles in my cart wondering what my father would have to say about the choices.

Rolling down the pasta aisle, I stopped. Kate Swift and her mother were mulling macaroni options. I approached. "Excuse me."

They turned and smiled. Kate said, "Detective Luca. How are you?"

She'd gained some weight and had good color. "I'm good. How are you doing?"

"Doing much better, thank you."

Her mother put an arm around her daughter. "Katie is back to her old self."

Katie shrugged. "I'm making some progress."

"You'll get there."

"They keep telling me it'll take time."

"You've got this, Kate. You're a special woman."

"I don't know about that."

"Well, I do."

She flashed a smile, and I returned it, saying, "Well, seeing you really made my day. Have a good night, ladies. And if you need anything, let me know."

Seeing the girl I'd rescued from captivity lifted my spirits so high, I didn't get annoyed at the cashier talking with customers instead of scanning goods. Walking through the parking lot, I passed a man wearing a Mets T-shirt.

It reminded me of going to Shea Stadium to see them play. My mind shifted to Rachel Shea.

She was a good person, and as I drove home, I forced myself not to dwell on how we'd dragged her into the investigation. Turning onto our street, I thought about the woman who accused her of killing Natalie West, her mother, and a boyfriend.

It turned out the missing woman had taken a five-year assignment in Singapore with Microsoft. She wasn't missing, and Shea's mother had suffered three heart attacks, dying of cardiac arrest. There was no reason to look for Kenny Green.

Shea wasn't Mother Teresa, but the woman who'd made the allegations against her wasn't in full control of her faculties.

Flipping through the mail, I pulled out the American Cancer Society envelope. Since I'd gotten cancer, we'd been sending in two hundred dollars a year. I took it into the den and did a quick search on charities. The American Cancer Society was rated high, but the Leukemia and Lymphoma Society spent more of the dollars they took in on research.

Fishing out the checkbook, I wrote a check to them. Then I penned another check. This one was to Ocean of Love, the New Jersey charity Rachel Shea worked for. We'd thrown her life upside down, and I felt I had to do something. Besides, it was for kids with cancer.

A hundred dollars was all we could afford, but I would see what the Gulf Coast Police Benevolent Association could do. The Preserve Killer case had generated a lot of good press for me. I wasn't above using my good standing, while it lasted, to help Shea.

The next book in this series is, No One is Safe. Find it in eBook & Paperback.

I hope you enjoyed reading this book as much as I enjoyed writing it. If you did, I'd appreciate it if you would write a quick review on Amazon or your favorite book site. Reviews are an author's best friend and even a quick line or two is helpful. Thanks, Dan

OTHER BOOKS BY DAN

<u>**THE LUCA MYSTERY SERIES**</u>

Am I the Killer

Vanished

The Serenity Murder

Third Chances

A Cold, Hard Case

Cop or Killer?

Silencing Salter

A Killer Missteps

Uncertain Stakes

The Grandpa Killer

Dangerous Revenge

Where Are They

Buried at the Lake

The Preserve Killer

No One is Safe

<u>**SUSPENSEFUL SECRETS**</u>

Cory's Dilemma

Cory's Flight

Cory's Shift

OTHER WORKS BY DAN PETROSINI

The Final Enemy

Complicit Witness

Push Back

Ambition Cliff

You can keep abreast of my writing and have access to books that are free of discounting by joining my newsletter. It normally is out once a month and also contains notes on self- esteem, motivational pieces and wine articles.

It's free. See bottom of my website: www.danpetrosini.com

ABOUT THE AUTHOR

Dan is a USA Today and Amazon best-selling author who wrote his first story at the age of ten and enjoys telling a story or joke.

Dan gets his story ideas by exploring the question; What if?

In almost every situation he finds himself in, Dan explores what if this or that happened? What if this person died or did something unusual or illegal?

Dan's non-stop mind spin provides him with plenty of material to weave into interesting stories.

A fan of books and films that have twists and are difficult to predict, Dan crafts his stories to prevent readers from guessing correctly. He writes every day, forcing the words out when necessary and has written over twenty-five novels to date.

It's not a matter of wanting to write, Dan simply has to.

Dan passionately believes people can realize their dreams if they focus and act, and he encourages just that.

His favorite saying is – "The price of discipline is always less than the cost of regret"

Dan reminds people to get the negativity out of their lives. He believes it is contagious and advises people to steer clear of negative people. He knows having a true, positive mind set makes it feel like life is rigged in your favor. When he gets off base, he tells himself, 'You can't have a good day with a bad attitude.'

Married with two daughters and a needy Maltese, Dan lives in Southwest Florida. A New York native, Dan has taught at local colleges, writes novels, and plays tenor saxophone in several jazz bands. He also drinks way too much wine and never, ever takes himself too seriously.

He puts out a twice-a-month newsletter featuring articles, his writing and special deals and steals.

Sign up at www.danpetrosini.com